Talking (

Sleeping Dogs

David Hudson

1

Couches chairs and beds used to be firmly out of bounds. But she always wants to be where he is, and he's decided that to persist would be to go against nature. And who would be daft enough to do that?

Of course, he still makes a determined effort not to let standards slip. But the importance of barriers has diminished alongside the barriers themselves, and their accidental co-dependency has become, well, precious. More precious than he ever dreamed or is prepared to acknowledge, even to himself.

Outsiders would view their closeness as beyond odd and this troubles him. But then he thinks that there are as many unlikely combinations as there are implausible things to combine, and who's to say what passes for 'normal' anyway. Kitty is a housemate who doesn't crave the television remote, watches and manages to enjoy whatever programme he chooses, doesn't covet the latest fashions and fads, and doesn't possess a mobile phone let alone the latest model. She doesn't have friends he can't take to or a mother that interferes, she doesn't ask questions to which there is no answer that won't offend, and she doesn't tell him how to behave or what not to wear. Kitty is a confidante whose one ambition in life is to please her owner, and so in every way that matters, she is the perfect companion.

He can sense that she'll dart towards the sound of his key being turned and that he'll have to squeeze past her just to gain entry. And he can already hear the hum of the microwave and see himself standing at the worksurface scooping his evening meal direct from its plastic container and watching her antics. He knows that, just like that microwave, every part of his being will soon be aglow, and the very predictability of their life together is exhilarating, heartwarming, even life enhancing.

Nevertheless, he can't seem to escape the intense anxiety that accompanies his Kitty enhanced life. He didn't plan for and certainly didn't want their rhythmic reliance, and he knows that he should throw the whole thing into reverse. But he can't bear the thought of losing the happenstance that now defines him, even though he recognises that the confining chains that come with the soothing oil will break him when the time comes.

Tea bag steeping in a mug labelled 'The World's Best Dad,' he sighs contentedly as, nose buried in premium tuna and sea bream sold as 'almost human grade,' Kitty chases her skidding bowl along the smooth linoleum until it strikes a kickboard. Inevitably, her water bowl gets in the way and there is spillage, and he meets her concerned look with a frown that ought not to be but is tongue-in-cheek. Later, bellies full and ridiculously thrilled to be watching a repeated repeat of a mediocre period drama, Kitty purrs under his strokes before he lifts her lips up to his and kisses her.

'You still love me, don't you Kitty?' he asks.

'More than ever,' comes the reply.

2

The headteacher of my daughter's school is the love of my life. No debate. No doubt. But *(there's always a but)*, I can't seem to shake the ever-present brain niggle that, thirty years ago, Michael Lloyd cold bloodedly executed a horribly disabled and defenceless fifteen-year-old boy.

I'm more than ready to concede that not too many detective chief inspectors wake up each morning next to a suspected killer, *(there will be a good reason for that)*, but my life is so close to being more perfect than I ever imagined it could be, and, though the niggle is following me around like a pissed off prophet of doom, it is just the one, and in my game niggles are ten a penny and come with the badge. So why can't I just bloody well woman-up and cope?

Other people know when to leave well alone, but not Julie Marsden. One moment I'm determined to catch the bouquet regardless of all manner of obstacles barring my way, the next I'm rendered motionless by indecision, riddled with doubt, and telling myself 'Don't tiddle on my leg and tell me it's raining.' Fact is, no matter how wonderful my life becomes, especially at the count on the fingers of one finger times when it's idyllic, everything that matters is destined to throw itself off a cliff. Why? Because for Julie Marsden, they always do. She sees the precipice long before it's too late - example: marrying Dennis - she knows fine well where the brake is and yet she presses accelerate every time - example: marrying Dennis and getting knocked-up before she could even begin to savour the knocking, so to speak - and when inevitably she's disappointed and depressed, she eats.

Collecting the girder masquerading as a chocolate éclair and my three sugared Grande Flat White, I spot recent CID recruit, Detective Constable Samantha Jardine looking sleek in her skintight black leggings - which on me would evoke two frisky ferrets fighting in a sack - gleaming white trainers and sloppy white top, all alone, occupying one of two armchairs, and chuntering.

'Daddy's chequebook got him into Cambridge, and he's only in the cabinet because he went to Eton with all the other chinless wonders.'

My petite young colleague has clearly relaxed enough for one day off, so I slide unseen into the vacant armchair and declare,

'Talking to yourself is okay, Sam. It's arguing with yourself that's a bit of a bugger.'

I'm known, well notorious, for my jocularity, but I might have misjudged this intervention – not like me at all – and full cream moustache bulging cheeks and saucer eyes looking everywhere but at the boss' rapidly decomposing black variety, Sam Jardine is suddenly a hamster caught in a headlight trying, as any off-duty foot soldier unexpectedly confronted by their superior officer would, to pull off polite whilst clearly repulsed by what is suddenly up close and way too personal. I help by pointing to the offending body part and announcing loud enough for all in Costa Coffee to hear,

'Stenton Cornthwaite! Or 'Crime Wave' as I like to call him!'

Thirteen-year-old Stenton is what seasoned professionals like me learn at detective school to call 'a pain in the arse,' and abandoning all hope of respectful restraint, Sam is soon laughing at her DCI's tale. 'It had been just another short and stress-free day in my opulent, ambient-temperatured office, getting paid shedloads of money for doing very little, and I was on my way home when a suspected shop break-in in Wickersley comes over the radio and I happen to be the nearest car. Well, I knew from the off that it'd be kids, all stick thin and fit as butcher's dogs, and that they'd be long gone before I rocked up. And if they weren't and I did manage to nab 'em, both bloody big ifs, I knew all too well that they'd be back on the streets minutes after I got 'em to the station. An exercise in futility if ever there was one … but I went anyway.

'So, it's pitch black, I'm round the backs amongst the garbage bins used condoms and dog shit, my flickering torch is in dire need of new batteries, I'm freezing my tits off, and I'm furious with myself for not being able to think of a half-descent reason not to have responded in the first place. When, resigned to giving up and going home, I fall over Stenton - the little sod was on his own lying doggo in the shadows - and we both end up on the ground, hugging.' Sam is now laughing noisily, and other Costa customers are openly intrigued. 'He's breaking his curfew, again, and he's no idea who's got hold of him. So, he does what comes naturally and he nuts me. And 'Mandy the Mound' erupts into view ... well not my view, obviously. Glasgow Kiss manages to sound romantic, Wickersley Whack, not so much.'

'Poor lad,' says Sam, seeing an opportunity to play along. 'He would have been so upset when he realised that he'd hurt you of all people, ma'am.'

'I'm glad that you're able to sympathise with my attacker, Samantha. Though it's a skill that you're unlikely to require as you look to further your career.' I grin, winking with the eye that's still in wink condition. 'But you're right of course. He was full of apologies when he realised it was me, and he got into my car like a dejected doggy that's done yet another doo-doo on the duvet. But all that doesn't alter the fact that he'd be back being mollycoddled at the children's home hours before I finally put my feet up at chez Julie. And we both know that he's far too young for us to legally keep him tied down and behaving.'

I emphasise my point by biting off an iceberg sized chunk of éclair just as Sam asks, 'how's Rosie, ma'am?' Needing chewing time, I gesture favourably towards her lilac streaked, honey blonde hairdo whilst grinding like a bullmastiff until, at length, I'm able to continue with the driven aplomb that my story deserves,

'Overnight my beloved sixteen-year-old daughter has gone from Devil's Disciple to a Big Boned Mother Teresa, and the transformation is all down to the new boyfriend.' Suddenly and inexplicably uncertain of myself but feeling the need to explain, I add, 'and that's good. 'Course it's good. But ... the thing is, Sam ... he's more than ten years older than Rosie, and even with a man as devoted as John, I can't help wondering what in Heaven's name they're ever going to find to talk about? It feels wrong, Sam. It just feels wrong.

'Michael is advising that I let it run its natural course or she'll rebel even more. And he keeps telling me to enjoy the calm while it lasts. But ... I don't know ...' Momentarily lost in a quiet moment of reflection, it's a while before I think to point out, 'and it's Julie when we're not working.'

Rosie's been a worry from her first deafening, delivery room demand, so, what's new? And despite daughter doubt that has boiled over ten times a day for sixteen years, I'm feeling perked up - all down to Sam - and Michael's alleged inclination to off the young and incapacitated is, for a while at least, on the back burner. Head at a disconcerting tilt and probably looking more pigeon than police officer, I decide on cheeky banter. 'And, Samantha dear, I can see that you're dying to know how my love life is progressing.'

'Sam?' The voice that comes from behind seems to impact on Sam Jardine every bit as much as my exploding bomb appearance did just minutes ago. Fascinated, I attempt to look up and focus but, inevitably, I over-swivel and manage neither. 'I thought it was you, Sam,' says the voice, 'it's been a long time. Too long. Much too long.'

*

Carly Simon's 'No Secrets' L.P. is Sam's grandad's favourite vinyl record, and despite her having it digitalised for him on his seventieth, it's never off the record player.

Sam hates it - one track in particular - with a passion.

In the song, Carly's next-door neighbours 'The Carter Family' move away suddenly and without warning, and she and Gwen Carter - still girls of the same age and best friends *from ragdolls through brassieres* - are forever lost to each other. Gwen had begun to annoy Carly, and as Gwen departs, she must *'fake her tears.'* But Carly finds that she misses her *'more than she ever ... would ... have ... guessed.'*

The song upsets Sam every time she hears it because she also had a childhood soulmate from ragdolls through brassieres, and that friendship also ended abruptly. But unlike Carter, Sam's soulmate didn't move away, in fact, in school, the pair continued to squander reconciliation opportunity after reconciliation opportunity before, years later, they both went their separate ways.

The friendship that had been so strong was instantly, and as it turned out, irrevocably, dissolved when, with minutes left to get home before the stipulated deadline, the two twelve-year-olds were standing waiting for a non-existent bus and were confronted by a taxi driven by an Asian man older than their father, and who was expecting the kind of payment that nice girls should refuse to pay. Sam's best friend in all the world had jumped in and left cold alone and far from a bus stop, home, her friend, and from ever being able to forgive, Sam has never since been able to forget.

Not asked to join the pleasant coffee shop police officer camaraderie, there is a messy pouring of consume on the premises coffee into a 'to go' cardboard cup, and Elaine Fenell once again leaves behind her erstwhile best friend.

And Sam misses her ... more than she ever ... would ... have ... guessed.

3

Today is turning out way better than expected. My Full Council, Rotherham Centred, Crime Report PowerPoint is over for another three months, I can return to putting distance between myself and puffed-up-politicians asking banal questions that are all about looking good in the newspapers, and I can get on with catching bad guys, and coffee with Sam was an unforeseen delight. What to do about Michael is still hanging heavy on my mind, but I'm feeling more optimistic by the minute.

Leaving my beautiful young colleague to try to enjoy the rest of her day off, Big Bag making Big Coat shoulder ski jump slant, and taking ages to remember where I've parked Izzy my sparkly purple Mazda RX8 with natural hessian reproduction leather seats, I'm walking through Parkgate Retail World carpark and texting always texting. Then, looking up and finding myself within a hair's breadth of t-boning an octogenarian driving her walking frame without due care and attention, I spot a very recognisable Stephen Gutowski coming out of Asda Living of all places.

And that's interesting.

But not half as interesting as the fact that he's not alone.

Running alongside Gus Gutowski is Borough Councillor Jeff Chapman ... and he shouldn't be.

Holy Jeff, local politician soon to be mayor of Rotherham who pretends to loathe his 'The Bishop' moniker but does all he can to promote it, is being chummy with a lowlife and so I fold into the all-glass foyer of Primark, to watch, perchance to learn.

Stephen 'Gus' Gutowski is all over the saintly politician and both look to be heading towards a silver-grey Bentley Continental with cream and tan real leather seats and blinged-up radiator that's standing out like a purebred Arabian amongst Skegness beach donkeys. In the car's passenger seat is a man who, I'm chuffed to say, I also know.

Queen Victoria was said to be rounder than she was tall, and the photographs of her in no measure - the correct word I think - contradict this curiously fascinating 'fact.' Albie Holroyd, who is the passenger in the Bentley and whose height I've yet to accurately apportion, always makes me think of the old queen because I'm convinced that Holroyd is taller sitting down than he is standing up. As soon as I can zap him into the nearest cell - I live in hope - I'll take great pleasure in proving what, for now, must remain a hypothesis.

As always, he's dressed as Hollywood's distortion of a 1940's Chicago gangster - something miserable Queen Vic did only rarely - and I can't resist a smile when Rotherham's very own Micky Rooney cracks open his window but doesn't bother to get out. Gus and Jeff have no choice but to bend awkwardly, like two giraffes brought low by an umpalumpa, to hear what The Man has to say.

The monologue is curt and is ended when, with no warning, Holroyd closes his window, and the Gutowski/Chapman handshake - a two-hand-under-and-over from The Bishop - is perforce, rushed. As Gutowski drives Holroyd past in the purring Bentley, I'm left pondering whether I've just clocked two villains, or three.

4

A stair carpet considered an unnecessary expense for a fourth-floor attic converted into an 'office,' the barked command of 'Veronique!' induces unavoidable clatter before, eyes down, teetering on falling apart ridiculously high heels, and not yet aware of how she's at fault, she tumbles into the small space mindful that the extent of her injuries will depend on her quickly and accurately evaluating this situation. Nervously fingering her elbows and the brown roots of her short-cropped, in the process of losing its crimson colouring, hair, and shivering in a skimpy faded blue bra and pink pants, her angular forty-year-old flour white body looks seventy.

'You 'ave to do exactly what Anthony tells you, darlin',' she whispers, her French accent many years mottled by a thick, Yorkshire brogue. Remembering just in time, she adds, 'wizout answering back.'

The focus of Veronique's attention, a pretty young girl still not out of her teens, gives no reply, and assessing the situation as bleak, the older woman starts to beg.

*

The three other new girls are very nice and very friendly, but they are already naked, and Katia - a name considered by her captor to be sexier than her real name of Kausar - is listening to Veronique. And she understands and empathises. But she can't do as instructed because she knows that if she doesn't take a stand her life will forever be ruined, her personality will be crushed beyond repair, her self-esteem a distant memory, and she will become this poor woman in front of her and imploring other poor sufferers to comply.

Sending hard-earned money back to a defeated family had been the excuse, but escaping debilitating tradition and tolerated poverty to join a world where a young life could be lived free was Kausar's real goal. And the idea of coming to England had excited her ever since she could first dress herself. Indeed, she and her friends talked of nothing else. In this small room in this

10

foreign country, and in the power of this intimidating man, she can't believe that she was so naïve.

Two of twenty-year-old Aisha's sisters had successfully sought their fortunes in England, so Aisha was the go-to resident expert that was just like her; and Kausar's friend pulled no punches. She made it clear that selling sex - not the story they'd peddled to parents and grandparents - is every bit as unpleasant as it sounds, and she repeatedly emphasised that it would be no more than a business investment for the English Contact. 'In England,' she'd said, 'money is quick and big, and it flows as it never has, never would, and never could in Kazakhstan.' But she'd stressed that over-worked, underfed, and even dying foreign families are not the English Contact's concern, and so Kausar can't claim that she didn't know the score. She knew even before she left her home and family that she would just have to grit her teeth and work hard to focus on the bigger and more important plan, but she also knew that her friend Aisha would be travelling to England with her, and that she would have a friend to guide her.

An event invigorated by the smell of opportunity, in their world as rare and precious as diamonds and thus worthy of celebration, proud friends and even prouder relatives turned out to wave them on their way to pursue the wholesome and worthwhile calling of nanny to well-to-do middle class English families, the elation was real and heartfelt, and Kausar was more excited than fearful … until, sometime during their first night in Rotherham, Aisha disappeared with her passport and what little money had been in her grandmother's, threadbare but cherished, purse.

*

Veronique has worked with mainly eastern European girls for longer than she cares to remember, and she can tell that Katia knows far less English than perhaps she thought she did when she left Kazakhstan. Nevertheless, as she employs her long and skinny thumbs to smear away developing tears from the terrified seventeen-year-old's big wet brown eyes, Anthony's bitch can sense that this clever girl has worked out what needs to happen and why. Holding Katia's beautiful young face in her callused hands, Veronique is momentarily hopeful.

11

'You 'ave to, darlin'. 'Anthony 'as spent so much money getting you 'ere, and you 'ave to pay 'im back.'

No reply is forthcoming, and Veronique turns and looks towards Anthony who motions her to come to heel.

*

In the end, brute force is all that matters, and the blow that lifts Veronique off her feet destroys Kausar's resolve as a sledgehammer demolishes tissue paper. And without question, argument, or hope, she quietly starts to undress.

5

I know all too well that the breathless battle to extricate myself from Izzy's sleek lines is Mother Nature's way of telling me to re-visit my budgerigar's belly food regime, but I've already thought of six reasons why the diet can wait, and I've telephoned ahead so that newly promoted Inspector Bill Pridding can get out the Hob Nobs ... medicinal, obviously. And if I'm to digest the gory details of the schemes and scams of Holroyd and Gutowski, I'll need something to smooth the edges.

Box files pinched under each arm, recently boiled kettle in one hand his own mug in the other, and said Hob Nobs clamped between chin and chest, Bill is soon following a now less wheezy me into my office where he plugs in the kettle to bring already boiled water back to temperature. And as I hand him my already tea bagged red and white Rotherham United mug, my mood continues to improve.

'So, Holroyd and Gutowski?'

'Well, they're both rogues, ma'am, but we've got nothing to go to court with for either one of 'em.' Bill pauses to pour - a man who knows his priorities, a proper copper. 'Back in the day, Gutowski was a cut and shut man. At the bottom end of the market but making a good living getting crashed cars cheap or free and salvaging their best bits before bolting screwing welding and painting. And turning out boy racer death traps by the dozen to be sold on housing estates with the buyer thinking the seller lives in the house at the top of the drive where the deal was going down. A cash up front, once in a lifetime bargain with a full refund promised if dissatisfied, the car would soon be a knackered heap leaving the buyer with no choice but to return to the house he thought he bought it from, only to find that nobody's heard of the seller and now there's no way of tracing him.' Another pause to hand me my milky cuppa. 'We never doubted that we'd get Gutowski eventually, but the jammy bugger hit the jackpot by marrying Becca Thompson, the daughter of very rich and very respectable local haulier called Henry Thompson, and he seemed to quit crime while he was ahead.

'But word is that he just pressed pause, and has been on the fiddle, one way or another, ever since.

'Feet under the Thompson table, he must have thought all his Christmases had come at once, and even though Henry Thompson had the look of a man who'd outlive his undertaker, all Big Gus had to do was bide his time. Then, completely out of character, Gutowski's hard as nails new father-in-law dashes like Usain Bolt with diarrhoea to commit suicide.'

'Now that's suspicious!'

'Yep,' says Bill wrinkling his bald pate, which on such a big man's man is for some reason surprisingly sexy, 'Thompson Transport becomes Gus Logistics overnight, and a bit part spear carrying extra called Gutowski becomes lead actor, writer, producer, and director of his own show. And now he's a powerful and on the face of it legitimate employer and businessman with big trucks carrying goods all over Europe.' Bill's big bushy black eyebrows frown before, like sunrise over Barnsley, his square jawed face morphs into a grin exposing, fanning outwards from more vintage brandy than brown eyes, a plethora of laughter lines. 'Though people like him always think that they can bend any rules that they decide need bending, and that's why it's only a matter of time before we nab him.'

'And Holroyd?'

'Well, Holroyd is much more your regular thug. He's violence and intimidation … and emaciated teenage girls to cater for every feasible, and not so feasible, sexual need. Unlike Gutowski, Holroyd's done Fines, Probation Orders, Community Orders, and he's been tagged, and a long time ago he did a bit of time in Armley Prison for Possession with Intent to Supply Class A. But despite trying hard, we've not been able to lay a finger on him since.

'We know he does no paid work and that he's had his benefits stopped. And yet, despite having no obvious source of income, he still manages to live in a three-bed detached house in Kiveton Park that he owns outright, and he drives a one-year-old white Range Roverr Sport - ALB 1E - that isn't on finance and that he bought new. There is no wife and no kids that we know of, and he lives with a big guy - bigger even that Gutowski - who everybody calls Marvin after Marvellous Marvin Haggler, the boxer. The big bloke's real name is David Smith, and David/Marvin has been Holroyd's live-in bodyguard since they shared a cell together nearly twenty years ago.

'Marvin puts people in hospital for fun, again hard to prove in court, and Holroyd rarely goes anywhere without him. That said, Marvin is not what you'd call a friend. In fact, apart from Gutowski, who's more of a partner, Holroyd seems to have no real friends.' Bill suddenly develops another smug grin. 'The really interesting thing is what pops up when both names, Holroyd and Gutowski, are inputted into the computer, together.'

I've been thoroughly absorbed until now. But when Bill says 'Darren Bates,' I'm sceptical and can't stop myself showing it.

'You're not serious, Bill? Gutowski and Holroyd would have only been teenagers themselves at the time'.

'Yes, ma'am,' says Bill. 'When seventeen-year-old Darren Bates murdered eleven-year-old Abigail Hardcastle, fifteen-year-old Stephen Gutowski and fifteen-year-old Albie Holroyd were, as you say, teenagers. But they were teenagers together, and they were there.

6

We were both too tired to cook, so Michael's just returned from the Happy Cantonese with way too much egg fried rice, chicken and cashew, something sweet and sour, and a beef and tomato, and we're mixing and shovelling like a brickies' mate on a building site.

'Tough day?' I ask,

'Yeah,' says Michael looking shattered, 'tough day.'

Clearly, it's been a day much worse than 'tough' because Michael's desire not to re-visit earlier stress and frustration is mushrooming from him like a welder's flash. He just wants to unwind and make small talk, but he can't stop himself adding, 'Jeff Chapman kept asking cheap shot questions about finance because Michael Waring's been daft enough to tell him that if things stay as they are we'll have an outturn figure of minus sixty-three thousand.' The tension is destroying his face and making me regret asking. 'Of course, things won't stay as they are because I'll sort it! And what kind of headteacher would I be if I made wholesale, needless cuts just because, as per usual, Jeff Chapman's winding up the school governors.'

'He had his Rotherham Council hat on then?' Chapman is just as much of a smart-arse in Police Committee meetings and I'm finding it easy to empathise.

'Yeah. More worried about upsetting the Leader of the Council than helping the school he's supposed to represent. And more interested in thinly veiled criticisms of me. Arrogant bastard.'

Now looking irritated that he's let Holy Jeff get up his nose in his own house and in his own downtime, eventually Michael smiles and that's my signal to sidle closer. 'But he's not sitting at home talking about us,' Michael says, at length, 'so he can shove his criticisms where the sun don't shine.'

Head now on his chest and my nyloned shoeless feet pulled onto the couch, I'm pleased that Michael's anxiety has crowned and faded ... but I'm still finding relaxation hard to come by. Fact is, I like talking shop, and right at this moment I have things, police things, that I want, need, to share. One 'for instance' being whether the man whose heartbeat I can feel, and who's hand is stroking my hair, has, for thirty plus years, gotten away with snuffing out the life of his best friend's helpless teenage brother. It's a subject that's worthy of discussion, that's for damn sure!

So, my choices are simple: I could snuggle doze and not utter a word, I could just tell him about my day like he's told me about his, or I could accuse him of cold-blooded murder. It's a tough call.

'My Town Hall PowerPoint presentation went well, and Chapman was also part of that little get-together.' My words strike a happy note, and I can feel him chuckling. I look up, also giggling.

'So, we both had the pleasure of his company then. A red-letter day.

'He's like bindweed. Pops up everywhere and chokes the life out of anything that's doing well. But in my meeting, he never opened his mouth except to eat and drink. For the whole hour. None of 'em did. I can't win. Hate it when they talk, can't stand it when they don't.'

'What? They didn't mention ...' Michael presses his strong chin to his hair tousled chest, exaggeratedly points to his own face, and, film trailer fashion, breathes out a deep refrain of 'the eye?'

'Not even, 'the eye,' I ape - not successfully due to my lack of hair tousled chest - 'but something very interesting did happen afterwards.' I pause dramatically. 'Imagine a drum roll, Michael. Can you hear it?' He steadies his tea and nods seriously.

'I hear it.'

'You ready?' He nods again, this time less seriously. 'I saw Chapman in Parkgate Retail Park car park, and he was being very friendly with Stephen Gutowski and Albie Holroyd.' I attempt a sphinx-like smile. 'And Gutowski and Holroyd are very naughty boys.' Michael has taken a sip of his tea and overacts a fake spluttering - not too much because of his aversion to any form of mess.

'Every school assembly should have a hymn and a prayer Jeff Chapman, talking with crooks?! And no thunderbolt from the heavens! What is the world coming to?'

I sit up and tell my Gutowski and Holroyd story and, inevitably, Abigail Hardcastle's death is mentioned. Suddenly, Michael is melancholy.

'It was a big thing in Rotherham,' he says, 'took some getting over for our school. Cathy Jerrom told me all about it a couple of times before she retired. All these years later and she remembers everything, every detail, it must have been horrendous.'

The pained expression is back and he's deep in thought. Then, gradually becoming aware of the silence, he turns to find me staring. 'Now wait a minute, my darling,' he asserts whilst managing to be anything but assertive. 'You can't ... we can't ... not at this time of night.'

Flashing what I'm claiming to be a coquettish grin, 'worth a phone call, my dearest, don't you think?' I purr.

*

For reasons I can't begin to explain, women whose homes are spotless, know their way round a soufflé, and can rustle up feather-light homemade scones and butterfly buns at the drop of a hat, intimidate me. And yet, it was a pleasant three hours spent in delightful conversation and I'm telling myself that Mchael's retired colleague not only didn't mind the late-night phone call and visit, but that she was grateful for the company.

It turns out that Cathy Jerrom's knowledge of Abigail Hardcastle's death borders on encyclopaedic, and back staring at Michael's 'artistic' overpriced clock with no numbers and almost invisible hands showing what I'm guessing is 11.27 p.m., and noticing every spill stain dirty plate and cobweb, I'm better fed than is good for me and I'm bursting in more senses than one. Desperate to share what I've learned with my team, I come up against an immoveable object.

'Normal people have normal lives,' says Michael. 'And midnight telephone calls from your boss expecting answers to questions that could and should perfectly well be asked after clocking-on and getting paid time, are entirely unreasonable and amount to bullying, even harassment.'

Despite synapses firing like a machine gun, my penchant for a man who knows his mind and isn't afraid to show it wins through. It's late. Bedtime in fact. And suddenly, work can wait.

18

7

My phone alarm is set to 7 a.m. and I ring Bill at 7.05.

'Hello, ma'am, I'm glad you rang,' he says, 'I've been digging into the Abigail Hardcastle case and there are things that you need to know.' Good old Bill. Not born but quarried.

Desperate - more than I realised - to throw off the self-imposed shackles, I assert, 'me too,' and a pressure release valve turns as I begin telling the gist of Cathy Jerrom's information.

'Gutowski and Holroyd were thugs and bullies even at school, Bill, Big Gus the muscle and weaselly rat the brains. And this you won't believe, back then, Little Albie was a pretty boy!' Bill splutters and I stifle a laugh. 'I know! According to Michael's ex-colleague who knew 'em well as kids, that shrivelled still waiting for a growth spurt wizened excuse for a body was lusted after by obsessed schoolgirls.'

I can hear Pam Pridding muttering in the background. 'Seven in the fucking morning, always said she was crackers.' She has a point, but I'm enjoying myself and don't miss a beat. 'Cathy Jerrom taught 'em all and she described Abigail Hardcastle as eleven going on twenty-eight, thinking she's streetwise, already knowing everything, dismissive of advice, fundamentally self-destructive, and with parents you wouldn't wish on a cuckoo. In fact, a younger version of my Rosie ... apart from the bit about parents ... obviously.

'Obligatory shorter than short skirt and over-the-top make-up, Abigail had set her sights on vacuous-blonde, and she was a sassy kid, well developed for her age, and according to Cathy who I think would know, she was a looker. Popular with a certain type of girl and with all the boys, she was mouthy and disobedient, she could twist her dad round her little finger, and her mother was about as effective as a liquorice wheel brace.

'Louise Bates - sister of Darren - was Abi's bezzie-mate and Cathy said that Louise followed Abi around like a little lost puppy.' I'm imagining Pam Pridding rolling her eyes and pointing at her watch. 'Darren was a big lad for his age, for any age, even bigger than Gutowski. He'd left school at sixteen the previous year and he was far too nice and much too soft. He would walk away rather than fight even though he could sort out most of 'em with one hand tied behind his back. He wasn't the least bit academic, but he worked hard, and his teachers loved him. Unfortunately, other kids saw him as an easy target. Even the little 'uns called him Willie Wankalot - Master Bates/masturbates - and he was too easy-going to stop 'em.

'Louise and Darren's mum died in a car crash and their dad, poor sod, couldn't cope and had a nervous breakdown. The powers-that-be decided that they had no choice but to commit him to a secure mental health institution and so the kids had to go into the care system. For some reason that I can't fathom, even though I can't help thinking that the reason matters, really matters, the people in charge thought it was a good idea to uproot Darren and Louise, eight and fourteen at the time, from their home in Leicester, and ship 'em out to a long-term foster home way up here, in our neighbourhood.

'They chose Enid and Eric Leather and their farm in Harthill, and by all accounts and against all the odds, Darren took to the hard physical graft of farm life like he'd been born to it. He learned to drive the tractor and the Leathers paid for driving lessons and bought him an old car as soon as he turned seventeen. Mr and Mrs Leather were heartbroken when the whole murder thing exploded.'

A sudden wave of empathy hits and Bill takes my pause as his cue to report.

'According to the notes, ma'am, Albie Holroyd had a free run as a kid because his mum was always out screwing for pennies or comatose in their train wreck of a family home. He could do whatever the hell he wanted, whenever he wanted, and the likes of Abigail Hardcastle and Louise Bates were easy prey.' Suddenly, and out of nowhere, I'm overwhelmed by steam hot anger ... and I'm shouting.

'So, fifteen and permanently ready to shag a lamppost in a snowstorm, Gus and Albie are in amongst these green as grass little girls like shit off a shovel and nobody gives a bugger!' I can hear Granny, who I'm hearing a lot these days: *do you kiss your mother with that mouth?* ' 'Sorry, Bill,' I say, dripping contrition that I don't remotely feel, and then, 'not had my 'who needs bacon sausage fried egg fried bread and hot buttered toast,' grapefruit and muesli. Once I get myself outside of a sizeable amount of plant matter, I'll be a different woman.'

'Doesn't make you wrong though, boss,' says Bill who I can sense is grinning. 'Louise and Abi were medically examined, with parents' and foster parents' permission, and both were conclusively shown to have had underage sex with at least one male. Louise refused to name names and no forensics were available to prove identities, though Louise was clear that there was just the one, male that is, and that that male was NOT Holroyd or Gutowski.

'In interview, both Gutowski and Holroyd claimed to be scared of Darren who did admit to threatening them with a baseball bat when, late one night, he burst into Holroyd's house and marched the two girls out and into his banged-up Toyota Corolla before driving them back to the farm, where the Leathers allowed Abigail to stay for two nights until her parents came home from a weekend last minute break in Edinburgh. They grounded Louise. Abigail probably talked her way out of any kind of punishment.

'Three weeks after the baseball bat incident, Abigail came home from school to an empty house as usual, and even though she had no plans to go out, she changed out of her uniform and into a skimpy bare-belly-button outfit before caking on the makeup. Standard Abigail behaviour according to her dad. Then she went to the chippie where she had a season ticket and brought back chips and scraps which she consumed with half a bottle of tomato sauce, a river of vinegar, and a mountain of salt. All of which she washed down with a can of coke.

'Her parents came home from work, and she was still in the house, so they went to the pub. Leaving at closing time and collecting their own fish suppers, mum and dad were back home around midnight and went straight to bed without looking in on their only child. Abigail always sorted herself out in the mornings, so the parents didn't realise something was up until about 6.30 p.m. the next evening when they bothered to look to see if she was home from school.

'Six days later, a bloke out walking his dog found a shallow grave in a small copse near Chesterfield. Stomach contents showed no other food eaten after the chips, and so it was assumed that Abigail went out minutes after her parents did, and that she died that night. There was evidence of alcohol - vodka was her mum's tipple - and it was thought likely that Abi had gotten used to at least one nip most nights.'

'So, what did Darren say had happened? Did he confess?'

'Well, in a manner of speaking yes, ma'am,' says Bill, enigmatically. 'But, had the case been heard in court, his story might well have added up to manslaughter, not murder ... and he might even have got off.

'Darren said that he went to Abigail's house to apologise for the baseball bat incident and for getting her and Louise into trouble, and to make sure that she understood that Albie and Gus were dangerous and to be avoided. He said he wanted to warn Abigail's parents about the two older lads, but that the parents were at the pub, so instead he found himself suggesting that he and Abi go for a ride in his car. He said she went willingly and that they drove out towards Chesterfield because it was 'a nice run.'

'They spotted a kind of kid's playground that was deserted and stopped, and then they began larking about. Darren said that, 'just for fun,' he slung a towrope that he had in the back of his car over the cross-piece of the swings, and he said this was Abi's idea. When asked why he had a towrope, he said that it was an old car and 'breaking down was 'likely'. He also kept a foot-operated air pump permanently in his boot, 'just in case.'

'He claimed that Abigail wanted to loop the rope round her waist so she could spin and make herself dizzy, and somehow the rope got round her neck, and before either of them realised what was happening, it had strangled her. He said that he panicked and bundled Abigail's body and the rope into his boot, then he drove to a reasonably deserted area and buried her. He had a spade in his boot because 'spades are useful.' Traces of Abigail were found in Darren's boot, and on the towrope which was also in his boot, and the soil on the spade matched that at the copse.

'But the cause of death was not strangulation. Abi's spinal cord was broken between the second and third cervical vertebrae and death would have been instantaneous. And for this to

22

happen, her head would have had to snap forward with extreme force.

'The rope had a sturdy metal ring with a hinge fastening at both ends, and the CPS said that the two ends joined creating a big circle around the cross bar of the swing would mean that Abigail accidentally getting her neck caught, as Darren had described, was tremendously unlikely. And they said that, in any event, dropping with enough force to cause the injuries that she sustained was impossible.

'To break her neck as it had been broken, the rope must have been thrown over the crossbar and threaded back through the metal ring with the hinged clip closed forming a small circle around the crossbar. Then the other end would need to have been connected back to the rope with the other clip forming another small circle. This second circle would have to have been placed around Abigail's neck. Two small, closed loops at either end of a line of rope, one loop around the crossbar and the other placed so that the unyielding metal ring could flip to the back of the young girl's neck and snap it violently, and fatally, forward. Somebody needed to set the rope up how it needed to be, and by his own admission, Darren was the only other person there.

'But this is where things start to get better for Darren, and we get to manslaughter and not murder … and possibly, the lad proven guilty of burying the body but not of causing Abigail's death.'

Bill begins to outline exactly what I'm thinking.

'Lifting Abi up and putting her neck in the loop, the other end of which would have had to already be fastened to the cross-piece, is no mean feat, and would probably have needed her to be unconscious, or remarkably, many would say unbelievably, complicit. He might have been strong enough to do it even if she'd been struggling as opposed to being knocked out, but there were no injury marks suggesting either of these two scenarios. So, the smart money is on the CPS going for Abigail putting her head in the loop voluntarily. A daft lark between two daft kids who didn't think of the possible consequences. So, manslaughter and not murder.

'But setting the whole thing up would have taken ages and real effort, and surely, one or both kids would have had second thoughts and would have realised it was incredibly dangerous. Abigail never gave those around her any suicide concerns, and while Darren was a bit slow at school, he wasn't bloody stupid. It stinks, ma'am. It stinks.

'Police investigations were ongoing, and I'm not convinced that the CPS would have, in the end, pursued the charges against Darren.' Suddenly there's a sadness in Bill's voice. 'But the case never saw a courtroom.

'On remand and awaiting trial, Darren rubbed the handle of his toothbrush against a stone windowsill until the plastic was razorblade sharp. Then, after lights out, he used it to cut his wrists, and the poor lad on the bottom bunk woke covered in his cellmate's blood. They found a note which is in the file and available.

'Eric and Enid never forgave themselves, and despite farming in Harthill for thirty years, they sold up and moved to London where their other two, grown-up kids were living. And Darren's sister, Louise, began a downward spiral. Two kids dead and so many other lives ruined, the whole thing makes depressing reading, ma'am.'

'I'll collect any letters and probably take them away to read, Bill,' is all I can think to say before ... 'so, we're supposed to believe that the mild-mannered immature and unworldly teenage boy with a record of avoiding all things remotely violent, was horny for the eleven/twelve-year-old, self-opinionated, know-all young madam, and that the gregarious party girl who couldn't wait to be grown-up fancied the pants of this awkward lad and bore him no ill-will for interfering and spoiling her fun with the much more sophisticated Gus and Albie. And that, in the end, passion got the better of them both to the extent that, on their first date, they decided that traditional back of the car tit lifting was far too prosaic, and they instantly hit on dangling from a great height autoerotic asphyxiation as being just the thing.'

'That's about the size of it, boss,' says Bill.

'Bollocks.' Sorry Granny ... again. 'It didn't happen, Bill, and it's about time that we found out what did, why, and who else was involved.

'We're going to discover what Darren Bates was hiding and why he thought that killing himself was better than simply telling the truth because you're right, Bill, this stinks, and even after all this time, we'll find the answers if we follow the smell.'

8

Despite the early hour, his coffee is two hours cold, and even though he moved to this rented one-bedroom duplex a good three weeks ago, 95% of Stan's possessions are still in three medium sized boxes and one small suitcase. Holding the unopened letter that arrived yesterday morning between thumb and index finger of both hands, he's fully aware that he's down, and that he may already be out. And while he knows that sitting here all day is not an option and that he needs to stir himself, for the life of him, he can't. Why? Because he doesn't want to. That's the top and bottom of it: he just doesn't want to. Last night's decision to stay home today licking his wounds because he couldn't cope with work was designed to help him sleep. It didn't.

But pathetic behaviour does not define Stan and these kinds of shenanigans are not like him at all. He's a man of action, he attacks things head on, he's a man from whom people seek advice, a man whose relationships only end because he ends them! And screwing the letter into ball and throwing it with all the vigour he can muster, Stan can suddenly feel the blood coursing through his veins; and he's on his feet shouting, 'not me!'

A man with much to do, it's time that Stan Russell made a start.

*

Postage-stamp, lemon-yellow panties peak out from tight, blue jeans, and pert, shamelessly uncovered breasts are provocatively turned in his direction. Stephen 'Gus' Gutowski likes that she dresses upwards. Becca dressed top down, a source of irritation at the time. There is no doubting that Tammy knows instinctively what to do and how to be and he knows that she's perfect in so many ways … but she's not Becca.

Slinking her way up the bed on hands and knees, she straddles his legs, leans, and kisses him gently.

'I don't need to ask what you want for breakfast,' she whispers, but Gus can only stroke auburn hair away from her hazel eyes and sigh.

'A lot to do, love. Early start. A nine o'clock with Albie in Sheffield. We'll even have to go in separate cars. Sorry.'

Reluctantly easing her off him before quitting the enormous bed and leaving her rolled onto her back, hands stretched over her head and smiling, he stands for a moment, admiring. Skin like ever so lightly roasted almonds and long legs stretched wide apart, every inch of her looks flawless, is flawless. If only she was Becca.

*

Constant William George Russell is unrelenting in his claim to be working class. He is in fact the son of a prosperous London solicitor and he went to an expensive, if minor, public school where, lazy and disinterested, he somehow managed to get a place at the University of Sheffield to read, of all things, Mathematics.

So, the flying-buttress-nosed, fake-tanned, cockney jack-the-lad invaded Yorkshire's second city parading Native American, shoulder length, jet-black greasy hair; always red skin-tight corduroy jeans; a white polka dotted navy blue shirt with sleeves constantly up-turned no matter the weather and permanently unbuttoned to expose a hairless chest, and several heavy gold necklaces and countless multi-coloured string bracelets. The white with black stripes Adidas trainers gave a false impression of athleticism, and the cream sheepskin inside-out gilet labelled him odd but interesting, daft but dangerous, and different enough to be noticed wherever he went. He boasted, only partly in jest, that his thin lined Salvador Daly moustache was reconstructed daily 'using an eight-inch Bowie Knife,' and even his green with pale wood coachwork mini traveller seemed to be doing its best to mimic a South Carolina mustang. Stan's joint convictions, borne of exquisite first-hand evidence, that a good lie beats an obvious to an any sane person's truth, and that he is always the only person of significance in any room, meant that he was always destined to come out on top.

He was aware then, and he's aware now, that most would say his student appearance and behaviour were ridiculous, indeed back in the day many gave voice to that opinion, but twenty-year-old Stan Russell was a walking talking pulling machine, and he would have had to remain unwashed for months, suffer from terminal halitosis, and fart for England not to get laid anytime, anywhere, and with anyone he chose. His male peers got drunk, threw up, dreamed of women, and laughed at him: 'nice enough bloke for a southerner, knows his football but can't hold his beer, bit of a twat,' but he was the guy offering meaningless fornication before encountering the heavily mogulled black run that is marriage kids and grownup responsibility, and so it was Stan's wedding-tackle under constant assault from women of all shapes sizes ages and backgrounds, and others were left to look on and wish, and wonder why.

He thought that he was exploiting 'his girls' and that gave him perverse pleasure. Now, all these years later, he's finally starting to realise that they were exploiting him … and it is that thought that stands every chance of destroying everything that Stan holds dear.

His third class, pass degree qualified him for several career paths, but labouring on building sites left plenty of time to party and to use and abuse women, so, for the next eight years, Constant William George Russell mixed mortar and concrete and carried bricks. He saw no reason to tinker with a winning formula and getting older just meant that 'his girls' had to get younger, and then, pushing thirty, he met twenty-two-year-old Tamsin (Tammy) Alderson, and everything changed.

Tammy was already pursuing a profitable modelling career when, for the first time in his life, Stan decided that he might quite like an exclusive and committed relationship. The thought that he should move from his functional but soleless bedsit bolthole in favour of her comfortably furnished apartment followed quickly, and re-visioning his hair, clothes, and outlook on life seemed to happen in the blink of his previously jaundiced eye.

And then he had his Road to Damascus moment.

Stan concluded that he'd never really enjoyed his former debauched existence, and that this growing up lark should have happened years ago. So, when Tammy swept his past life into their new, only one in Rotherham and personally delivered by currier from Harrods chrome flip-topped designer disposal unit, he was more than pleased, he was relieved.

28

After several years of invisibility his bosses started to recognise his analytical capability - this coincided with his significant other beginning to pick Stan up after work - and within days he was riding a desk. He'd been fool enough to think that he was happy mixing mortar and toting a hod, and so, his ambition burgeoning, he now had no time to waste, and becoming a graduate late starter with a new profession career path and pension was the obvious next step. Now aged thirty-seven and after just a few years as a police officer, Stan Russell is a newly promoted police sergeant, a man of substance, the man that Tammy always said he was destined to be, and, ironically, the one man in the entire world that Tammy is certain that she no longer wants.

In a bad place but refusing to be weak, Stan won't allow himself to become the object of other people's - other men's - pity. He made rookie error after rookie error, and he should have known better … but the important thing is that he knows what he did wrong. Somehow, he developed an actual interest in what his girls had to say, and, God help him, he turned into respectful listener! And as a result, Tammy is the willing possession of a man who now really does have everything, and the decree absolute that he knows to be enclosed within the now scrunched envelope is confirmation that, for the moment, he has lost her.

But he's a free agent - he doesn't want to be, but he is - and he intends to feed like a lion drowning in antelope so that he'll be in the kind of womanising shape needed to get Tammy drooling again. And when she's back where she belongs, he'll rip the heart, lungs, and spleen from the slack belly of Tammy's new lover.

Sergeant Constant William George Russell strokes his stripes, smiles, and sets off for work. Stan the Man is back, and Tammy will soon return to him … and Stephen fucking Gutowski is a dead man walking.

9

First her handbag, then her scarf, and now her car keys, she's repeatedly locked and unlocked, turned the alarm on and turned the alarm off three times, and this time she's determined to push on to her car patiently waiting at the end of her garden path, no matter what. Her tiny front lawn looks like a neglected wasteland, the thought of spending her down-time gardening is sticking in her craw like an unexploded bomb, and she's just at the point where actual steam might burst forth, cartoon fashion, from both ears, when nice Mr Butterell doffs his trilby and begins wagging a long, thin, arthritically bony finger.

'In a hurry as usual, Sam. And I bet you haven't had a proper breakfast. Most important meal of the day, you know.'

In Charlie Butterell World, Sam would be on her way to the nice warm office she shares with the nice warm young man who'd given her two nice warm children, one of each. She would eat well because of the loving care provided by this wonderful human being, and, pursuant to her delicate young thing status, she would have a job that would never ever put her in any kind of physical danger.

'I'm not hungry at this time in a morning, Mr Butterell,' she says, causing thick as Amazon rain forest foliage eyebrows to raise high on an elderly forehead. 'I mean Charlie.' Calling a man older than her granddad by his first name doesn't sit right, but this lovely man who's quickly become her perfect next-door neighbour insists.

'Are you off to Rotherham Hospital … Charlie?' she asks, knowing already that he is.

'Those trolleys won't push themselves, Sam,' he beams. 'Trolly pushing is highly skilled work, you know. Us pushers are a bit like the doctors in that respect, well like consultants anyway. Needed a six-week course. Six weeks! You've got to study wheels: how many, where they're best placed, going forward, going back, corners, we had ten days on corners, and not killing patients had a mention, maybe two – mentions not patients. And you're looking at an operative who is adept at alignment, and alignment is advanced trolleying.'

They're generations apart but age seems to be trumped by a shared sense of humour, and even though she knows that she's already late, retired but sprightly Mr Butterell's deep and silky, warm spa voice is hypnotic, and Sam is suddenly disposed to linger. He fits her idea of Roald Dahl's Big Friendly Giant, and the effect is remarkably enthralling. More than once, she's thought of suggesting that she scissor the white bushy eyebrows and silver side-hair that's too long too thick and too straggly. But Mr Butterell is Mr Butterell, and wanting to change him is even more unthinkable than routinely calling him Charlie.

Most mornings Sam sees him oozing vitality from every pore and loping off to work with the small red backpack that inevitably will be carrying a beaten-up old flask and the same polythene box overflowing with his corn beef on white, and he pulls at her heartstrings every time. After a lifetime delivering other people's letters and parcels - backpack red is no random choice - Mr Butterell's energy, though something to behold, is just one of the qualities possessed by the rangy old man with the long nose and flappy ears, and the characteristic that Sam most admires in Mr |Butterell's is his resilience. She can't imagine having to cope with the shock of losing his wife Ronnie, let alone doing so without self-pity, and whilst building, with no other family to lend support, a new life miles away from everything he held dear. As far as Sam is concerned, Charlie Butterell has the art of living all figured out, and working so hard for so many hours just for his expenses at his time of life is a measure of the adorable old man.

Finally reaching her car and giving Charlie a farewell wave, she sits in and turns on the ignition … and is immediately confronted by a flashing, engine light. Just one more thing to fix that has no right to need fixing, and not for the first time, Sam thinks that to live in Charlie Butterell World would be no bad thing, no bad thing at all.

*

The car park at Main Street Police Station is full to bursting and, attempting to squeeze her mini into a left-over space not remotely designed for that purpose, Sam is blaming herself for

31

arriving after the 'legal' spots have all been taken. And then her embarrassment skyrockets as, just her luck, she spies Sergeant Russell striding towards her car. He stands and watches but doesn't help as she does way more shuffling than remotely necessary and, balancing the double jeopardy of a cock-eyed car placement versus a full fifteen minutes more of manoeuvring, eventually Sam settles for what she considers the best of a very bad job and yanks on her hand-break. Gracelessly clambering out, she clicks on central locking, turns, straightens ... and finds herself looking up with difficulty at her unexpectedly up close and personal sergeant. All she can do is say 'good morning' and attempt a smile before his Dean Martin sleepy-eyed facial expression suggests incoming jokey banter and she begins to relax. Suddenly, her hand is subjected to a cobra-like strike and placed in a tourniquet grip and Russell pub-lothario-whispers, his lips touching her ear,

'Careful, Sam, can't have anything upsetting our best girl.'

'Sam!' She turns instinctively in the direction of DC Colin McNamara's shout, and when she turns back, her sergeant is already disappearing through the police station doors. Trotting over and talking breathlessly all the way, Colin is bursting to tell.

'Had a bloody marvellous weekend, Sam. Went to Brighouse. The cold weather was to be expected, but no rain and the sun was shining and that's all we needed. Took the Royal Scot. Ran like a dream. Loads of kids asking for rides. Couldn't have been better.'

With no apparent need for anyone else to be listening, the model steam train enthusiast talk continues - fixed the clack, light on its feet, meaty chuff - until he finally realises that his friend and colleague is preoccupied and unusually quiet. And when he does, Colin immediately looks towards the police station doors, and Sam thinks, makes a link with Sergeant Russell. But the young DC changes the subject and enquires after Sam's day off and she loosens a little, though even then, her replies are perfunctory at best. The two soon settle into a comfortable trusting silence as they walk into and through the station building.

My immediate superior, who is very married, who I like, and who I work well with, has made an inappropriate and offensive

sexual advance.' The thought is searing Sam's brain and she's starting to panic. Then collective colleague laughter about Colin and his trains, and talk of the DCI's eye and Stenton Cornthwaite, break the spell and she begins to question: has Sergeant Russell really done a bad thing? Was it just a daft, blokey joke? Has everything changed or am I reading it all wrong?

10

Albie Holroyd's six-foot-six-inch elongated heavy with the giant shiny black shaved head big nose cantilevered forehead and craggy face is as incongruous as a hippo in a chicken coop. One eye focussed on his newspaper and one across the room on his boss, taking up space when standing but barely able to secure one tenth of one arse cheek on a woefully inadequate teeny-tiny chair, Marvin is well used to having no reason to be there other than being there. So, for fun and to pass time, he fabricates the occasional hostile glare.

He finds that he doesn't mind being a paid enforcer whose primary function is to scare the begazes out of folk, or having to always be ready to prove that he can hurt just as much as he looks as though he can hurt, but over their many years together, he's grown to detest Albie's motionless dullard staring at life passing him by and making other people feel uncomfortable shtick, and from that he has developed a deep hatred of Holroyd himself. He must watch him, that's the job, but not being able to stand the sight of him has become a problem. The monk-like bald patches that elbow their way into view from under the bloody ever-present fedora irritate Marvin more than they should, and he's sickened - amazingly there is no more apposite word - by the wizened little body that seems incapable of fully occupying its adult male casing. Skin that Marvin remembers, just, as once being cashmere smooth, now stockpiles at the neck and folds and sags at the jowls, and Marvin is increasingly repelled by the grotesque vision that he's paid to preserve and protect. But the kicker is that what nauseates most is that he, big strong tough Marvin, never even thinks about leaving the employ of the despot that he despises. Institutionalised for the rest of his life and aware of it, Marvin is doomed to be wherever and to do whatever Holroyd chooses, and it's the big man's own fault.

There was a time, before he perfected the persona, that Holroyd wasn't so omnipotent, and in the beginning, he depended on Gus Gutowski's car money to pay for the drugs that were later sold on at a four hundred percent profit. Pimping the addicts that were now prepared to do anything for their next fix then doubled and trebled his assets and it was Holroyd, not Gutowski, who soon had his own private army permanently mobilised and ready to do as instructed at a moment's notice. Since then, Albie has sailed close to the wind and ridden his luck, and, crucially, worked hard to ensure that all links to wrongdoing are well hidden, and so these days, Marvin's brand of gentle persuasion is rarely required. A booming voice suddenly fills the tiny Crusty Cob café and Marvin eases back his poor excuse for a chair.

'I'll have a black coffee and croissant like my friend here, love. Make my croissant almond, please darling, and I'll have it warm.'

Shining in his sharp pewter grey three-piece herringbone suit and sporting solid silver union jack cufflinks and a peacock blue waistcoat with pocketed gold watch and heavy gold fob, Gus Gutowski is waving manicured big girl hands and, as always, he's trying to look like an important time-is-money man. But Marvin sees a fop that he's never taken to trying to compete with a loose eyed and unblinking lizard who's recharging in the sun but ready to strike. The big enforcer knows what's coming and he folds his Daily Star and waits.

His 'how do, matey' eliciting no reply, Gutowski sits noisily across from Holroyd and after just a few seconds of inactivity he moves the fake rose in its tiny 50p from the market vase from the table between them and onto the floor. A further minute passes before he picks up and scrutinises the stained and out-of-date menu and puts it alongside the vase. Then, he stretched flat hands on the easy to clean linoleum tablecloth and, using a breaststroke action, he sweeps the cloth three times. Finally, he sits back and exhales loudly and Marvin smiles. 'Pecking order emphasised.' He loathes him and everything he stands for, but Holroyd is 'The Man,' and a master at work is a master at work.

A full five minutes of silence later, high-pitched, and girlish, Holroyd speaks.

'We need to talk about Veronique.'

'Game on,' thinks Marvin, *'game on.'*

*

Bouncing through life, Stephen 'Gus' Gutowski does everything at pace. He tells anybody prepared to listen that compromise and settling for second best are for the feeble minded, and that even as a young boy he'd decided that he would rather starve than routinely take orders from anyone ... except Albie Holroyd.

Too hefty to facilitate quick feet, good in the air but too slow on the ground and with an even slower turn, no matter how dedicated and committed, he was never going to make money from professional football, and the taste of that first failure has stayed with him. After football came a well-devised and comprehensive business plan developed from his idea to import and sell vintage cars. He recognised that high unit costs needed financial backing, that the product must fly quickly out of a flash and expensively put together showroom, and that cash flow was going to be an issue from the get-go. Nonetheless, he had every reason to feel that the selling of these cars to its niche market would prove a goldmine, that investors would recognise potential when they saw it, and that they would be queuing to give him money. But, after months of ultimately pointless work, the realisation that no financier was ever going to stump up for an untested, very young man, hit like a wrecking ball. It was fiasco number two, and he should have known better ... Albie would have known better.

Suited and moneyed older heads had discouraged his energy and enterprise, and crime was to be a temporary measure to get much needed funding. Once he had the readies, he would revisit the vintage cars and show them all what fools they had been. But dangerous living and the possibility of being caught turned out to be ridiculously exciting to a testosterone fuelled young man *(who'd have thought)* and it soon became the only fix that made Gus' adrenalin pump. The means to an end had morphed into a career path without him realising it and, temporarily, he was able to fund Albie's nefarious schemes instead of his own lawful one. The cash rolled in and there would be plenty of time later to launch his vintage cars business, and then one day, preoccupied by a need to get on a sure thing at the bookies before it was too late, he carelessly opened the blood-orange door of his illicitly parked and financed to the hilt classic Ferrari across the square-metre of pavement occupied by Becca Thompson, heir to Thompson Transport. Dumping a sophisticated woman on her neat posterior and sending her parcels flying is an event that no one plans for, and the horse came in at 25 to 1 but went unbacked. Instead, he took the time to make it up to Becca, and suddenly, just like that, he had reason to grow up, sober up, and to operate within the law.

Albie is talking again.

'Anthony has become a liability. He punched Veronique. Veronique, Gus! Could have killed her ... but he didn't. Instead, she's in hospital and having operations on her face. Damaged but not dead. Police'll be sniffin'.'

Top lip pulled back in a parody of Humphrey Bogart, hoodlum accent attempted but nowhere near achieved, interminable time taken to say anything, and the inept jinking of a 2p coin across the fingers of his right hand, index to pinkie, and back again, everything about Albie Holroyd is preposterous but somehow chilling. Highly tailored navy-blue double-breasted suit with red pocket square, shiny black shoes with tan spats, red tie and sparkling white shirt, light grey fedora with a red band, and a wooden toothpick in his mouth and worked hard, the effect could not have been more idiotic. But Gus is terrified and has been since he was fifteen ... since Abigail Hardcastle.

The hat raises agonisingly slowly, and Albie's eyes ascend into view. 'Veronique knows everything, and she can damage. Cut him loose, Gus. If you're not man enough to control your brother, then I will.'

It's an order. The first one in over twenty years that Stephen Gutowski knows he cannot and will not obey.

11

I knew fine well that Sam was trying to deflect her boss' interest in the mystery Costa Coffee woman, and that she chose to bang on about her neighbour, Charlie Butterell, because he was as good a diversion topic as any. However, my desire to know had been roused, and me being a detective of sorts, I've already found out that the coffee lady almost certainly lives in Thurcroft, went to school with Sam, and was, perhaps still is, more than a tad notorious. I've given myself forty-eight hours to come up with a name, and, as it turns out, talk of Charlie Butterell has sparked what I think is a bloody good idea.

Ringing Sam whilst on my way to interview a hospitalised assault victim, I've suggested that she and I tag team the patient and that she meets me at Rotherham General. I could do this on my own, but it will be good experience for Sam, and I like working with young bobbies. Makes me feel young and that's a sensation I'm craving more and more. But, truth be told, my cunning plan of engineering an accidental on purpose bumping into Charlie who works there as a porter so I can run my eyes over the old man ... so to speak, is the real reason for dragging the poor lass into the impossibly overcrowded excuse for a car park, and, ever the optimist, I'm not so quietly confident that it'll prove to be a master stroke. We're just entering the foyer of the hospital when, despite the noise from yet another Costa, this time situated in the hospital entrance area, and the comings and goings of patients' visitors' and staff, we hear what has all the makings of a music hall double act.

'The fellah says, "doctor I'm very upset because I woke up this morning with a strawberry growing out of my forehead." And the doctor says: "Not to worry. I've got some cream for that."' Charlie Butterell is twenty-five yards away and pushing a wheelchair whose occupant, who we subsequently learn is called Janice, is obviously in pain and desperate not to laugh. And even from this distance, I already have an even warmer feeling that my long shot will come good. Charlie's lively patter is still in full flow.

38

'How do you know when an elephant's been trapped in your fridge?'

'Footprints in the butter!' I yell. 'Now leave that poor woman alone before she has a relapse.' Charlie turns towards the voice and Janice works herself into a position to see. Spotting Sam, the old man shouts,

'Sam! How lovely!' Then he leans conspiratorially over his patient and stage whispers, 'girlfriend, Janice. Can't keep away. Body like mine, who can blame her?'

'Can't you do something with him, love?' laughs Janice. 'He has us in stitches, and I've got twenty-six of them buggers already!'

'Well, I am a police officer,' says Sam, 'so I suppose I could arrest him. But then I'd have to pay for my own telly license. I'd lose the fuel allowance and bus pass, not to mention life membership down the bingo. I'd be on my own at the beetle-drives and …'

'You're as bad as him!' shouts Janice, laughing even more. Then, spotting Quasimodo's Hump where my Angelina Jolie peeper once held sway, and pointing at his own eye in the way I'm finding to be universally accepted practice, Charlie twinkles,

'Much bigger and that'll be having kids and selling its story to the BBC.' I can sense a punchline, we all can. 'Badass Bruise Corporation!' A collective sigh and a 'bless him' giggle follows as Charlie Butterell laughs himself silly.

*

Walking and wheeling along cleaned to the brink of extinction corridors, the four of us chat comfortably, and by the time we part, I've already arranged for Charlie to pop round to Sam's place after work 'for a gossip,' and Janice has succumbed to a well-earned doze.

Enjoying the visit is a nice surprise and I can tell it is for Sam, but once inside the closed double-doors and standing alongside Ward A22's ubiquitous hand gel dispenser suddenly it's a proper hospital, and that 'I'd rather be anywhere but here' sensation begins to overwhelm. Then I spy a spread-legged snow-haired uniformed officer called Malcolm 'Chalky' White and, as always happens when Chalky is around, I feel comfortable relaxed and 'at home.'

Me and Chalky go back a long way, in fact to the beginning when we were trainees together. My age but never seen in a jacket even when conditions are arctic, Chalky still sees short sleeved shirts as his most effective bit of kit, and it's generally accepted down at the station that after just one glance at his biceps, Johnny Criminal does still tend to confess remarkably quickly and incredibly often. Standing next to the mountainous copper, Sam, who went ahead while I was sanitising, looks like Tomasina Thumb trying and failing to get Hulk Hogan's attention,

'So, what's the craic, Chalky?' I shout from fifteen yards away,

'Bloody 'ell! Which gorilla did you piss off?' Chalky never did have much time for rank and seniority.

'Long story, Chalky. Wrong place, wrong time.'

'Well, if it's any consolation, this lass,' he left-hand thumbs in a North Easterly direction, 'makes even your face look good, and believe me that takes some doin'.' He chuckles before making a big thing of remembering to say 'ma'am.' Hands on hips that I contend are more curvaceous than childbearing, I wait until, good copper that he is, Chalky goes into report mode.

'Half-starved woman with face bashed in found wandering in vest and pants on Mafeking Street in Brinsworth. Traffic Warden, Beth Nixon, the first to clock her and be public spirited enough to do something about it, sat her down and called for an ambulance. Concussion and a couple of teeth loose or lost, fractured cheekbone and eye socket, badly bruised jaw, plastic surgeons'll work on her later today. All she'll say is that she doesn't want any trouble. Her name's Veronique Sabet - French I'm guessing - and she says she walked into a door. We need to find that fuckin' door and arrest it! Doctor says she's been assaulted, no shit, Sherlock. They've sedated her and she's a bit dozy, but they say you can have a word if you don't push too hard. Can I go now?'

'Got a hot date have you, Chalky?'

'Yeah, right. Everybody's a smart arse,' grins Chalky as, on the hunt for some proper police work, he takes a series of very long strides and is soon through the double doors and away.

Turning and walking the short distance to the state of the art but thoroughly uncomfortable looking computer-designed bed, I confront an image that makes my car crash of a face look fabulously beautiful. Tracing paper skin struggling to confine brittle bones that wouldn't look out of place on the corpse of a ninety-year-old, the realisation that the woman in the bed is someone about my age hits hard, and unless the afore-mentioned door was masquerading as a steel toe-capped boot, or a two by four piece of timber, or a very big fist viciously swung, these injuries were not self-inflicted.

'What bastard did this?' I ask - honest if not tactful – provoking a tired flicker of the patient's lids. Then, like sapphires in soot, her revealed eyes are gateways to a world of pain, and, even though she's sedated, I can sense that this woman is not angry or despairing, she's relieved.

Veronique gestures that she's thirsty and points towards her bedside table, and, eager to help, Sam rushes to pour water from a plastic jug to a plastic cup before holding it against dry and flaking lips. The act of drinking is clearly painful, and Sam waits for the injured woman to settle before she says:

'My name's Samantha Jardine and I'm a police officer. I'm sorry, but I need to ask some questions.' Again, the flutter of eyelids and Sam hesitates before asking, 'can you tell me your name?' The question isn't ignored, but time and effort seem to be required to work words into a coherent pattern. The response when it finally comes is French accented.

'Veronique. Veronique Sabet.'

'Thank you, Ms Sabet,' says Sam. 'May I call you Veronique?' The slight nod causes all three of us to wince. 'Well, I have to say, Veronique, this wasn't done by a door.' Veronique manages a grin.

'You two are ... not as ... dumb ... as you look.' The response breaks the tension, and, trying to grin, she continues, 'I'm sticking ... with the door story. I ... know it's a ... a lot to ask, but I need to get ... where I can never be ... found before I can say anything.' Veronique is clearly determined to do what she thinks is best for her own safety, and knowing how scared she must be, I keep my response short and to the point: 'we'll make some calls.' Then, squeezing past Sam and the morphine drip, and leaning over the bedridden woman, I add 'it shouldn't take more than an hour or two to get you a place that's secure and secret.' We exchanged smiles and I say, as if to a good and long-standing friend,

'You'll have noticed that Sam here, poor lass, is in desperate need of as much beauty sleep as she can get.' Veronique and Sam look surprised and not a little puzzled. 'So, I'm thinking that I should send her home, what do you think? Then, when she's not here to hold us back, you and me can go clubbing. With our looks, I reckon we'll pull.'

12

No more than an hour back in the office after her hospital visit, Samantha Jardine has already written and filed her report, set up a place for Veronique Sabet in a vulnerable women's hostel, and, on a roll, given a good deal of thought to a spate of recent burglaries in of Rotherham's Dinnington/North Anston area. One of those top mornings where everything comes up trumps, she places on Sergeant Russell's desk written notes linking the MO of the Dinnington burglaries to that of known drug addict and prolific criminal called Robert Bartholomew who she's nicked many times and she's feeling good about herself. Noticing that Bartholomew is out of prison early on license and that he's been at large for at least three months, Sam suspects he will be as drug dependent as ever, and comparing his availability with the burglaries, the dates fit. It feels like a breakthrough.

The next job is to watch a downloaded video labelled 'Stenton Cornthwaite' and sent to her email address from the school where Michael Lloyd is headteacher. She suspects that the Boss will have told Michael all about the incident behind the shops in Wickersley and he's obviously decided that some of his Stenton information needs to have a wider audience.

Filmed on a mobile phone then placed on social media and shared what seems to be hundreds of times, she sees kids of all ages shapes and sizes gathered in a field. No adults or buildings are in sight, but she can just make out a goal post, and judging by the absence of any school uniforms, Sam guesses it to be a Saturday or Sunday, perhaps even school holidays. A circle begins to form and, egged on by the jeering crowd, two fourteen or fifteen-year-old girls are pushed to the centre where they square up and get into it, one girl immediately getting the upper hand. The other girl's heart isn't in it from the off and, clearly desperate to get the preordained beating over and done with as quickly as possible, she does little more than cover up. Hair viciously pulled, head yanked left and right and up and down, dragged through the dirt, three or four stamps viciously administered, the 'winner' struts away and into the crowd and the loser is left sitting straight legged and dazed, and checking her nose and mouth for blood. Sam understands from personal experience that the poor girl had no choice but to turn up, and that back at school she will be laughed at, called names, jostled, pushed around, and required to carry out the victor's bidding as and when instructed ... but she won't be ostracised, and she will still have a place. On the periphery perhaps, but a place, nevertheless. Belonging is all that matters, and she will believe that she belongs, even though she doesn't.

After making progress on several fronts, Sam was on a high, but suddenly depressed, even fatalistic, she can sense that there's more to come. Another collective wave of anticipation gathers amongst the children whose significant adults are conspicuously absent, and then, to Sam's absolute horror, the architect of her boss' facial disfigurement is suddenly on her screen and centre stage. This must be a recent recording because Stenton Cornthwaite looks the age that he looks now, and as she watches the diminutive idiot shape up for a bareknuckle battle with a much bigger and clearly older boy, Sam's heart is in her throat.

It soon becomes obvious that kicking and hair pulling are clearly things that only girls do and that this will be a more organised and tactical affair. Their hands shoot up, Georgian pugilist fashion, and several over-stylised punches are quickly thrown and easily dodged. The taller boy is leaning back and protecting his face as he swings, Cornthwaite is lunging, intent on inflicting damage, unconcerned about taking a hit himself. Almost immediately, Sam notices that the older boy is cut; and not just once. Three, no four, what look like shallow stab wounds have appeared on his face and blood is streaming down and onto his shirt. A girl screams: 'Stenton's gorra knife!' and the crowd moves in to separate the two boys. And Sam hears the boy filming say, 'fuckin' 'ell! Stenton's barmy.'

An attached note to Sam from Sue Thackery - one of Michael's pastoral team - says that they'd interviewed every schoolboy or schoolgirl that they could recognise from the video, and that they've told their parents all of whom had no idea what had been going on. She also says that the staff at the children's home searched Stenton's room while he was out at school, and that they found and confiscated a short blade set at a right angle

44

to a small wooden handle and designed to protrude between fingers curled into a fist. Every time Stenton punched or even brushed his opponent's flesh, a cut would ensue. Remarkably, Sue's note also says that the injured bigger boy is nearly eighteen, left school over a year before, and is now working as an apprenticed plumber. And that, even though he could have been blinded, his parents don't want the matter pursued and won't press charges.

Suddenly Stenton's future trajectory is hammer-drilling inside Sam's head. *He thinks he'll live forever, uses weapons without a second thought, routinely causes criminal damage, breaks into places, ignores his curfew, gets into fights, stabs people, and the law seems to be telling him that, whatever he does, there will be no consequences. He'll be dead or locked up for life before he's twenty!*

'What you up to?' Sergeant Russell is behind Sam, his hands on her shoulders, and she never saw or heard him coming. His cheek touching hers, he's gazing at her laptop. 'An organised set-to, eh?' He leans further in, 'just kids,' he says dismissively. 'While they're knockin' seven shades out of each o'ver, they're not boverin' us. Leave 'em to it, we've go' better fings to be doin'.' Moving around to Sam's side, easing one buttock onto her desk and looking down on her like a praying mantis his leg touching hers, her only thought is that his white socks look ridiculous.

'One of the two boys fighting is Stenton Cornthwaite, sarge,' she says finding it hard to look him in the eye. 'He's the one who damaged the DCI's face. I thought I'd just pop round to the children's home and have a word.'

'Nooooh!' he rails in mock horror. ''e might do the same to you!' Russell is loud, his arms are flailing, and she's convinced that every colleague in the room is staring. ''armin' that gorgeous face would deserve the death penal-y,' says Russell, and, before Sam can react, he has her face in both hands and she can feel the warm moisture of his breath, and smell the peppermint. 'Blue green and set in twenty-four carat white gold,' he grins. 'I'm an expert in female anatomy, Samanfa. And trust me, I'm … not … a doctor.'

Releasing his grip as suddenly as it had been applied, he self-satisfied swaggers from her desk towards his own and Sam is left in shock. Taking a moment to compose herself before standing and making her halting way to the door that leads to the freedom of a familiar and permanently noisy corridor, which, though busy as always, somehow today seems quiet and unpleasantly confining. Clearing the corridor and stepping into the bright but chilling outside air, she's affronted and humiliated ... and she's also frightened, and that makes her very angry.

My married sergeant is hitting on me, and it will only get worse.

She knows that she must do something, but what? Every possible course of action casts her as a weak and unable to cope victim and she can already hear Russell's responses.

'Sam fought I was coming on to 'er. Surely not. I was just larkin' abart. 'avin' a larf wiv a colleague. If I've done anyfin' to upset 'er, I'm mortified. I'll apologise, course I will.'

They'll call her po-faced. Can't take a joke. Not a team player. They'll feel sorry for Russell, and they won't want to work with Jardine. Imagining everything and certain of nothing, she knows that until she decides what if anything to do, she must tell no-one ... absolutely no-one.

13

In her mid-forties, carrying too many - thankfully evenly spread - pounds, and dressed like a pensioner who's ceased to care what anybody else thinks, Dean House Children's Home camp commandant, Jess Simcox, is utterly focussed on helping and protecting the children in her care. She may have long been a stranger to make-up let alone the beauty parlour, but she has a face made pretty by optimism and Jess is easy to like. If I can't cheer up down in the dumps Samantha, then Jess will, and she's been forewarned about the reason for our visit.

'I know that he can be a little shit,' says Jess, 'but you've met his mother.' I have indeed spent time with the not so lovely Kylie Cornthwaite and, enough said, Jess is spot on. Deciding to be cheeky, I ask if Jess is aware of whether Stenton is 'in' or not. The housemother's eye roll and shrug are, I think accurately, translatable as 'fuck knows,' and she goes on to explain that the school rang this morning to say that he was with them at the time of the call. And that that means he should have arrived back at the care home by now. However, if he's bunked off early because he's decided that today feels like a good day to create havoc in Rotherham Town Centre, then there's bugger all that Jess or anybody could have done to stop him, and Julie and Sam will have had a wasted journey.

'I've not actually seen him,' says Jess, 'but, if he is in, I'll need to ask if he's willing for you to go up.'

'His permission? We need Stenton's permission?' All part of the expected banter and Jess' grin is an indication that she's aware of what I really think.

'I know, I know,' she says. 'But it's his room, his space, and this is his home. It matters, Julie, as you know very well. If it helps, I think on this occasion I can waive the need for a responsible adult, me, to be present throughout.'

Leave for us to speak with Stenton, who is in, taking Jess just a couple of minutes to secure, two police officers are soon knocking and politely waiting for a spoken invitation to enter the little scrote's inner sanctum. His come in, Miss, sounds eager,

47

and we step inside to find the telly blasting, remote control owned and vice-like gripped, and the five-foot-two-inch cherub in jogging bottoms and t-shirt and lounging on his bed; and my immediate thought is 'pre-John Rosie!' Then, walking over to sit on his armchair - the only other item of furniture apart from a small and unused desk and desk chair - I look around at a basic but clean and comfortable room, and my spirits lift ... a little.

As Sam forgoes the desk chair and perches on the bottom of Stenton's bed, the lad switches off the TV of his own volition and sits up straight. Then, head down, he says,

'I'm sorry, Miss. I didn't mean to hurt you.' My response sounds singsong, as if to a toddler, even to me.

'If you lash out, Stenton, somebody will get hurt. Stands to reason.'

'But I wouldn't hurt a girl, Miss,' he insists, 'I wouldn't hurt you. You've been good to me you have, Miss. You Miss, and you Miss, and Miss Simcox.' He raises his head, his fluorescent eyes startling, and the close-up view of my wound suddenly seems to hit him much harder than anything he inflicted on me. He's genuinely appalled. 'Oh Miss, did I do that? I didn't know who it was. I didn't know it was you.'

'Do you think you owe me a favour, Stenton?' I ask, 'because I do.' Suddenly suspicious, he opts for silence. I start to press, 'you say that you're sorry, but I'm the injured party here and you need to make things right. You can't take back your attack on me and make me not hurt, so it makes sense that you have to compensate me in some other way. That means that you must do something for me to even things out. What do you say?' Still not sure where this is going, Stenton makes no comment. 'Are you sorry?' I ask.

'I am, Miss. I'm sorry. Really, really, really, sorry.'

'Would you like to try to put at least some of it right?' Stenton's contrition stops short of dropping himself in it, but he squeezes out a 'yes'.

'Do you trust me, Stenton?' There can be only one answer.

'Yes, Miss. I trust you more than anybody,' he says, and he means it.

'OK then. I've got somebody I'd like you to meet.'

14

Sam and her DCI met at the children's home, and they arrive back at Main Street's car park in their separate cars at roughly the same time. Sam makes a detour to the toilet and so arrives in the shared work area after Julie, who she immediately spots talking with Sergeant Pridding. Clearly delighted with the meeting and with Stenton, the boss gives Sam a wave and a smile … and Sergeant Russell's booming reproof carries to all four corners of the busy room: 'Good of you to turn up, DC Jardine!' and hits like a two-ton buffalo. Sergeant Pridding and the DCI look almost as shocked as she is.

Intimidated into feeling that she has no time to hang up her coat, she throws it instead onto the back of her chair before diving headlong into the deep pile of paperwork covering her desk. A folded and steepled sheet of A4, like her name in black marker pen, is hard to miss. She opens it and the words 'Looking Good' strike like a pissed off cobra. Her eyes shoot recklessly and without her authorisation to the desk of her sergeant who, chair turned half-facing her and half not, legs spread wide and wet grinning, is hesitantly touching his desk and pulling his hand away as if burned before shaking his fingers and mouthing 'hot.' It ought to be comical, not to be taken seriously; but it's not funny, not funny at all.

It's a good hour before she feels able to look up from her work let alone speak, and even then, her vocabulary only extends to a thank you when Colin brings a hot drink and gives her a 'when you're ready to talk I'm ready to listen,' look. Sinking deeper and deeper into files, reading page after page and remembering none of it, and feeling even worse because her friends and work colleagues are noticing her private dilemma, she's in a panic because this whole thing is spiralling out of her control and threatening to go public when she not remotely ready. Then, as suddenly as she appeared at Costa Coffee, Detective Chief Inspector Marsden is standing over her and looking concerned.

Colin is worried, no doubt Sergeant Pridding is worried, and now her DCI is worried. Sam has become the object of other people's pity and it's all too much, too much for her to bear.

*

'Long time no see, Police Constable Jardine.' Predictable and not remotely amusing, but I'm wearing the warm and friendly smile that has stood me in good stead for many a year and I'm hopeful that it'll do the trick. Sergeant Russell is out of order, and later, in private, I'll tell him so, but this counts as the normal toing and froing of a busy workplace and Sam needs to develop a thicker skin. I know from personal experience that, in the long run, the odd set-to with a testosterone tosser will help not harm, and Russell is just another daft bloke trying to run a tight ship and overdoing it. It'll be a steep learning curve for them both. Suddenly, Sam's on her feet and her coat-weighted-chair is tumbling backwards and clattering to the floor. 'Sorry, ma'am, got to go.' Hands pressed firmly against gathering vomit, she pushes past, and I have no option but to follow.

Hunched over one of the five sinks in the thankfully empty women's toilet, the cold tap gushing and spilling on to the floor, she's turned away, but the tear-stained eyeliner-streaked snotty and splashed face is still visible in the mirror. And upon further observation, I can tell that this turmoil must be caused by something way more worrisome than I originally thought. Sam is clearly not just extremely distressed, she's tearing the heads off new-born-chicks with her teeth, livid.

'Can I help, Sam?' I ask, aware that I mustn't rush or push. 'Is it work?' It's a reasonable question and, after a long silence and still facing the mirror, Sam un-locks a little.

'It is work, ma'am,' she says, her voice flat. 'Kind of. But it's something that I've got to figure out for myself.' Sam turns. 'It's not the job.' I can tell that, to Sam, the most important thing is that I know it's not the job. 'I really enjoy every bit of the job. And it's not my love life, I haven't got one.' We both grin: nervous, brief, and not with gay abandon, but a step in the right direction. 'I'm bloody furious,' she says, 'and I need somewhere for this rage to go.'

I wait for the big reveal but Sam volunteers no more information, and the pause long past pregnant, I decide that I have no option but to take charge.

'Well let's get you cleaned up and back at your desk. You'll have to run the gauntlet, but the women will be empathising their hearts out, and the fellas will assume it's your time of the month and be too scared to ask. It's a good job that men are so full of shit or up and coming young females like you and me would be stuffed.'

I know from personal experience that after a very public embarrassment, entering a familiar room full of long-time work colleagues is like anaesthetic-free root canal treatment performed by a three-year-old with attitude, but I think Sam pulls it off. And good old Colin not only brings two more cups of strong tea, but applies the biscuit rank protocol: Rich Tea - constable; Malted Milk - sergeant; Milk Chocolate Hob Nobs - inspector and above; Plain Chocolate Hob Nobs - inspector and above that you don't rate; if in doubt and/or civilians - custard creams. So, Rich Tea is replaced by Milk Chocolate Hob Nobs, and it should be plain sailing from here on in. Sergeant Russell is looking concerned about his young constable - another good sign.

After sufficient time has elapsed, I ask if Sam would like to walk with me out to Izzy to pick up some notes that I've left on the passenger seat. We both know that it's a tactic, and as we walk, I say,

'You know Sam, you could do worse than run your problem past your sergeant. That's what he's there for.' The young DC looks aghast, and despite wondering if I've said the wrong thing, I feel the need to press my case. 'Why not?' I ask. 'Oh, I know that he ballsed up just now. But I reckon that he has your best interests at heart and he's a smart cookie. He was telling me about those Dinnington burglaries that have been worrying us and I think he's come up with what looks like a winner.' Sam is still shocked but looks more interested, and I sense progress. 'Apparently, Bobby Bartholomew is out.' Sam is now astounded. 'I know!' I say, 'released on good behaviour. Good behaviour! Can you believe it? It's only minutes since we nicked him and sent him down. I would have assumed that he was still banged up had it not been for your sergeant. Stan Russell not only noticed the release date in the bulletin, but he also put Bobby Bartholomew in the frame for the Dinnington break-ins. It's Bobby's MO, and as Stan Russell pointed out, he's bound to be still using so he'll really need the dough. Takes nouse to put all that together, Sam. Your sergeant will go far.'

Sam has stopped walking. She's stiff as a board and now breathing like a severe asthmatic mid attack. She looks ready to faint ... and a blindfold is suddenly ripped from my temporarily incompatible eyes.

There's a link between Sam's problem and Sergeant Stan Russell!

Does he know what her problem is? Is Sam upset that he knows?

Then it hits.

Sergeant Russell IS the problem. Now there's a thought.

15

Home at least a couple of hours and yet to take off her coat let alone slough off the day's hypertension, Sam is pleased to see her neighbour despite not because of the promise she'd made to Julie. Still in his hospital porter gear, Mr Butterell must have seen the note pinned to his door and come straight round. He's on good form.

'So, favourite police officer, what can this sad and lonely old man do to lighten your load?'

'Come in, Mr … come in, Charlie. Good of you to pop round. I've not been home long myself.' A white lie, but easier than explaining what a bloody awful shift she's had. A 'nice cup of tea' is offered and accepted, and Charlie settles into Sam's small but cosy front room.

'Same layout as mine, Sam. Much more tastefully done, of course. A woman's touch is a wonderful thing.'

Charlie could perk up a corpse. But by the time she's prepared the refreshments and is standing, tea tray in hand, in the front room doorway, she's ridiculously nervous and certain that her DCI's idea is a very bad one. And Charlie's big wet brown trusting eyes aren't helping.

'It's a favour,' Sam declares, more forcefully than she intended, 'though I think I'm probably asking too much … and you must say no if you want to. I know how hectic your life is and how much you do for others already … and it's not as if you owe me anything. I honestly won't be offended if you say no.' Offering acceptable escape routes is still fulfilling her duty to Julie, and just for a moment, Sam feels better. The more she things about it, the more she can't believe that she's let the idea get this far, and while this making a habit of disappointing her bosses is driving her to distraction, she suddenly sees no alternative, and so, nothing else for it, 'tell you what, let's forget about it altogether. Daft idea.' Then, carefully balancing her flowery tray, bought by her mother, thoroughly detested but destined to forever be a fixture, on her fashionably tiny and much-loved coffee table, and moving cups saucers milk jug and sugar bowl from A to B and then back again, Sam asks, 'how's everything at the hospital?'

'The favour, Sam?'

'No, it's alright. I can …'

'The favour, Sam.' Typical Charlie. Firm, inoffensive, and always can-do. 'Let me judge whether it's a daft idea or not. I'm a big boy now, you know. Can dress myself, walk and talk at the same time, in fact everything but work my video recorder.' He stops staring into space, turns and looks directly at his young neighbour and commands, 'so spill.' Clearly amused and not annoyed, he's somehow making what she's about to suggest even more disrespectful.

'I haven't offered to take your coat. And I haven't taken mine off either.' She's stalling and they both know it, but Charlie stands to help her off with hers before removing and handing over his; and Sam is quickly away from the old man's wet eyed stare and in her small hallway, where, hanging coats, she decides that her work attire isn't helping. Rushing up the stairs and returning ten minutes later sporting a very smart white blouse, black cardigan with a white blaze at each pocket, tight fitted black peddle-pushers, and fluffy slippers with rabbit ears that flap as she walks, she feels more like herself and she's as ready as she'll ever be. Returning to her living room, she finally gets down to business.

'There's this teenager, thirteen, called Stenton Cornthwaite.' Charlie coughs into his China cup. 'Yeah, you're right,' laughs Sam. 'They never seem to have sensible names, do they? He's got the mum from Hell who's called Kylie. Kylie Cornthwaite, would you believe? And Cornthwaite is her maiden name, so Stenton's dad could be any fertile male living within a five-mile radius, or further if he rides a bike. The lad has never really had a father figure in his life. Or, depending how you look at it, he's had too many father figures.

'Stenton sometimes behaves like a twenty-four-year-old thug, but most of the time he's as polite well behaved and adorable as any kid you could wish to meet, and he's better off living anywhere other than with Kylie. That said, there's no getting away from the fact that he's in a children's home mainly because nobody with any sense will foster him.

'He nicks cars and fights, and he has a season ticket to the Magistrates Court,' Sam is determined that Charlie be fully informed, 'and he can be a little bugger. But his school says that he's no trouble when he's with them and that he's very respectful. They judge him as a bright lad who has low self-esteem and precious little self-worth, and they're very worried that he's on a path with only one outcome.' Coming to the crunch, Sam steels herself. 'We think that the school is right, and we think that he needs a positive, male, role model. Someone like you.'

There's no reaction from Charlie, and, feeling like a fool, Sam starts to ramble … again. 'Now I describe the lad, I can see that I'm letting my heart rule my head and I'm wasting your time into the bargain. I've got to learn that some cases are beyond help, simple as that.' She slaps both hands on her knees and is quickly on her feet. 'Let's have a biscuit,' she says. 'Or Battenberg. I've got Battenberg and it's got our names on it.'

Charlie is completely focussed on what appears to be the most delicious cuppa he's had in many a long day, from his expression, perhaps ever. And then, just as Sam if about to disappear in search of cake, he says,

'Battenberg would be lovely, my darlin'. Perhaps you can fetch it while I figure out how Stenton, stupid bloody name, mother should be shot, can help me at the hospital and the allotment and still find enough time to go to school.'

He holds his empty cup up for her to take. 'Perhaps I can have another,' he says. 'In fact, I'd like to think we've graduated to mugs.'

16

When she's confused, my mum still says things like 'I don't know if I'm on this earth or fullers,' when any kind of sharp object comes anywhere near any part of a younger person's anatomy, she'll remark: 'you'll have your eye out with that,' and she's straight in with 'he'll not get there any quicker' when she thinks somebody is speeding. If I'm ever daft enough to find something she's lost, it'll be 'hiders can find;' and she begins any kind of announcement with 'if you're sitting comfortably, then I'll begin.' I already know that I'll end up looking just like Mum looks now - a scary thought - but the Mum mannerism and quirk is, like Mum herself, a treasured friend.

Savouring Colin's over polite attempts to understand what Bill and I find so amusing, I say, 'if you're sitting comfortably, then I'll begin,' and then, tradition satisfied, I get on with the job at hand. 'I think we can all agree that the accepted version of events surrounding the death of Abigail Hardcastle is bollocks.' Nods and smiles from the boys. They're good lads. 'So, Colin, what have you found out so far?' My young DC straightens his tall and unhealthily thin body, flicks ramrod stiff mousy hair causing a rise and immediately fall and no further discernible change and begins his report.

'Well, ma'am, such was, and I think still is, the lack of affection for Stephen Gutowski and Albie Holroyd, that plenty of people were ready and willing to tell what had been happening. And at the time, Gutowski and Holroyd had no choice but to admit to making Darren Bate's life a misery, though Louise Bates said very little. That Darren got very upset every time his sister had anything to do with Gutowski or Holroyd was common knowledge, and the big brother constantly trying to look after her looks to have really irritated the sister. Darren seems to have been kinder to her than she was to him, or he was to himself.

'After Darren's death, Social Services re-fostered Louise with a Mr and Mrs Green and she was given a complete name change, something that they rarely, if ever, do. They must have thought that she was extremely vulnerable and in danger, perhaps from Holroyd and Gutowski, and that a drastic and atypical intervention was needed. However, the strategy doesn't seem to have worked, and little Louise Bates/Jane Green became wilder and wilder, and there's documentation to say that she was even considered for a move to a third foster home. Finally, the Greens relocate to Adelade, Australia, and Louise pops up as Louise Bates living and getting fined for soliciting in Leicester where the Bates family came from in the first place.

'Louise and Darren's father, Donald Bates, was sectioned after his wife's tragic and unexpected early death in a car accident, and then, years later, he was released into sheltered accommodation, again in Leicester. He seems to have worked in a warehouse and stayed well out of it all.

'When he recovered sufficiently to leave sheltered housing, he rented an ex-council house on a rough estate for which he later got a mortgage, and he seems to have started to sort himself out. However, even though Louise is living in the same city at that time, she's not shown as living with or near her dad. After a few years, Donald sold up and moved out of that ex-council house. This was about two years ago and we're struggling to trace him after that. Louise disappears from the records just after she's done for soliciting.

'The spade used to bury Abigail Hardcastle was found propped up against the Leather's farmhouse for all to see, and the soil on it tested the same as that where the body was found. So, we can assume that Darren Bates did bury Abigail Hardcastle's body, and that, perhaps, he didn't care that others could trace the burial back to him.'

'Very clear, Colin, and very useful,' I say, fighting the desire to fill the chasms defined by the lad's high cheek bones and razor-sharp chin with a decent meal. He's noticeably pleased with his performance, and I'm chuffed. 'When you factor in how Holroyd and Gutowski turned out, good-natured Darren Bates looks even less like a murderer.' Bill Pridding nods his agreement with my assertion before taking up the story.

'You're not wrong, ma'am. In fact, put Holroyd and his known associates in a room and blow up that room and our crime figures would improve by 50%.' Too near to the truth to be funny, the three of us share resigned shrugs. 'Holroyd hasn't done prison time for many years, but we suspect that he tops our drugs pyramid, and the word is that Gutowski dishonestly secured sole control of his transport business. He maintains his association with Holroyd even though he's loaded, and he doesn't need to, and the word on the streets is that they can't stand the sight of each other.'

'Let's start there.' Bill's 'blowing them up' comment has made me even keener to prioritise these two villains. 'If we can prove Gutowski is corrupt, then we might just open flood gates and swamp Holroyd as well as his long standing oppo. Can we afford more of Colin's time, Bill? Perhaps a couple of days a week for a couple of weeks?'

'I think we can manage that,' says Bill and, yet again, Colin's reaction warms my heart. Oh, to be young and keen. He jumps and Bill laughs when I scream, 'Samantha!'

The antithesis of in keeping with destined to rise to chief constable, the shriek is, however, effective, and Sam arrives quickly, if less exuberantly than the pocket firebrand I know and love. She's visibly pleased to see Colin whom she favours with a smile.

'A spot of hospital visiting is just what the doctor ordered, Sam,' I state as enigmatically as I can, before adding: 'how's your French?'

*

Enveloped by the dark shadow of a behemoth, Sam and I can't stop staring at the colossus whose middle name must be 'outsize' and who is showing no awareness of our presence. Perhaps he genuinely can't see us without super-human distance vision. Perhaps like a polar bear spotting plankton, he sees but considers us unworthy of note. Whatever he's thinking, for reasons that I'm finding hard to come up with let alone justify, I'm pleased that Sam and I are in civvies and not uniform. Having him close but not caring who's watching is, I'm considering, no bad thing.

Massive head snapping left right and left again, mammoth legs wanting to move but having no sense of direction, he has his back to Ward A22, he's staring at long corridors all of which look identical, and despite his size, he looks distressed. Just the kind of thing that would normally tap into my 'must help' reflex. But wrapping this guy in a motherly hug, even if it was physically possible, is the last thing on my mind, and when he finally makes his move, I'm shocked though not remotely surprised that, without seeking the opinion of her boss, Sam sets off in pursuit. He's a very big guy radiating menace, she's right to sense trouble, and I have no option but to follow.

Six-feet-five, each leg thicker than my young colleague's body, heavy hanging hands and gargantuan quads causing a sway, keeping up is anything but difficult and I'm guessing that, even though he looks no older than late twenties, running to fat is the only kind of running our target has done for a very, very long time. Wearing what he can and not what he wants, a hairy slab of belly hanging over his crotch like a half-unfurled window blind and peeking out below a black loose-fitting tee-shirt that's big enough to cover a small car, must be shaming. The fashionably shaved head is perhaps an indication that he hasn't completely given up caring what he looks like, but ultimately, we're tailing a sad case of self-neglect, and he must know it better than anybody. His anger is self-evident, but it could well have its origins in his awareness of his own lack of willpower.

Arriving at the packed hospital car park, we watch from a safe distance as he pulls himself into a Mitsubishi tank - black with 'Warrior' emblazoned in gold on the side - before sitting for a long moment and catching his breath. Knowing without need to ask that Sam suspects that this man has been visiting Veronique, I put the car registration number into my phone just as, having made no attempt to pre-pay for parking, he destroys a colourful and much cultivated flowerbed by driving around the still closed barrier, and out onto the main road.

*

Thanks to Samantha, Veronique's safe-house placement is already set up, and we were looking forward to visiting a patient optimistic for her future. Sadly, the sight of a trembling and starey-eyed shell of a woman quickly disabuses us both of such a romantic notion and confirms that we're seeing the result of an encounter with a not so jolly giant who holds everyone and everything – including beautiful flower beds – in low to non-existent esteem.

59

When there is no reply, Sam repeats her question. 'Who is he, Veronique?' Still no answer. 'The police can protect you. We can lock him up. Even a big bastard like him. But we need you to tell us who he is and what he's done to you.' Veronique still can find no words, but she attempts a 'thank you' smile. Despite being as shocked as Sam, time's money and I'm determined to make progress.

'Well, you're looking better. Last time you looked like a mangled corpse hit by a train. Now you look like a mangled corpse hit by a Ford Fiesta, maybe even a Smart car, or a bike. A big bike ... obviously.' The pause hangs, but the laughter that comes eventually provides a much-needed pressure release.

'You're better than any med...medicine,' says Veronique at length, tears starting to flow, 'it's so ... so nice of you both to come and visit.'

'Your place in sheltered accommodation is being held for you,' says Sam. 'As soon as the doctors give the go ahead, I'll come and collect you and I'll take you there in my own car.' Sam leans conspiratorially. 'Only you, me, and DCI Marsden know and we're telling nobody. You mustn't either. He'll not find out, and when you're fully recovered, we'll see, eh?'

'Ey'up, Miss!' The shout is coming from the other end of the ward and it's loud enough to disturb a hearing-impaired pensioner who's forgotten his aids and is standing next to a ready to take off jumbo jet. 'It's me!' Pleased to see that Veronique and the other patients visitors and nurses look to be enjoying Stenton's eagerness, I decide to play along.

'Ey'up, Stenton!' The lad starts to shout his reply but a nudge and quiet word from Mr Butterell lets him know that he's having his leg pulled, and his mentor in tow, he's soon standing by Veronique's bedside and next to his favourite DCI.

'It's great here, Miss,' he gushes all arms and legs excited, 'and Mr Charlie has been looking after me and telling all his sick people what a good boy I am. And he tells funny jokes all the time.' Then, head bowed, 'I won't let you down, Miss, promise.' The attention span of a gnat and noticing Veronique for the first time, before anybody can stop him, he blurts, 'bloody 'ell! You look 'orrible.'

'Stenton!' shouts Charlie, finding it impossible to stifle a grin, 'you can't say things like that. It's ... well, it's rude.' Suddenly, like night and day, the old man goes from jocular to uncomfortable. 'Come on, lad, we've got work to do.' And in a flash the two are leaving, Stenton working hard to match his mentor's footsteps and gait.

A plan coming together is a wonderful thing, and Sam and I look at each other sharing a warm feeling. Then, turning from the Cornthwaite/Butterell bromance and back to Veronique, we're astounded to see that the terrified victim that we faced when we first arrived is back. Deciding that the medication is pulling her all over the place and that our presence isn't helping, we make our excuses and leave.

*

The number plate of the SUV soon generates an address and it's not long before Sam and I are sitting watching a stream of visitors, all male, outside a house in Brinsworth. We can tell that it's a brothel, something that the locals must know all too well, and we're not surprised, and the need to put this injustice right is burning hotter than ever.

17

A nose broken more times than a politician's promises, bull neck tree trunk legs anchor tattoos and one gold tooth, Nathan Guy - aka Barry Gascoigne - circles his purpose-built, professional hair-stylist's chair like a loose hipped cha-cha dancer sure of the glitter ball trophy. The bejewelled mirror artistically held between stubby index fingers and angled thumbs shows back, left side, and then right, before he swirls the protective cloak around an eddy of unwanted hair. Twenty years in the business has taught Barry a thing or two, and in Stan Russell - a copper with a fit wife - he sees an arrogant arsehole.

*

Cards and a suitable present for people who already have everything at Christmas, having to put petrol in the car, grocery shopping, especially grocery shopping, are all never-ending chores that chip away at a person's three score and ten and they irritate Sam way more than they should. But Morrisons' eggs, brown bread, skimmed milk, low calorie plain yoghurt, Crunchy Nut Cornflakes, coca cola, crisps, and chocolate, are all staples, so she's busy in the supermarket and fed up. And just as she decides that things can only get better, she spies an approaching trolley bulging with booze and cream cakes, and, too late, she realises that it's being pushed by Elaine Fenell. And, apparently, the coldness of their last encounter has already been forgiven.

'Sam! Lovely to see you! Twice in a matter of days, who'da thought. It's a sign, that's what it is. A bloody sign! I hate coming here. Not the same as shopping for shoes or a nice top, is it? Still, I'm nearly done, thank God! Tell you what, why don't we get a coffee and a cake? You can tell me about all the fellas you're fighting off. In fact, why don't we get together tomorrow evening at my place? A proper dinner party, just you and me. I'll get a couple of chops, they're cheaper here late-on and I need to come back to Parkgate to pick up some dry cleaning anyway. We can have a girl's night in. What say?'

Elaine's monologue is machine-gunned, and Sam's reply of 'I'd love to' probably surprises them both. Producing a crumpled fag packet and biro from her handbag, Elaine says, 'write your number on here' before adding, sheepishly, 'I'm down to three a day.'

They finish their shopping together, Sam noticing Elaine's gold card payment, and cheek air-kiss in the car park before Elaine says, 'I'll text you the address. Shall we say seven?' Then they go their separate ways, Elaine bouncing like Tigger towards what looks like a very expensive sports car, and Sam shuffling like Old Mother Hubbard to her clapped out Fiesta with its engine light showing fault.

18

Head full of 'proper dinner parties' Elaine Fenell and Russell, Sam is home lethargic and miserable, and responding to the doorbell ring as if she's at the end of a forty-mile hike and seeing her worst nightmare leaning against the doorjamb, suddenly every nerve ending is demanding her immediate attention. Legs crossed at the ankles and feet extravagantly trainered, Russell is relaxed, carefree, and holding a bottle of red and a bottle of white by their necks in one hand whilst pointing at them with the other. He football-chants 'Sammee!' before whispering, 'I'm rostered to be stakin' out Bobby Bartholomew's 'ouse, so, better get the white in the fridge and this red open, pronto.' Pushing his shoulder against the jamb, he straightens and makes to enter before, spitting blue lights furious, her strong flat hand on his chest abruptly halts his progress. *He must think I'm available to anything with a penis.*

'This is my home! Mine!' Sam spits. 'You don't get to come here uninvited. Nobody does!'

Disappointment tempered by understanding, he segues from stud about to service a grateful filly to kindly uncle. More important, he seems unaware that his voice is rising in pitch and intensity.

'Oh Samanfa, Samanfa. We're not goin' to play this game, are we? I know I should 'ave let you know that I was comin', but I've gotta be careful. Surely you can see that. I'm your sergeant. Your sergeant for Christ's sake! We've got to play cute. Take our chances whenever we can. AND WE HAVEN'T GOT TIME TO PISS ABART!'

Now certain that he's taken something, she's at risk of harm from a work colleague. From her boss. In her own home. And guessing that he's too out of it to notice and thinking to scare him just enough for her to lock and bolt her door with him outside, she reaches her mobile from her back pocket and quickly takes a picture. However, though temporarily startled, he doesn't take the expected backward step, and all that she's managed to do is further aggravate a predator.

He lunges forward, and this time, she has no option but to retreat further into her hallway. Then, just when she thought things could get no worse, her immediate work superior, a man whose good opinion she's hardwired into coveting, is having seizure, on her doorstep, alongside two bottles of wine, and at a time of night when there is no acceptable reason for him to even be here. He's collapsed in a heap at her feet, and all she can think is that, thankfully, the wine bottles hit the carpet and didn't smash. And then, over the crumpled mass that used to be her sergeant, she spies a primed and ready to strike velociraptor resembling Stenton Cornthwaite. Already ridiculously surreal, he's doing a cringeworthy impression of Clint Eastwood.

'Don't make me angry. You won't like me when I'm angry.' Russell tries to move. 'Stay down! Get up and I'll put you down again and again until you do stay down, for good. I've got a big carving knife.' Convulsing with glee, Stenton looks towards Sam and silently mouths, 'I haven't really.' 'So, do yourself a favour and stay down. Sound like a plan?' Sound like a plan! Sam is in a parallel universe. Bizarre World where only the impossible can happen. Then, seeing for the first time the heavy chain that Stenton is holding, she quickly scans her sergeant's head, praying not to see blood. The teenager is unfazed. 'Soon, I'm going to let you try to get to your feet. It'll not be easy because you've had a smack on the back of your knees. But coppers are supposed to be fit,' again the look to Sam, before, this time, he mouths 'sorry, Miss.'

'I'm going to talk and you're going to listen. You are going to listen, aren't you?' The aggressive power play is all coming from the thirteen-year-old. A pained, pathetic, little boy whine of 'yes' emerging from the grown-up.

'I can't hear you!' shouts Stenton, flicking Russell with the chain.

'Yes! Yes, I'll listen.'

'Good boy.' Good boy! Sam can't believe what she's witnessing.

Then, suddenly and with teeth bared, Stenton looks as if he desperately wants to kill and Sam's blood pressure soars. She must do something before the lad goes even further than he has already, but she can't think what.

'Miss, and Miss Marsden, and Miss Simcox are my very best friends,' the boy snarls. 'Can you hear me?'

'Yes!' Russell shouts, clearly expecting cold steel to pierce his exposed back.

'Anybody who hurts Miss, hurts me. So, if I let you live, you will be nice to her from now on and you won't try to get off with her anymore. If you mention what has happened tonight, I'll tell everyone why I had to teach you a lesson. Do we have a deal?'

'Yes,' snivels Russell.

'I want to hear you say that we have a deal.'

'Yes! We 'ave a deal!' He bellows, and then, like a spirit whose earthly task has been successfully completed, Stenton fades into the darkness.

Sam immediately moves to help her sergeant but is forcefully shrugged away as, desperate to recover some dignity, Russell struggles to get himself upright before, right leg thrown forward and barely able to take weight left leg pulled after like a scurrying late-comer, a man on stilts minus the stilts and with a pole up his backside, he ricochets through Sam's door and part hobbles part falls towards his car, where he leans, exhausted. Then, yanking it open - aggression in evidence too late, way too late - and collapsing in, he fires the ignition and rabbit hops down the street. And, only when out of sight and not before, a shaken and stirred Sam feels able to retreat into her house.

She's just started to fill her kettle when the doorbell rings, again. This time more than ready for a fight, she growls, 'oh no you don't,' and, fists clenched, chest squared, she's at her front door in seconds. Throwing it open, she's not confronted by Russell but by Stenton peeping out from behind Charlie Butterell, and Sam can immediately sense that the old man knows that things have gone too far.

'Stenton stayed late at the hospital today, with Mrs Simcox's permission of course,' he says, 'and we got carried away discussing plans for the allotment over a hot chocolate and bun. Then we couldn't resist popping to the allotment on our way back to the children's home to check on some of the planting we've done.

'That was a mistake. It was too dark to see much let alone do any digging, and it meant Stenton was going to get back to Dean

House much later than agreed with Mrs Simcox. But we had some good ideas that we needed to talk through, didn't we, mate?' Charlie looks to his young acolyte whose still more Border Collie wallowing in sheep than little boy who has just committed a serious assault, and who is nodding vigorously. Spotting that Sam is about to explode, Charlie quickly gets back to his excuse masquerading as a narrative.

'It's easier when you're there and can point at stuff, even when it's dark, and I was giving him a lift because I don't like him going on the bus, especially when it's dark. And I'd promised to let him take some plans I'd drawn up back with him so that he could look them over. That meant that I needed to pop into my place to sort out a couple of things ... and that's when we spotted your unwelcome visitor.' Sam is amazed to see that Stenton has now reverted to his polite kid listening to grownups persona. A game. Just a bloody game. 'I went to my house and got this.' Charlie pulls a heavy-duty metal spanner from behind his back. Seeing his neighbour's eyes widen, he quickly adds, 'I know it was stupid, but I was just going to use it to threaten, and then only if necessary. But Stenton had seen the big chain in the car ... and it seems the lad decided not to wait.'

Sam says nothing because Charlie is making full use of the big, moist eyes, the albatross wing eyebrows are soaring like hang gliders, and all the words coming to mind are so predictable as to serve only to make her sound like a spoilsport harridan. Taking advantage of the pause, the old man asks, 'perhaps you could ring Mrs Simcox to say he's alright? Please, tell her it's my fault because it is.'

Still livid, Sam remains motionless and silent. And then, with what Sam could swear is a pleased with himself look, Charlie adds, 'the lad and me could murder a nice cuppa, my dear.'

19

Outside doors locked and so never outside. Off the furniture and away from windows. Eating and drinking only what he allows, from her own bowls, on the floor, in the kitchen. Rules make him happy. And when he's happy, she's happy.

It's so much better than it was, and he lets her sit alongside him more than he ever did. The lovemaking that used to be so painful has become much more tender, and sometimes he even allows her to touch him before he has touched her. And that's a breakthrough that she never in her wildest dreams imagined would happen.

She knows that she's blessed.

But the thought that he will sell her on to another owner, or that she will have to share him with another pet, is terrifying. And if he does decide that their living arrangements must change, it will be her fault, because it always is.

20

Her shift at the Council Offices began at nine and she's already late. But Elaine Fennell doesn't flap. Instead, she languidly throws one arm across the double bed, considers giving work a miss altogether, and marvels at how difficult sleeping without a man - tall, short, fat, thin, old, older - seems to have become.

Most of her men, and there have been a lot, have treated her well, with many making it their business to save her from herself. But at school, other girls called her names like slag and prosy, and she agonised before deciding that she didn't need their friendship, or her parents' indifference, and that she was going to follow her own instincts no matter what.

Getting into that first taxi driven by an unknown, exotic, and so un-Rotherham, Asian guy, began the conveyer belt of men and it was a mistake. A twelve-year-old's decision that introduced her to the astonishingly addictive 'grown-ups treating kids like grown-ups' drug; a drug that Brownies Girl's Brigade and Girl Guides who preferred instead to focus on rules, didn't have. Rules that helped her to discover only that she was a natural rule breaker. That she was extraordinary. And that her friends weren't.

Making new friends who were also rebels, she found herself on the outside where she wanted to be, and she wasn't isolated as she'd feared. Then, one by one, her new friends turned into part-time rebels only interested in defying their parents, and before long she was unique, one of a kind, on the outside but notorious, and therefore alone. She could have conformed and become ordinary. Re-joined her gang of friends who still considered themselves rebels but weren't. Or she could graduate to breaking rules that were weightier and carrying more danger. She chose to take the different, higher-level path, and she elected to swim solo in a sea of men.

The increased bitching and name calling was a test of her full-time rebel status, and when subsequent taxis took her away from single male territory and into the zone occupied by groups of men that she'd never met, she was determined to overcome her panic.

69

And she enjoyed the false eyelashes, bright red lipstick, suspender belt tights, fancy things to put in her fancy pencil case, and the Big Mac Meals with Chocolate Milkshakes available anytime she wanted. But most of all she liked the attention, and their obvious need for her body gave her a buzz. Little Elaine Fenell was the powerful one. She was in charge. And the physicality was like an injection: painful and unpleasant but over with quickly and thought necessary and good for her by those old enough to know.

Twenty-six-year-old Elaine feels no anger towards the men who took advantage of her youth and lack of sophistication. It was what it was, and now it is what it is. But, terrified of racist labelling, the police let her slip under the quicksand and, crucially, they made it easy for the child that she was to legitimise her own dysfunctional life. Their indifference was after all, proof positive that she wasn't worth saving.

And then in he walked, and, with little fuss and no resistance, fourteen-year-old Elaine and two other equally obedient females were sent to live with five other women in a house that he owned.

Told that he had her parent's permission to take over her guardianship and not bothering to ask a mum and dad who had shown little interest thus far, Elaine now had something approximating to kindness. She couldn't have boyfriends, but she could have friends that were boys. She was to be exclusively his, but he insisted that she still went to school every day and that she completed her GCSEs, and when she did well, he was pleased, even proud.

His only demand of her as she got older was that she would show interest in the things that he liked, and he began to allow her, pay for her, to go to gigs discos and parties. He seemed to take pleasure in buying her fashionable clothes. He even consented to her getting a job.

Now living on her own, rent-free in a house that he owns, he still gives money whenever she asks for it, and her council salary is considered an allowance to be used for luxuries that she must still seek his permission to buy, but that he seldom refuses to permit. She's a twenty-six-year-old bird in a gilded cage, and she's surviving, even thriving, by not attempting to fly.

Or she was, until recently.

Six months ago, he shocked her by directing that a man in his employ, a man that she had never met called Joss Rawlin, was to be her live-in boyfriend with immediate effect. And last night was the first in all that time that Joss Rawlin had not shared her bed.

Reversing policy and insisting that she has a boyfriend had to be a punishment for something that she's done wrong, or something that Joss Rawlin has, and she's wracked her brains to think how she has misbehaved. She can think of nothing, and Joss says he can't think of anything either. She knows that Joss must be lying but she doesn't care. Because Elaine Fenell has fallen in love with Joss Rawlin, and amazingly, Joss Rawlin has fallen in love with her.

21

Legend has it that a Canadian Mountie always gets her man. And allowing for the fact that I'm not Canadian and I'd need two big lads and a fork-lift just to get me on a horse, I like to think that I'm cut from the same cloth. However, there comes a time when single-mindedly gnawing at what has become an all-encompassing objective is an indulgence, pure and simple, and nailing Holroyd has become an obsession. I'm neglecting other work, and it's getting out of hand. Then I'm told that Councillor Jeff Chapman has a window in his busy schedule, and without a second's thought, I send for my trusty steed.

Riding to the town hall in Izzy with Sam, I can hear myself jabbering away about my Michael Lloyd dilemma. I know that the prattle is rambling and dripping self-pity and I hate it, but almost as worrying, I can't for the life of me seem to stop. Sam just smiles and nods when she probably can't wait for the short journey to end, Izzy bless her tries harder than usual to avoid potholes, and I can tell that both are thinking that I'm crazy to even contemplate the idea of Michael being responsible for a death that is thirty years old and was judged at the time to be from natural causes. In no position to tell me what to do and probably wanting to politely point to the fact that no court would touch the case with a barge pole anyway, and that, killer or no, grown-up Michael is not the same person, and his distant past is irrelevant. Sam looks to be racking her brain for a non-judgemental response, and as soon as she can get a word in edgeways, she gives it her best shot.

She begins by agreeing that Terry Makin, the older brother of Joan Burlin, the kidnap victim who has been unable or unwilling to speak since we got her back, and who is under twenty-four-hour care at Middlewood mental hospital, deserves the Michael is a killer hypothesis to be rigorously tested. Michael was one of two devoted childhood friends of Joan, he remained in close contact until her recent kidnap, and he remains a mainstay of support now she's been rescued. His accuser was a now dead kidnapper who stated that, as a 10/11-year-old, he was seen, by another now dead kidnapper, coming out of Terry's house on the day of the severely disabled boy's death.

Sam is quick to remind me that the so-called witnesses are not only dead, but even if alive would not be the most reliable, and I must admit that what she's saying makes perfect sense. But Sam wasn't there when I was told. She didn't see the facial expression, hear the tone, pick up my informant's certainty that what she was saying was the absolute truth. AND SAM DOESN'T KNOW MICHAEL LIKE I DO. Protecting his friend that he loves from a wasted life of selfless caring for a brother who can do nothing for himself and is barely alive anyway, is just what Michael - 10/11 or at the age he is now - would be prepared to go to any lengths to do.

And then Sam reminds me of the exact words used.

'He was seen coming out of Granddad's yard. Chris Winterbourne and Roger Huddart were watching, and when they heard that Terry had died, they put two and two together. They didn't say anything then, but years later, Chris Winterbourne told his new love, me.'

It's a chilling voice from the grave and the words spoken by Sam, a young woman not much older that my original tormentor, cut deeper than I thought that they would. But Sam is on the button. Two people are supposed to have seen Michael near the scene of Terry Makin's death at the time of Terry Makin's death, and only one of them is dead.

A possible solution to my uncertainty has always been available, and my avoidance strategy has been unmasked. Nagging doubt is just not going away, and for Michael and me to have a future, I must track down Roger Huddart and ask him if Michael Lloyd killed Terry Makin. He might say that didn't witness Michael leaving the scene, but he thinks that Michael killed Terry, and I will have to decide how my knowing that changes anything. I suspect that it doesn't. He may say that the sighting never happened, and that the accusation is just a lie designed to inflict hurt on Michael and/or me, and in that case, Michael and I can have the life together that we both want. Huddart may on the other hand confirm word for word what Winterbourne is alleged to have said, and if that's what happens, my secondary source will have become a primary source. Still not conclusive, but enough I fear for Michael and me to have to go our separate ways. One way or another, talking with Huddart will close the file.

*

Well past retirement age and still irritatingly sophisticated and immaculately turned out, Sandra Pocock has worked for the council for about a hundred-and-four years and she is yet to crack a smile. She makes no secret of the fact that public accessibility to and public accountability of politicians is only pretend; and even then, only comes out to play at election time. As far as Pocock is concerned, apart from the one day every few years when they become voters, ordinary people are to be endured and not encouraged.

'Good afternoon, Sandra, you're looking well.' It is, if I do say so myself, a valid attempt at being magnanimous, but, offended even when paid a compliment, Pocock tightens, and turning on infuriatingly stylish heels, she strides towards an imposing oak door at the end of a short corridor. Sam and the fat lady who regularly ignores advice not to sing, are left to follow.

Councillor Jeff is sitting alone in the conference room with his Waitrose Club Sandwich organic coleslaw and low-fat sea-salt crisps, and he's occupying the chairman's chair - the only one with arms - normally at the end of eighty-seven-year-old, twenty-four-place, mahogany, worth more than Terry Makin's dad Les made in his entire lifetime, conference table, but now placed in the middle, just for Jeff. A bone China cup with matching saucer and half-filled by camomile tea is sited lovingly nearby his manicured left hand, and parallels with the cabinet table in Ten Downing Street are as obvious as they are predictable. Pocock locates her two police officers across from the good councillor whilst pointing a fortnightly nail parlour fettled finger at a geriatric hot-drinks machine, a disorganised rabble of paper cups, and a recycled coffee jar that is one third full of broken biscuits. Despite feeling that I could devour a dead rat, on behalf of my colleague and myself, I decline Pocock's offer.

All angles and with Red Rum teeth, Holy Jeff's greying, severely shaped, ginger hair frames a ship's bow face that would come in handy should he ever be iced in. And in a box-lined

74

tweed jacket and waistcoat, light-slate shirt and Burberry tie, tope trousers, highly polished brown brogues, trademark gold pocket watch chain and fob favoured by the equally stylish Stephen Gutowski, he's every inch the well-heeled toff. He wants everyone to know that he could be making shed loads of money running a blue-chip company but, out of the goodness of his big heart, he has committed his life to doing good works on behalf of the seriously smelly poor.

'Detective chief inspector. What a pleasure. How can I be of service?' As always, The Bishop is professionally respectful as, well into his fifth decade, he sips his tea delicately whilst managing to keep his long thin digit out of the cup handle and a well-scrubbed pinkie constantly pointing skyward. The painted-on smile never reaches his eyes and Holy Jeff manages to make my skin crawl without even trying. His substantive job is pearl white gloving the taxi doors of the rich and occasionally the famous, whilst standing outside the five-star Hilton hotel in Sheffield in all weathers and in his fancy doorman's livery. And the nearest he's come to being country gentry, or to the white-hot heat of big business, is being ignored one evening by Sir Alan Sugar who was no doubt in a hurry for a hot shower after a hectic day firing people. An insignificant part of Hilton Hotels Limited's contribution to Local Government, Jeff receives his monthly door attendant's salary despite not professionally opening or closing a door for the last ten years, and I suspect that the company regards having him anywhere but in front of their hotel as money well spent.

'So, councillor, tell me all about Stephen Gutowski and Albie Holroyd.' My lack of servility and preamble has Sam's hand shooting involuntarily towards her mouth, and the disgusted Pocock huffing loudly.

*

Instantly grabbing Chapman's full attention is good, Sandra Pocock running the two of us outa Dodge in less than fifteen minutes is not. Nevertheless, the short visit has been enough for me to find out all that I needed to know. Apparently, Gutowski is a pillar of society providing work and pensions for the hardworking people of Rotherham, Jeff has never even heard of Holroyd, and he suspects, neither has Mr Gutowski, and if all of this is true, I'm a five-foot-eight size ten who's in line to be the next face of Vogue.

22

Russell was late in work, and when he finally arrived, he was limping. He's said nothing about the incident, in fact he's said nothing at all. But police officers are naturally curious and colleagues are looking. Sam will have to decide how to proceed, and the clock is ticking.

Insisting last night on personally driving Stenton back to Dean House meant that she could deliver the explicit warning about the dangers of knives, a warning that he was clearly expecting ... and a heart-felt thank you that he was not. She knows he's a loose cannon - not always his fault - but when she left him, he'd seemed compliant and desperate to get back into Miss's good books. And just to hammer home the point, she'd made clear that he'd be walking with a limp and destined never to father children if he said anything to anyone about any of the whole sorry affair.

He'd listened intently, and, while this is proof of precisely nothing, driving home she found herself verging on optimistic. However, now that she's had time to think, really think, the idea of containing an issue of sexual harassment, superior officer on junior officer, when that containment is dependent on Stenton Cornthwaite, is so preposterous that she can't believe that she'd even considered not telling the DCI. But how to tell her boss that their thirteen-year-old protégé bicycle chain attacked her sergeant, after working hours and outside Sam's house, is like choosing noose or electric chair, and on her way to Elaine's dinner party for two, she's trying not to allow herself to wallow in why me?

Having seen the contents of Elaine's shopping trolley, Belgian chocolates and red wine seemed like good choices, good choices confirmed by Elaine's reaction.

'Booze and chocs! Just the job. The diet can wait, eh Sam. Not that you've ever needed to diet in your life.' Effusive as ever, Elaine leads her former best friend into a small entrance hall before turning into the cosy living area with a pushed back settee and formally set out table. The host has gone to a lot of trouble and she's already looking nervous, and Sam's 'this is nice' while expected is so gratefully received. Petite blonde - which Sam hears as short and stunted blonde - and leggy elegant brunette reunited after such a long, long time, anxious Elaine is as beautiful as ever, and Sam drinks in the moment that she had begun to think would never come. Tight, black, fake silk pants and cerise top, what looks like a real but can't be diamond necklace and matching earrings, professionally made-up - again can't be - and recently worked on hair, Sam's erstwhile best friend could always have the boys salivating, and little dumpy Sam never failed to be left, like now, impressed, and yes, wishing that she could be just like Elaine. Water has still to flow under their ridiculously wide bridge, but they've made a start, and what Sam really wants to say to her former best friend is relax before adding: 'you can have him. You and Joss are the perfect fit that me and Joss never were.'

'Joss Rawlin is with Elaine Fenell.' Facebook's blunt reveal, on balance, left Sam relieved. She doesn't think that she and Joss have fallen out, and they never actually broke up, but now that their 'item' status is no longer even a long-distance pretence, Sam is telling herself that it would be good to see him again, not awkward at all. However, when Elaine mentions in passing that he isn't at home, using freshening up as an excuse, she's barely able to lock herself in the downstairs toilet before losing control. She's suffered a couple of panic attacks in recent days, and she knows that she needs to pull herself together. Yes, her job dominates her every waking hour she has the love life of a tailor's dummy and she's never likely to meet anybody, but that's okay, it's always been okay … at least it was before Russell. Now doubting her choices in life and so doubting its meaning and relevance, she can't seem to stop wondering whether giving up so much has been a tragic waste, whether losing Joss was a tragic waste. 'Enough!' She tells her reflection in the mirror. 'Enough.' And the Sam Jardine that exits Elaine Fenell's downstairs loo is back in control and determined to stay that way, at least for tonight.

The obligatory tour of the ex-council semi gives her opportunities to make all the right noises and to feel better as each home improvement made is fully explained and justified.

The blinged-up bathroom moved upstairs and replacing a built-in cupboard and a quarter of the master bedroom to make space downstairs for a high spec open-plan kitchen diner and sitting room. The Jacuzzi/hot tub in the landscaped garden visible through the French windows that generates over the top squeals and laughter from the two of them. Hilarity designed to indicate that possessions aren't, at the end of the day, what's most important in life, when clearly - two enormous integrated sound system TVs and at least three shiny new laptops strategically placed to be seen - they are. And the truth is that it's all tremendously impressive and Sam is genuinely pleased for her childhood friend … but she's also worried. Despite trying to switch off her day job and just enjoy her night out, she can't help wondering where the mountain of money to do all of this came from. And knowing Elaine as she does, it could have come, God forbid, from criminal activity.

Elaine is looking wistful.

'I like it,' she says as if she's trying to convince herself as much as persuade her guest. 'I do like it. Who wouldn't? But I can't stay here, Sam. I've got to think of the future.' Suddenly guilty, she adds, 'when … when Joss and I,' *no need, not mine, probably never was,* 'have our babies. Well, my kids can't grow up in Thurcroft. Not bloody likely! They'll end up only interested in Reality TV, tattoos, fake tans, hair products, sex, and beating up old ladies for their pension money.' Elaine sets herself. 'No, Wickersley's the only place good enough for my bairns.

'Course, it'll be a wrench. Should'ah seen it when I arrived. Hardly anything spent because the people before me intended to pack up and disappear to run a bar in Alicante. Then the husband goes and glasses a drunk in Parkgate, and forty-eight hours later, the wife does a moonlight with Tyrone the teenager from next door.' Again, they laugh. Just like when they were twelve and had their whole lives stretching out in front of them. Elaine sighs. 'Still. A blank canvas is no bad thing.'

According to Facebook, Joss is a kind of rent collector and Elaine works for the council. But all of this costs serious dosh, and unless they've both changed out of all recognition, any money they do make will be badly managed. And Wickersley prices are half as much again. It doesn't add up, literally, and

Sam is starting to get that uneasy feeling, again. Complications around her childhood best friend and the man she always thought that she would marry, coming at her now, at this moment, when everybody else's crap seems to be raining down on her, is a joke. 'Why me,' thinks Sam, 'why the fuck, me!'

23

The first in the family to go to university, his mum and dad embarrassingly determined to sing his praises at every opening, his neglected twin brother suffering by comparison, Red Beard, aka Kevin Caldwell, was flying high but has come down in the world. And his once-proud parents and brother now could well be thinking about him in the same way as he's thinking about Sandra. Her destroyed body is half on and half off the two-seater nicked in the dead of night from outside the backdoor of a house two streets from their squat, and that makes Kevin doubly sad. It's the family, the loved, those that are left behind, that suffer most.

She was such a beauty, and she was going places, they both were. Now the filthy and ripped vest is failing to cover empty, sagging breasts. Her bare buttocks are lying in vomit and her mouth is loose lipped and oozing. And her once shiny hair, degraded into patchy clumps of grease, is dangling lifelessly across opaque eyes countersunk deep into gravel grey, twenty-six-year-old skin. He knows that she's been out to score, probably from Black Danny, but it could have been any one of ten dealers that know her, that know them both. There's no point in trying to find out what she's taken because it will have been cheap, low-grade crap, because his wage and her ruthlessly curtailed prostitution money won't cover much. He re-checks her pulse - neck and wrist - just to be sure, and he decides that she won't die … this time. But any kind of recovery will take a miracle and he's at his wits end.

The deal, the one-off, take it or leave it deal, is Sandra's only hope and he had to accept. A slim chance is better than no chance and he's out of options. He's been out of options from the moment that that first needle pierced that first vein. He should have listened to Mum and Dad. He should have been more like his brother.

24

One-day you wake up and tall and ridiculously handsome with intense hazel eyes, strong jaw, and a facility for the nimble repost, are no longer enough. You're up-for-fun and prepared to party, but your friends are pairing off and talking about career mortgages and pensions ... and your girlfriend has chosen university over you. Suddenly, you have time but nobody else does and you're drinking alone, or with older men whose wives don't understand them, and, like you, still laugh at fart jokes. Drunk and throwing up at sixteen is easily dismissed as a rite of passage, drunk and throwing up at twenty-six is a portent of a tragic future, and you know it.

Until recently, Joss Rawlin had led a charmed life, and even though there were no obvious reasons for compatibility, he and Sam matched, a couple from the moment Mrs Scanlon sat them together in Early Years' Class. Quiet, thoughtful, and motivated to achieve from the moment of conception, Sam grew up planning a career around improving the lives of others, and staying on at school and then going to university was always the plan. Garrulous and loud, and a winner without the need of interest or exertion, Joss saw school as blocking his ability to earn money, and he swapped full-time education as soon as possible for a plumbing apprenticeship with his dad's friend. One month later he replaced blue overalls with the sharp suit and sharper patter of a trainee estate agent. He didn't want Sam to go away, but he was proud of her ambition, and Durham wasn't so far in the grand scheme of things. And he had clean fingernails and his own car.

Helping her to settle into her Hall of Residence was an opportunity to look grown-up, but traipsing north every weekend when cool stuff was happening in Rotherham was a bore. Sam's crowd were all stuck up types talking about politics and economics, and courses and lecturers that he'd never heard of. In Durham he wasn't pack member let alone pack leader. He journeyed to Durham five weekends out of Sam's first ten ... and then not at all.

Nobody mentioned that trainee estate agents don't get their own office with phone and secretary and aren't swamped by overt displays of respect from colleagues. And told once too often to make the tea, his kneejerk career change to call centre employee just proved that he could sell ice to Iceland. But a mind numbingly easy job, no girlfriend or friends of either gender, money that stayed in his pocket, days and nights that dragged, and the memory of how good his life used to be, tormented him, and Joss' search for excitement began. A regular flutter on the horses and the dogs seemed a harmless pastime until something better came along, and the world of casinos with its smart dress code and beautiful people was that better alternative. It was the world that he was born to inhabit, roulette and blackjack the things that kept him sane.

Cash was never an issue but somehow cash flow became a problem for which payday loans was the solution. And for a time it worked. After all, he was just bobbling along whilst waiting for Sam to finish at university so that real life could resume. What could possibly go wrong? Then, with no warning, he was working overtime in a job he hated, to repay creditors he was barely aware that he had ... and then Albie Holroyd bought his debt. As rent collector/property agent/house renovator for Mr Holroyd's big and ever-growing property portfolio, Joss owed less money, but what he did owe, he owed exclusively to Mr Holroyd, who was now also his employer. The penny took a very long time to drop, but when it did, it dropped like a depth charge, as Joss finally grasped that he belonged, BODY AND SOUL, to Holroyd.

And it took Daisy Winton to make him realise that he had to make a stand.

Expensively transformed into a high-tech hospital ward, fourteen Parkside Close was five-year-old Daisy's home, and it provided round the clock care for the little girl. Robert and Melissa were not able to be in paid work and so were behind in their rent. The amount outstanding was relatively insignificant for a man of Holroyd's means and fundraising in the community had already started. But to Albie Holroyd, a debt is a debt, and all Albie's debts are paid, one way or another.

Hearing the never-ending backdrop of the constant drone of machinery and looking down on Daisy's frail body, boxed by cushions, hemmed by oxygen cylinders, impaled by tubes, and on a small settee downstairs in a tiny, converted living room because not being bedridden is important, Joss knew instantly that he had finally reached his rock bottom. Evicting Daisy and her family would be to let the little girl die knowing that the adults in her short life hadn't loved her enough, and he just couldn't do it. He had to change Albie Holroyd's mind. He had no choice.

They were in Mr Holroyd's living room. Marvin was standing, Joss was standing, and Holroyd was sitting as befits the man in charge. Marvin's look said it was a suicide mission and that Joss should take heed.

Toothpick flicking against his slug of a tongue, the 2p piece maladroitly worked from pinkie finger to thumb and back again, Holroyd's stare absolute proof that, as always, Marvin was right, and Joss faltered even though he had an ace card that would work … if he could summon the courage to play it. He would suggest that local press, perhaps national newspapers and even the BBC, might take up the story and become involved. And if they did, such a heart tugging tale would sell and would throw a spotlight on low rent and low maintenance housing in the north of England, and that would be bad for Mr Holroyd, very bad.

Joss played his ace and won the game. Daisy would get what she needed, and a little comfort would enter that family's heart-rending existence. And for the first time in a long time, Joss could feel like his own man, and proud of himself.

But *(there's always a but)* he'd made his boss look fallible. And that would demand a high price that he alone would pay. And keep paying, forever.

25

Albie Holroyd does not eat out, ever, and to say that Albie is particular about food and drink is like saying that the Marquis de Sade was 'a bit of a lad.' No-one would guess that Marvin's unprecedented phone call inviting Gus Gutowski to dine with Albie at Zizzi's has the big haulier terrified.

All Albie's meals are prepared elsewhere by professional chefs, are always consumed at home and butler served by Marvin, who eats exactly what Albie eats and drinks exactly what Albie drinks but does so first. Each day there are four identical deliveries: at 9 a.m., pancakes with maple syrup served with a milky, three-sugared, English breakfast tea in a slim and tapered white mug perched neatly on a flowery saucer; a second tea paired with one small Bakewell tart arrives at eleven; at twelve-thirty, a lunch of pickle and Wensleydale cheese on cut diagonally, crust removed, white bread, is washed down by a third tea; dinner is always at 7 p.m. and consists of four Westler's sausages with creamy mashed potatoes and gravy, HP sauce in an unused container, and a cold coca cola in an authentic bottle opened at the point of delivery. Apple pie, custard, and a fourth cup of English breakfast tea follow, and no more food or drink is taken until the whole thing starts again at nine the next day. So, whatever this is, Gus knows it's a trap, a Venus flytrap, and if he settles, he'll be eaten alive. He has minutes to understand what he needs to do to keep himself and those he loves safe. So, every inch the local big shot commanding attention, trophy wife on his arm and Maître-d waiting to greet them personally, Gus Gutowski lights up the room before it realises it wants to be lit … and is as ready as he can be when his partner's high-pitched and genderless shout lacerates the air and gets the attention of everybody in the room.

'Gus! Tamsin! Good to see you both. Come and sit, old friends, come and sit.'

Deliberately eye catching in a made to measure, biscuit coloured suit, chocolate shirt and shoes, and gold tie, is Gus' style. But in a tailored, navy-blue, double-breasted suit with red pocket square, black, shiny shoes with tan spats, white shirt that sparkles, and red-banded, light grey fedora that, despite being indoors and at the very best table the full restaurant has to offer, is still on his head, Albie's attire is so eccentric that he cuts a pantomime figure causing people that don't know to snigger. He dramatically points at the waitress who's clearly horrified by what she must have done wrong.

'This is Charlotte, Gus.' Holroyd squeals loud enough to be heard by everybody. 'Doesn't she look like Charlotte Bingham from school? Altogether prettier, but the spit of Charlotte Bingham, don't you think?' Despite having absolutely no knowledge of Charlotte Bingham, all the diners and staff seems to be considering the proposition as the waitress' smile grows ever more hysterically fixed.

And, months later, they will remember the moment. They will be able to describe the detached and disinterested, big black and bald Hell's Angel making them uneasy in his motorbike leathers and heavy biker boots. They will have talked about the suave and sophisticated celebrity couple who seemed happy to join the oddly disconnected group. And they will still laugh at the creepy little man with the lifeless eyes and folding face who dressed like a B film gangster, and who sounded like a teenage girl.

The thought that Able is creating an alibi hits Gus like a jack-knifing juggernaut:

Something unpleasant and very criminal is happening nearby and now.

Must warn Anthony, before it's too late!

26

The brutal strike to the back of his legs instantly transforms a mountain of muscle, head-down arse-up, into a foothill of fat. Five, crisp, clean punctures applied to shoulders and upper back, mighty arms inefficiently thrown against the elbow bend and towards the area that hurts, down and bleeding, Anthony Gutowski is reacting to symptom and not cause. He will know that upright is the only way that he will survive, but though his legs are improving, they won't yet be ready to hold his considerable weight and he's panicking. Terrified that his injuries are life threatening and aware that his attacker has not run away, he needs desperately to be doing something. Hence the giant chest pushed upwards, head craning, back arching, and the straining to become as upright as a man with no legs can be.

Plan A was to cave Gutowski's head in with the scaffolding pipe used to disable his legs, and applying a deep slash from behind would be an improvisation, which is intrinsically not a good idea. But the unexpectedly accessible throat is just too available to ignore, and when, like a Giant Redwood, the big man falls forward onto his face, his blood pooling forming a grotesque pavement halo, the attacker becomes Clint Eastwood as he says,

'You're big but there's always somebody bigger. Or somebody smaller with a massive knife.'

*

A porter in regulation hospital uniform pulling a curtain around a patient's bed is unusual but far from unheard of. No reason to ask why, so nobody does. Here because he must be, killing because he has no choice, he's soon suffocating his prey along with all possibility of any kind of future happiness.

Hyperbole will flood the airwaves and he'll become notorious. The carer that kills. The sinning saint. The fiend masquerading as a friend. He'll be seen as a contradiction, a challenge to the universally held 'bad people look different to good people' viewpoint. Finally pigeonholed as born wicked or the result of overindulgent parenting, chanting 'this must never be allowed to happen again!' will serve as a soothing balm ... until the next time.

*

Night Nurse and Doncaster Ladies rugby player, Siobhan Callahan, shows an impressive turn of speed and she's astounded to see Charlie Butterell where Charlie Butterell should not be. Several questions are fighting for space, but her first duty is to make all necessary checks of a panicked Veronique Sabet, and this she does until she is forced to break off to prevent the hospital security team creating another medical emergency by attempting to headlock the old man. The additional panic caused by a group of fired-up young men who ought to know better, and who have forgotten every minute of their training, is 100% unhelpful, not least because it prevents anyone noticing the confused and probably concussed 'other' porter sitting like a tranquil frog on the wet lily pad that used to be Ward A22's spotless floor.

The Rambo wannabes finally spot suspect number two who's away with the fairies, surrounded by water, bits of earthenware pottery, and beautiful flowers bought at the franchised in-hospital florist by DCI Marsden and DC Samantha Jardine, and who is clearly posing no threat. The flame red matted beard and bleeding head and right ear a clear indication, even to them, of what Charlie Butterell did with the vase.

*

Time passes, Veronique and the understandably frightened other patients have been taken care of, police have been sent for, and Veronique has been left to the peace and quiet of her own company. Red Beard has been carted away, Siobhan is dividing her time between paperwork and telephone, an auxiliary is mopping water and picking up flowers, and the old man who is on a ward that he visits rarely, and whose shift ended hours ago, finds himself momentarily unobserved and aware of a short window of opportunity to escape. Instead, Charlie Butterell tentatively eases aside the newly arrived screens and then the curtains back surrounding Veronique's bed and squeezes inside.

Looking down at the sad but remarkably serene face, he's heartbroken to realise that, for Veronique, this ordeal is just one more in an on-going tsunami of suffering and thought of the

88

extent of the abuse that she has been subjected to throughout her young life sets his emotions soaring out of control. He does the unthinkable, he reaches out and holds her hand. And as he does so, her eyes open.

'Hello, you,' she says. 'It's been too long … and I'm so sorry.'

27

Last night, Elaine was even more 'inventive' than usual and Joss suspects that the meal with Sam went well. These days all he ever wants is for Elaine to be happy, and he's pleased that the two women in his life might have buried some sort of hatchet. But he's also apprehensive, even frightened, because this new arrangement with Elaine originated with Holroyd. And even though he's sure that he feels more for Elaine than he's ever felt for anybody, including Sam, he can't help thinking that his boss is setting him, them, up for a fall.

Bringing some small comfort to Daisy Winton and her family was a turning point, and Joss knows Holroyd well enough to realise that The Man won't forget, and he will never forgive. Fitting in with what Albie Holroyd wants, even when it's also what he wants, is likely to be a mistake from which there may be no recovery.

So, he's planning. For the first time in his life, he's planning. Planning for a future for himself and his family. He's more than frightened, he's terrified … and he must be ready.

*

According to the books of Barbara Cartland, lurve is the gateway to a trouble-free world of pink pleasure and yet the pursuit of true love has led me to a shed load of pain. I reckon that, in addition to a gazillion of books, Babs has sold me a pup, and finally reaching Heaven only for it to feel like Hell is driving me crackers.

And the kicker is that it's all my own fault.

Fact is I can't stand the agonising about action and I'm craving the action itself. And getting on with accusing Michael of cold-blooded murder is starting to look inevitable.

So, with all the patience of a six-year-old at the fair with a pocket full of tokens, I decide to hurtle towards a showdown meeting over which I have no control with the man who is and always will be my soulmate… and then a recovering addict cohabiting with a near death, dyed-in-the-wool addict, in a squat so filthy that the rats are on speed dial with the council housing officer, saves the day. Interviewing Kevin Caldwell is a cowards sidestep in any language, but I grasp the opportunity with unabashed relief ... and I feel dreadful. A woman of my own age, that I know and like, and who has had a life you wouldn't wish on Vladimir Putin, has had a pillow pressed on her face while sleeping, has barely survived, and my first thought is 'thank God for that!!'

When I get to the station, I'm told that Caldwell has a severely cut ear, a two-inch laceration to his scalp, and likely concussion brought about by having a heavy water-filled vase cracked over his head. Apparently, the cracker is Charlie Butterell of all people, and whilst the crackee, Caldwell, is likely to be okay and could probably cope, I nevertheless decide to let him talk to his lawyer, and for all involved to get a good night's sleep before an under-caution interview is even attempted. It's a decision that proves fortuitous because, in the meantime, Anthony Gutowski gets on the wrong end of a well-deserved seeing to - *mustn't say that, not out loud anyway* - and suddenly, I'm relieved to say, I've got enough urgent stuff stacked high on my plate to make an early set-to with Michael impossible.

Anthony Gutowski won't be missed and that's a fact. Indeed, the runners and riders who might have taken it upon themselves to provide him with a one-way ticket to a chinwag with St Peter will be plentiful. But he's dead. I hated his guts, but he's dead. And I know that I will have to be professionally determined to bring his murderer, or murderers, to justice.

Immense though he was, according to Dr Wong, Gutowski's body lay unobserved for over ten hours before this morning's bin men decided that he represented a category of waste that fell outside their remit - *oh dear!* He'd suffered a heavy blow across the backs of his knees and been stabbed repeatedly with a very big knife before having his throat cut, presumably with that same knife. Significantly, to me at least, the murder weapons are nowhere to be seen, and there was no sign of injury to the perpetrator or perpetrators. And that points to a much more difficult to handle problem. This has the hallmarks of a cool, calculating, ruthless killer and if that's the case, despite having potential Gutowski killers everywhere I look, I'm already sure that there will be no concrete leads.

Before Anthony Gutowski and the big knife became over-acquainted - *bloody hell!* - I'd secured a warrant and assembled a team to raid his brothel, and I had made up my mind that I would be part of that team. Considering intervening events, I've now added Sam so that I can visit the murder scene with Bill and still see Gutowski's place of business by joining the group later. DC Colin McNamara has been catapulted to Palace Gutowski so that Stephen Gutowski be informed and recruited to carry out formal proof of identity of the body; and the interview with Caldwell has had to be put back even further to 1p.m.

When I arrive in Brinsworth and see the heap of once human flesh against a very ordinary wall, that this victim deserves justice just like any other is reenforced, and leaving Bill and Jim Renavent with clear instructions, I walk with my thoughts the few hundred metres to what until last night was Anthony Gutowski's kingdom. Putting Anthony Gutowski out of business for a couple of months had been the best that I could have hoped for, and this early morning raid was to be no more than a cage rattling exercise. Making the big gorilla's life more difficult by rounding up a few illegal foreign nationals who were unlikely to say anything useful but would leave him with staffing issues was the primary objective. The faces and body language of my team are a stark reminder, not that I needed one, that this little foray has turned into much more.

I give Chalky the nod, and he bursts in as if finesse is a little-known Scottish loch before bounding straight up the steep and narrow stairway. Composed by comparison, Sam and Liz check the downstairs, and, bringing up the rear, I'm the first to spot an ill-fitting louvred door. Easing it open I'm confronted by an untidy and heavily tea-bagged kitchen area and two house-coated, very young and wearily apathetic, girls clutching stained mugs. Liz is deployed to sit with them, and Sam is told to interview the middle-aged, bespectacled, plump and Mumsie Madam in threadbare downtrodden carpet slippers found standing next to a makeshift shelf/writing desk that's screwed to a wall on the landing. The woman replicates her stiff and immobile hair and, unwilling to utter a word, she's eventually taken with the two house coated girls, and three others who had been in bedrooms and at their work, to a bedroom labelled 2.

The three - amazing given it's still relatively early in the morning - terrified clients are, in contrast to the females whose skill set they were road-testing, beside themselves with anxiety. They're kept with Chalky in bedroom 3 where I'm even more surprised to see that one of the 'men' is in fact a boy, probably a shade younger than his seventeen-year-old service provider. The lad has an 'I'm wagging school and using my dinner money for a guaranteed shag, rabbit-in-a-headlight, please don't tell my mum,' look. Boomerang chested and skimmed milk skinned, his hastily pulled too high underpants are uncomfortably occupying a spotty arse crack and he cuts a slapstick figure. I'm amused ... and immediately ashamed. Had he been a girl, I would have been appalled, not to say bloody furious, and I knows that I should know better. After his statement is taken, I want this young man gone.

It turns out that Number 2 Bedroom Client had just started his experience of a lifetime and Number 3 Client had just finished. So, they are both almost fully dressed and will be able to descend to the ground floor with a little more dignity than the boy. Mostly concerned about whether their wives will need to know, and desperate to get out of the mess they're in, I can guarantee that they'll shoot off at the mouth but will be reluctant to 'get more involved.' So, leaving Liz corralling the women in bedroom 2, the rest of the team and I ascend to the attic where a more cautious Chalky eases open the door.

The room is tiny and crammed with one short single bed, one small desk, and one dining room chair. How Anthony Gutowski got through the door let alone found space to live stretch or 'work' is a mystery, and his desk would have struggled to accommodate his massive backside let alone any quantity of paper. He would have had to sit side-saddle to use it. Thinking of him in this room conjures an image so ridiculous that it makes my memory of him, dead and alive, so much sadder. Menacing and evil, he was. Heartbreakingly pathetic, he was even more.

The desk-lamp has been on all night, and four pieces of paper and two glossy magazines - one for body builders and one for high performance cars - are on the tiny desk. Several such mags are piled to form a makeshift bedside table, and one of the pieces of paper on the desk has writing on it.

A not happy   watch ur back.
I look at Sam and translate.
'Albie not happy. Watch your back.'

*

Minutes after informing Stephen Gutowski of his brother's murder, and ringing hands-free from his car, Colin sends through an update. He reports that the next of kin of the newly deceased was 'noticeably irritated' by being disturbed by his initial knock, and that he was 'implacable' from the start of their conversation and throughout. Colin wasn't invited over the threshold, and his feeling is that Gutowski is a man who is 'quickly annoyed.'

My thoughts are clear and certain: Big Gus knows who killed his brother, somebody somewhere had better watch out.

28

Two very well to do looking lawyers appear within minutes of the Brinsworth brothel spilling its contents into Main Street Police Station, and it's all too apparent that some mystery big shot is footing their bill. The cautioned Madam, whose name is Gaynor Hart - *you couldn't make it up,* lifelessly parrots 'no comment,' and all five girls, now in shapeless coveralls, stand unconcerned but silent, and seemingly grateful just to be warm. Immigration officials are on their way, interpreters - just one local and present, and several available but unused on phones - are earning easy money, and the enterprising but very young man who saw getting his end away as a better use of his valuable time than studying maths, is still insisting he's nineteen when he's clearly not even close. His mother is not feeling the love and has refused to come to the station because 'he's no son of mine!' And she's promising that she will 'one hundred and ten percent guarantee that he'll be bothering no more women, ever!' Chalky is insisting that he personally takes the boy home so that the lad will at least have a fighting chance of seeing out his teenage years.

Noticing that one of the girls is standing quietly to one side and showing distaste for Gaynor Hart and the flash lawyers, I ask Sam to slither her and the onsite interpreter into a side room that immediately becomes a welcome haven from chaos for all four of us. There seems to be an instant and instinctive bond between the young woman and Sam.

Despite 1950's winged spectacles, black hair the consistency of a jellyfish, and an unsettling resemblance to notorious mass murderer Rose West, dowdy interpreter is helpful, empathetic, and ideally suited to the specific dialect required. The girl feels relaxed enough to takes the initiative and, as everybody seems to do, she touches her own eye to signify that she's noticed my rapidly blackening fried egg. In an unexpected display of hooker/ bobby comradeship, her smile says, 'I hope it soon heals,' and my reciprocated gesture indicates, 'I'm sure that it will.' Choosing her words carefully, and delivering them slowly and in batches so that Rose, who like Sam is living every syllable, can keep up, the young woman then says,

'My name is Kausar. I am happy that Anthony is dead. I want to be sent back to my home country as soon as possible.' It's a blunt beginning and it's soon clear that she has a prepared speech. 'All of the girls must go with whichever man had the money. But Anthony decided from the start that my spirit needed to be broken. So, I was always his woman whenever he was in the house. Never the others, only me.'

She goes on to tell us how, even though he evidently had little interest in what she termed 'normal' sex, her encounters with Anthony Gutowski followed the same pattern: she had to be completely naked and in full make-up, and penetration was never attempted. Instead, he would position her on the edge of the bed so that her head and shoulders dangled, before laying his full two-hundred-and-eighty-pounds weight 'square on top,' his big heavy rough hand on her throat. 'He enjoyed watching me panic as I struggled to breath,' she said, not attempting to catch tears splashing onto the tabletop. 'After a few minutes, he would sit on my chest. He seemed to need to see me suffer before he could …' Kausar mimes the movement and Rose says the word 'ejaculate.' 'The amount of suffering he needed to see was increasing and it was taking longer and longer for him to be satisfied. I knew that, eventually, I would be dead. So, I decided that I had to kill him … before he killed me.'

29

People are desperate to provide relief when faced with bereavement. It's natural. And Gus is grateful. But tender comments and affectionate gestures, however well-intentioned, only serve to diminish him further, and he has come to equate sympathy with torture. Yes, he's had to deal with disaster after disaster. But they've all been homemade. And he merits no compassion. So, despite being terrified of being alone with only guilt for company, in this inhospitable mansion, Gus insisted that Tammy keep her breakfast pedicure and manicure appointment with 'the girls' at Roget's Nail Parlour, whilst he sits in solitude, watching his gardeners - two strong young chaps and a supervising older man, as they help him to maintain the luxury he's connived and colluded to create.

Soil dug and grass cut. Greenery lopped and reaped. Short flurries of activity between long spade leaning pauses. He watches and envies men with purpose and despises his spineless self. All because of a man who drains and exhausts him. Who treats him like a pet dog. And who he first met as a schoolboy. A man for whom his trucks still import drugs, and who still deposits dirty money that Gus has long since ceased to need in the offshore account set up so many years ago. A man who used him as an alibi whilst having his baby brother killed.

Unable to concentrate, he doesn't intend to go to work today. Right at this moment, he doesn't intend to go to work ever again. If only he could switch off and then reboot his brain. But he can't. Staring across at men keeping manicured rolling paddocks and mature shrubbery in check and dissecting past decisions, it's been a life defined by incompetently navigated crossroads, Henry Thompson being the biggest crossroad of all. Gus knew from day one that he had a mountain to climb: a no-show at their wedding, two strangers cajoled to be witnesses, and the baby born just four months and three days after leaving the registry office, Henry did not attempt to hide his contempt. But many sons-in-law have successfully worked their way to an improved, even close, relationship with their father-in-law, and grandads mellow. Joy first talked and walked to Henry: 'go 'way, daddy, Grandad do it.' Henry laughed most at her Fairy Nuf on dressing up day. He cried most at her portrayal of 'the fried egg at The Last Supper.' And he most needed her reassuring hug when she broke her arm zip wiring. Gus would always be Joy's father and her love for him was unconditional. He should have been overjoyed that his daughter also loved her grandad. Henry could have become a kindred spirit. But Gus thought that he was playing the long game, and he couldn't see it. Henry wasn't supposed to kill himself, and Albie wasn't supposed to keep Elaine Furnell close, under control, and ready to weaponize should Gus, now a force to be reckoned with in his own right, ever chance his arm. Joy and Becca were supposed to grow ever more loving as befits a daughter and wife. And Gus was supposed to be his own man, his own boss, and the head of his own, happy family.

He no longer notices the indoor heated pool, sunken garden, summerhouse and tennis court, and his tears constantly blur the very best vista that money can buy. Soil dug, grass cut, greenery lopped and reaped, he watches the short flurries of activity between long spade leaning pauses, and he sees only Henry Thompson's sad, old eyes. And hears only his stupid younger self.

'I know she looks twenty-five, Henry. She might even have told you that she was twenty-five. But Elaine is fourteen and you've sexually abused a little girl. A little girl just like Joy.'

30

The sadistic ogre dead but my star witness feeling even less safe and still not talking, I've a murder to solve and all I know with any kind of certainty is that more people wanted nasty Anthony dead than turn up on a Saturday afternoon to watch United. Of suspects I have way more than I can handle. Of useful information, I have bugger all.

I believe Kausar when she says that she concealed a knife that she intended to retrieve and use to stab Gutowski to death. But I also believe her when she says that the opportunity, like Anthony's todger - *sorry Granny* - failed to arise. And, regrettably, wanting to kill a scumbag isn't a crime, or they'd have put me away long ago.

'Can I have word in private, please ma'am?' Sam has the haunted look of a woman with a secret to tell.

I'm pleased that she's finally decided to unburden, a trouble shared etc., but this suddenly feels like me being placed at the wrong end of yet another impossible to solve passion puzzle, and recent events have proved that, not only am I crap at solving passion puzzles, I'm also crap at life. Whilst I'm searching for a change the subject strategy, her words begin tumbling like autumn leaves in a blizzard, and it seems that I'm 'it'.

Having listened carefully, and surprisingly, to me at least, understood everything that Sam has said, it's immediately obvious that my young colleague needs a coherent slab of useful advice. But, as I suspected, I'm caught slabless. So, I try to formulate a response somewhere between 'adversity is a good thing, and in the long run you'll come through this tougher stronger and more able to live the life you want,' and 'all you can do is learn to live with damage that will never completely go away.' But, a combination of my afore mentioned ineptitude, and the fact that murders and attempted murders are stacked like a Jenga tower with no obvious stick tp pull, causes me to quickly lose patience, abandon all thought of a measured response, and to let rip and see what develops.

'What in Heaven's name did you expect to change, Sam? Did you think that he'd flip from chauvinistic pillock to thoroughly decent chap overnight? Did you imagine that you two could ever continue to work happily together?' Sam's eyes and shoulders drop. 'I thought not.' My approach has become harsher than intended. Happens to me a lot. So, I tone it down. 'There are some things that you can't cope with on your own. Some things that require the help of other people.'

Dejected and hands clasped tightly in her lap, Sam murmurs, 'yes, ma'am,' before adding, 'I know that I must be more prepared to ask for help, but I don't want people to see me as a complainer. I want to be a team player. I ...' Words that clearly once burned hot and dangerous are now cold and serving no purpose, and all Sam can do is sigh. Once again, I take charge.

'Listen you. You've done nothing wrong. And you're worth a hundred of that narcissistic fucker. So, head up, shoulders back, chest out, we're going to show him and everybody else what professional, high calibre women can do.

'Can't be me, not in the first instance, so it'll have to be Bill that meets with you and your union rep. when you make your formal complaint.'

'But there's such ...' Sam is shocked by the cavalier use of the term 'formal complaint,' but her objections quickly die on her lips. 'Yes, ma'am,' she says. 'But before I do that, there's something that I must tell you. Something that's even more important. Something that you're not going to like.'

*

'STENTON HIT RUSSELL ON THE BACK OF HIS KNEES WITH A BLOODY BIG CHAIN AND THREATENED TO STAB HIM WITH A BIG KNIFE?' My screech is enough to shock us both.

'Yes, ma'am.' I can see that Sam is struggling to get this said and I indicate that, despite appearances, I am calm, and ready for her to continue. 'Sergeant Russell couldn't move, and he was helpless for long enough for Stenton to get the upper hand.' Sam's demeanour changes from nervous to terrified and I brace myself. 'Exactly as seems to have happened to Anthony Gutowski.' I knew it was coming but the statement hits hard.

'Before you contact your union and fill out your complaint form, Sam, I want you to ring Colin and tell him to swing by Michael's school and to pick up Stenton Cornthwaite, if he's in, and bring him here to see me. If he's not there, Colin's to find him.

'I'd like to interview Veronique myself - at least one of the two of us should do it, you, or me, ideally both. But it's all kicking off at once, Russell can't take part for obvious reasons, and Jim Renevant is snowed under with work that has a strict deadline. So, it looks as though it'll be you and Colin. We need time to put Bill in the picture and to give you the opportunity to go with Colin to the hospital. What do you say to the idea of delaying the complaint about Russell? Just for a day or so.'

*

In the end, the interview with Kevin Caldwell that was scheduled for the morning, that morning, took place at 2 p.m. with Paul Drury-Smith's 'no comment' advice followed to the letter. It was as disappointing as it was late. Disappointing but not a complete waste, because I noticed that the big lad with the enormous, enflamed beard has kind eyes. Not professional, logical, analytical, or even sensible, and unlikely to be found in 'how to succeed as a detective' textbooks, but I just can't see Caldwell as a cold blooded, calculating killer.

Bill agrees, though he fails to mention the eyes, and the two of us decide that somebody else is pulling Kevin's strings. And that we need to find out who.

*

Now 3 p.m., interviews fast becoming my least favourite thing - and I've got more least favourite things than most - this one, the one involving Stenton, is well on its way to planet fruitless. Desperately wanting to please his bestie DCI, and Jess Simcox who is acting as the responsible adult, Stenton can't stop commenting. The odd 'no comment' would be a relief. 'Yes, I did whack that bad sergeant,' 'no, I've not hit anybody else ... yet.' If every sensible word that the lad uttered was laid end to end, it wouldn't reach the length of a gnat's dick, as Grandad, who Granny always blamed, poor sod, for my potty mouth, used to say. And the only thing pointing to the Boy Blunder is the MO. Why? Because it's a bloody big, pulsating, impossible to ignore

101

MO, that, at this moment, can't be explained. Nevertheless, just one link is nowhere near enough.

'The sergeant was going to hurt Miss, Miss,' says Stenton passionately. 'And I was outside, keeping an eye like. On Miss. For Mr Charlie. They live next door to one another you know?' My reply is 10% amusement and 90% exasperation.

'I'm aware of where they live, Stenton. But it was nine o'clock at night, pitch black and bitterly cold, and you're thirteen-years-old and on a curfew.'

'But you and Miss, Miss, have been good to me, Miss. Only right for me to protect Miss if I can. And Mr Charlie is a very old man.' Said as if Charlie Butterell should think twice before purchasing a fresh supply of toilet roll.

'Just don't turn up at my house to protect me,' I say, and the little boy who finds all sorts of unfunny stuff hilarious, laughs himself silly.

'You, Miss? You don't need protectin'. Nobody messes with you.' It's meant as a compliment, but somehow, I'm insulted. Fed up with failing to make progress, I decide to revisit the very specific back of the knee connection for a fourth and final time. This time I press the lad hard and Stenton waits a beat, thinking. Then: 'Mr Charlie won't get into trouble, will he, Miss?' I sense a breakthrough.

'Nah, you know me, Stenton. Trouble is always the very last thing on my mind.' Jess grins and so does Stenton. He likes it like this. Three grownups sharing 'insider' jokes. He seems to make up his mind.

'Well Mr Charlie told me about when he was a kid, and he was getting' picked on by bigger kids. He said that he'd wait until he could take 'em by surprise and then 'e'd 'it 'em on the back of their knees with a bike chain. You've got to 'it them sticky-out lines that go from the top of your leg to your muscle at the bottom of your leg. You 'it 'em hard just there.' Stenton has his trouser leg rolled up and he's pointing as he's talking. 'It gets 'em down and kinda makes 'em so they can't move, like quick, for a bit. Mr Charlie says you've got to 'it dead 'ard and on the right spot, first time, and then be ready with your next move before they've time to get their proper feelin' back.'

Resisting the temptation to ask how members of the male gender always seem to be able to source a bike chain whenever needed, I summarise.

'So, Mr Butterell, who lives next door to Detective Constable Jardine, showed you how to hit somebody you want to get the better of, on the back of the legs, and then you tried it out on Sergeant Russell?'

'Yes, Miss. Mr Charlie knows everythin'. Mr Charlie's brilliant!'

31

Stenton remained at Main Street Nick far longer than was necessary, and he had to be virtually pushed through the doors so that he and Jess could be police-car-taxied back to Dean House. He signed his statement with a theatrical flourish, Donald Trump style, and I had to remind him to return my pen. Only then did I tell Bill about how Sergeant Stan Russell has behaved towards Samantha Jardine.

Bill rates Sam highly, as a colleague and a person, and I was worried that he might let his feelings get in the way of his duty. And had that been the case, a wallop with a bike chain would have been the least of Russell's worries. But Bill reacts more calmly that expected, and his professional approach is a relief, not least because I'm now confident that he's the right man to conduct Russell's preliminary, fact-finding interview. I begin setting clear parameters as to how I wants the interview done: contemporaneous notes and Russell offered a witness of his choosing to be present; a no blame suspension on full pay with immediate effect and with no remarks added to his file; strong advice, given and repeated, to talk his union rep before the meeting, the same rep to be present at the meeting; and Russell clearly informed that he can have direct access to me, his DCI, should he want or need it. Delegating this tricky issue to safe hands means one less thing for me to deal with. But it's Russell's word against Samantha's, the hastily taken photo only proving that he visited her house not that it was both unprofessional and unwanted, Stenton an unreliable witness easily accused of misreading the situation and overreacting, and Mr Butterell only arriving at the end. Nauseating though the thought is, a mutually agreed, brush all wrongdoing under a thick carpet, voluntary transfer to a distant force, might be the best option.

I'm glad of a quiet period to try to get all my ducks in a row, and for a better solution to the Russell issue to pop into my head. But every pop involves Veronique not Russell or even Sam and generates yet another question. Why would the victim of a life-threatening attack insist on giving credit for her rescue to someone who clearly was not involved, whilst denying someone who most certainly was? Charlie Butterell not Night Nurse Siobhan Behan performed the heroics. So why, especially now that Anthony Gutowski is no more, is Veronique, the woman I've come to think of as a friend, saying different? And why is Charlie Butterell backing up her story? Even Siobhan's own written statement is gushing in its praise of Charlie. But, when confronted with it, Veronique falls back on: 'well I was a bit out of it,' 'can't really remember,' 'didn't see much.'

Getting nowhere fast, I decide to revisit Darren Bates' file, and to reread the lad's handwritten suicide note.

Dear Dad,

The last thing you said to me was I had got to look after our Louise and I have not done very well. I tried dad but I have let you down a lot I am sorry. She got in with some baduns up here and two lads keep putting her in danger and I can not manage to protect her all the time. It is not our Louises fault dad. It is all my fault. I have tried everything and I can not think what else to do and now I have got to do the right thing even though I do not want to. I no that losing mum sent you funny and I do not want to do the same. But I think you will soon get back to how it used to be with our Louise. Eric Mister Leather always says that what I am going to do is a sin. I hope he is rong. Goodbye dad. I am very sorry.

Love

Darren your son

I want to exonerate Michael, nab Holroyd and Gutowski, and find Joan's missing ransom money. But each unevenly etched pencil letter generated by a lad I never met but feel like I know and can't bring back, fills me with deep melancholy, and I find myself thinking of another, new question that keeps repeating like acid reflux: is it all worth it?

32

Seven, black, Iron Maiden tee shirts; seven, black, trunk underpants; and seven, black, pairs of socks; all fitting neatly into one drawer, the second reserved for clothes awaiting their sink and soap, hand wash. Much resoled black biker-boots stand alongside his prison issue single bed. And his black leather biker-trousers and black Hell's Angels biker-jacket cling to one wire coat hanger nipping the picture railing that encircles his 10-foot x 12-foot room. Marvin owns a pedal cycle, drives Holroyd's Range Rover Sport, and has never in his life owned a motorcar or driven a motorbike. He believes that he lacks the necessary balance and co-ordination for two wheels moving at speed, but debilitating reticence crafted by recurrent embarrassment is really to blame.

Growing up big and black in Barnsley - 'a bit slow' according to his four-foot-eleven, white mother, 'a useless lump' according to his six-foot-four, black father - and standing out when all he wanted to do was blend in, Marvin's daily life was punishing until, age fourteen, he lamped a twenty-year-old bully, who was hospitalised for a long, long time. Respect had arrived, and existence got easier. But damage already done, and any kind of decision making still to this day has the power to generate heart-palpitating panic. So, teenage Marvin opted never to decide anything. And the habit, like his daft nickname, persists.

Looking like an enforcer ought to look, and slavishly following the judgements of those more mentally agile than himself, quickly led him to a prison cell, and the company of one Albie Holroyd who offered a life where all decisions would be taken for him. And from that moment on, he hasn't needed to remember to pay a bill, buy food, or think what he might do today, or tomorrow, or for the rest of his life. To pass the time, he crafts objects, mainly from wood, and they sit, seen only by their creator, in his otherwise bare room. He has a modest but regular salary that, on average, he dips into less than twice a year, and he has no costs. Plenty would give their eyeteeth for his bank balance, and he's given extra money as and when he needs it, which is never. And in return, he's become the never acknowledged and largely unnoticed non-person that he always wanted to be.

And that's how things were destined to remain until, recently, disappointment at not having what others regard as a life appeared from nowhere, and finally began to chafe. And now the big enforcer has reached a point where, given the opportunity, he would do something of his own choosing ... if only he could decide what that something might be.

*

Forced to hold his own jacket by the lapels and away from his body, the checking for weapons accomplished in silence, and left in no-man's land uncertain as to whether he's passed muster and can proceed to Albie's inner sanctum, Gus stands like a newly arrived, first time prison inmate, naked and dreading the internal inspection. His task completed, Marvin returns to sit on his hard plastic chair, next to his Formica table, and continues reading his Daily Star.

Having finally plucked up sufficient courage to ease open the connecting door and edge into the living room, Gus' agitation level soars as he sees Marvin put down his paper and follow him in. Three people are to be present in this meeting. A rare change in procedure that will have a distinct purpose that both visitor and bodyguard know they will not like.

In the normal course of events, seeing Gutowski in such discomfort would give Marvin pleasure. But knowing about Albie's penchant for young flesh is one thing, catching sight of pipe cleaner legs and plywood arms pushing at tissue paper skin disappearing upstairs in light blue nickers and yellow boob tube, is something else entirely. He can sense that Albie can smell Gus's 'that could be my Joy' thinking, and he wants to crush his boss' scrawny neck ... but he doesn't. Fighting not to retch, instead he scans his boss with a mixture of admiration and loathing. Marvin realised long ago that Albie's pantomime clothes and bad actor style are both armour and weapon because they shriek a confident pride at not caring what others think. Dressed as always in a tailored, navy-blue, double-breasted suit and red pocket square, black shiny shoes with tan spats, sparkling white shirt and light grey fedora with a red band, and red tie, The

107

Man wants the world to know that he acknowledges no boundaries. And by doing so, he is instantly able to inflate from disconcerting to incapacitating, giving him an edge that he invariably uses to game winning effect. Confronted by a proud paedophile pariah, Gus is already looking wretched. The sight of the urchin, however fleeting, has done its job.

'You think that I invited you to dinner because I needed an alibi while your brother was being murdered,' squeaks Holroyd before a timed to perfection linger. 'You're right, of course.' Stark, boastful, and stated before Gus has had chance to sit down. Delighted by what he has done, Holroyd wants Gus and Marvin to know it. The Man continues. 'On that night, at that time, a murder that I ordered was happening.' The second pause is electric and Gus glances towards Marvin who sets himself for action. 'While we were putting on our performance at Zizzi's, breath was being squeezed out of the scrawny body of our old friend ... Veronique.'

It's a straight left from Little Bo Peep and it has floored Big Gus. Mouth curling and fighting but losing to his urge to cry, he begins blubbing ... and Marvin is disgusted.

'You s-set ... me ... up.'

'I didn't kill Anthony or have him killed, Gus.' Albie is emphasising as if instructing a toddler.

'You ... used ... us, Tammy and me.'

'You don't seem to be listening, Gus.' The sneer is overflowing with contempt. 'Try to concentrate. I ... didn't ... kill ... Anthony ... or ... have ... him ... killed.' The corners of Holroyd's mouth rise a fraction, for a moment his teeth are slightly visible, and Marvin recognises the signs. His boss has surprised himself and thought of what he considers an amusing quip. 'Anthony's behaviour was opening floodgates that I didn't want opened, but that doesn't mean that I wanted him dead.' *'Now the gag,'* thinks Marvin. 'Somebody else jumped to the head of the long queue and got to him before I did. Who'd have thought?' Utterly humourless. A joke only to Holroyd who knows it and not only doesn't care but is pleased by the confusing effect. 'Your little brother never did much that was useful in his wasted life, Gus. But he did make me realise that Veronique could do us harm, and that she's become too dangerous to live.'

Gus is incredulous. 'So, Veronique is dead?' he asks. Albie's reply is shrieked irritation and Marvin takes a moment's pleasure from his boss' annoyance.

'No! She's not dead because the task was not finished!' His emotions back in check, Holroyd becomes more calculating. The fedora rises just enough for the leer playing on his wrinkled lips to become visible, and Marvin is suddenly sure. *This is why I'm in the room. This is a message for me. Not Gus. Me.*

The small, folded face is now consumed by an evil, not to be messed with, grin. 'Unfinished business, Gus.' He's looking at Gutowski but talking to Marvin. 'But not for long, eh, not for long.'

33

Charlie is getting handshakes and actual pats on the back, and there was even spontaneous applause when he Sam and Colin met up in Rotherham Hospital's reception area. Sam is delighted. Calling Mr Butterell by his first name feels easier today.

'What's it like to be a hero, Charlie?' Expecting a modest 'all in a day's work' smile, or a 'can't get any work done today for people wanting to say well done' self-effacing shrug, when the old man says nothing and looks like he's lost a pound and found a penny, Sam is more than puzzled, she's worried. A man in Charlie's position should not look miserable. They find a quiet corner to have a chat.

'Your shift finished at 5.30, is that right?'

'Yes, Sam. 5.30.'

'So why were you still here at 10 p.m.?' An obvious point to be cleared up, and yet Sam's neighbour looks scared, as if he has something to hide. And the answer to her question is still to arrive when the DCI takes a nearby chair. Gesturing an apology for interrupting, she signals Charlie to carry on and pushes slightly backwards, presumably to show Sam and Colin that she wants to be close enough to see and hear, but far enough away to keep her interference down to a dull roar. Her arrival is unexpected and bound to be a little disconcerting for all three of them, but Sam can see that it has terrified - no other word for it - Charlie. White bits have appeared around his dry lips, a sheen of sweat is coating his brow, and he's starting to look like yet another obvious perpetrator about to resort to 'no comment.'

'I ... er ... left my phone in ... er,' his eyes are everywhere but on Sam Colin or Julie, 'my locker. And I ... er ... I came in to get it.' Aware that his strange and unexpected manner is spreading concern, Charlie seems incapable of doing anything about it.

'Couldn't it have waited until the next morning, Mr Butterell?' asks Colin, who's meeting Sam's neighbour for the first time.

'I didn't ... notice ... I didn't notice that I ... that I didn't have it until about nine o'clock,' the old man says as if he's struggling to believe what's coming out of his own mouth. 'And I've got so I like to know what's on it.' Then, as an afterthought, '... and it's my alarm clock.'

'But the locker room is a long way away from Ward A22, Charlie. Opposite end of a very big hospital, in fact.' The DCI's intervention comes as a shock, especially by the look of her to the DCI herself. Sam can tell that Julie's intention had been to allow her less experienced colleagues to take charge, and the boss will be annoyed about her lack of self-control. But she needn't be. Sam is just glad that a senior officer is here, and she suspects that Colin feels the same. 'So, you forget your phone and you come in to retrieve it, got all of that, Charlie. But I still can't see how that gets you anywhere near Ward A22, and Veronique Sabet.'

*

The cosy café in the hospital reception area seemed appropriate for more of a friend's get-together than an interrogation, but it's a poor fit for questioning a witness who is being deliberately obtuse. I put on my kindly copper face - not difficult because I like the old duffer - and say, 'we're not trying to catch you out, Charlie. If it hadn't been for you, it's an absolute racing certainty that Kevin Caldwell would have killed Veronique Sabet. It's just that there are some inconsistencies that we need to clear up. Ts to cross and Is to dot, you know the kind of thing,'

Charlie is thinking much too hard and for much too long. Eventually, he reveals,

'When I first saw the young woman, Miss Sabet, I was saddened by the state she was in. Nobody deserves that kind of mistreatment and I wanted to know that she was all right. Couldn't settle at home. I know it's daft, but I needed to see her ... to reassure myself that she was okay.' Charlie is cutting a pitiable figure, Sam looks as though she's going to throw up, Colin looks like a man unable to recognise the nice old codger that had been promised, and I'm not satisfied.

'Thing is, Charlie, I've been looking into the files of a seventeen-year-old boy called Darren Bates.' There is no reaction from Charlie, but both Sam and Colin sit up. 'Almost thirty years ago, Darren was charged with an unlawful killing.' This time Charlie twitches. 'The victim was twelve-years-old Abigail Hardcastle.

'I've read and re-read Darren's case notes over the last few days, but, just today, I noticed something for the first time. Isn't it funny how you can see things but not actually see them?' Charlie Butterell is leaning and listening intently, his translucent, unbelievably sad eyes are now focussed and aware.

I choose not to elaborate.

'I think, Mr Butterell, we need to continue this conversation, under caution, back at the station, don't you?'

34

Charlie Butterell has politely declined duty solicitor Paul Drury-Smith's advice, which, predictably, was to say nothing, and he has already asked that Samantha not be present at the interview, because he 'couldn't bear to see the disappointment on her face.' He's also requested that someone tell Stenton why he won't be able to be his friend anymore. With Colin riding shotgun, I commence the digging.

'Thirty years ago, seventeen-year-old Darren Bates was involved in the suspicious death of Abigail Hardcastle, who was eleven/twelve at the time. Darren and his sister Louise, also eleven/twelve, were originally from Leicester. Their mum had died suddenly and unexpectedly, their dad was struggling to cope, there was no extended family to call upon, and so they were long-term fostered.' I pause before adding: 'and at this point the first incongruity appears.

'For reasons we haven't been able to fathom, the choice of foster parents was a couple called Eric and Enid Leather, who provided a perfectly acceptable foster home, in fact a very good one. But the Leathers home was a farm in Harthill, and therefore up in our area. An hour and a half's drive from Leicester. And the question is: why? I have no doubt that there are many excellent foster homes near to the people and places that the children already knew. Perhaps even close enough to their home so that Darren and Louise could have remained at their schools with their friends. And I can think of only one reason why Social Services would make the choice that they did. And that reason is that they wanted to get the children as far away as they could … from their dad.'

I'm disappointed to see no reaction and no change in Mr Butterell's expression. Sticking to my game-plan, I continue.

'Darren and Louise knew Abigail Hardcastle from school in Kiveton Park, and Louise would have considered herself to be Abigail's best friend.' Still no reaction. 'And when Darren was charged with Abigail's murder …' Charlie shudders. Only slightly, but I'm encouraged. 'He was remanded in custody,

113

awaiting trial. We think that the charge would have been reduced to manslaughter by the time the case came to court, perhaps even dropped altogether.' Charlie's head shoots up at this observation, and I wait before adding, 'regrettably, we'll never know, because, distraught and lonely, Darren cut his own wrists in his cell.'

Charlie Butterell is now grappling with a myriad of noticeable emotions and, realising that his solicitor could soon request a pause, I step up the pace. 'We're not happy that Abigail's death was as thoroughly investigated as it should have been and, despite not being satisfied that the gathered interview statements fitted the forensic evidence, the authorities at the time decided that, because Darren committed suicide, admitted burying the body and being the only other person present at Abi's death, and was not around to interrogate further, in the absence of any other more likely suspects, wrapping it up tight and much too soon was the best way to proceed. My team and I think that Abigail deserves better, so we've looked again at what was proved all those years ago, this time considering possible contemporary connections. And, today in fact, my brain managed to pick up on something that I should have seen much sooner.'

All by themselves, my words have fallen into a rhythm and, in contrast to Paul Drury-Smith who is desperate to say the right things to protect his client but clearly has not yet arrived at the races, Colin looks to have deciphered where his DCI's narrative is leading. 'I've read about Darren and his sister, and I thought that I'd learned all I could from the information available. But just today, I realised the significance of some of the names involved.

'This whole thing started when, tragically, Ronnie Bates swerved to avoid a child chasing a football, and hit a lamppost head-on. She died at the scene and left a family bereft and unable to survive without her. A family that disintegrated in the most horrible way.

'Well, today I noticed, I mean really understood, the significance of Mrs Bates first name.'

Charlie Butterell is rigid. Holding his breath. Seemingly aware of what I'm about to reveal and torn between wanting it said and wanting it hidden, forever. 'Ronnie is a diminutive of

Veronica. And the French Veronica is Veronique. But you already knew that didn't you Donald.'

Like a delicate crocus losing its battle for survival to the harshest of winter snows, the old man's rangy body seems to close in on itself, and Colin eases back into his chair. Paul Drury-Smith has the look of a man who's been hit by a train and still doesn't know how he got onto the tracks. I carry on.

'Any vaguely foreign accent will pass for French in South Yorkshire and rearranging the letters of Bates to Sabet allowed Louise to keep hold of her real self. But she took a risk. A big, unnecessary risk. She must have cared deeply for her biological family. That must have pleased you, Donald, that must have pleased you very much.'

'She's a good girl.' A few uttered words. Significant enough to consign Charlie Butterell to the shadows, there to remain.

'The kind of girl to make any father proud, Donald.' It's a point upon which we can agree, and I'm pleased that Bates is about to tell all. However, seeing the change in his body language makes me uneasy, to say the least.

'When Louise was seventeen,' his tone is transforming into the equivalent of a strut, 'she came to visit me at St Hilda's.' Suddenly eager for clarity, he explains: 'it's like an old folks' home for vulnerable adults. But it's really a sanatorium for the mentally ill.' He waits, needing to be sure that his audience understands. 'The people there managed to upset her.' Cheated. Mistreated. Owed. This is a theme of which he has experience.

'Everybody there was well paid to be nice, and to pretend that they had my best interests at heart. But my life ended the second that Ronnie was taken. And there was nothing that anybody, anybody at all, could say or do that would help.

'But their attitude was hurtful and cruel. And because of them, Louise's first visit was her last visit.' Donald Bates' eyes blaze and his fists curl. 'Because of them, I didn't see my daughter again until that day in a hospital bed. And I will never forgive them, never!'

He becomes chatty, conspiratorial. 'You're a clever woman, chief inspector. You've seen how everybody gets in line to make money from picking over the bones of honest people down on their luck like me and mine. First the Leathers let Louise and

Darren down so badly, then, loured by pound signs, the Greens arrive at the trough and change my daughter's name to theirs. Can you believe that! And Social Services agreed to it!' The resentment, replaced by lively resignation, is gone as quickly as it comes. 'I suppose I shouldn't have expected any better. Nobody cares about a Bates. Never have, never will. And from the moment that they called her Jane, Jane Green, the lives of Ronnie and me were ripped away and forgotten.' Nose rising into the air, he puts on a snooty voice. 'My keyworker kept telling me to "go with the flow, Donald. Don't fight against things you can do nothing about. Learn to accept. Look forward, not back." Easy to say, but each time I thought about Louise, a part of me died.' Suddenly, the chirpy chappie is back. 'But after years of hard work and sacrifice, I was able to get a job and so move out of St Hilda's. First, I went to sheltered housing because they insisted. Then, I graduated to a bedsit on my own - what a red-letter day that was. And finally, I made it the heady heights of tenant in a house.

'I've always known that I would never recover from all the terrible things that people have thrown at me,' he's sad again. 'Nobody could. But not knowing where Louise was and what she was up to was harming my already fragile health, and when they made me redundant at work and I got a payoff, I decided that there was nothing to stop me coming up to South Yorkshire to seek her out.' Too little and years too bloody late is on the tip of my tongue, but there it stays. 'I found out that the Greens had moved to Australia years before, and Social Services said that they could only give me information about Louise if Louise herself said it was okay to do so.' Just for a fleeting moment, Donald Bates looks like a man in the throes of a heart attack, which in one sense he is. 'I can only suppose that she didn't want me in her life,' he says, head bowed and beaten. Then he instantly becomes a big-eyed puppy playing cute to get extra food. 'I knew that her foster so called parents wouldn't have taken Louise with them, so, about three years ago, I settled into the house next to Sam. Time flies,' he says, his Charlie Butterell laugh extremely disturbing. 'I guessed that Louise would still be in the Rotherham area, and my plan was to live here, do some volunteering at the hospital as a good way of meeting people, and to get around the town so that I might bump into her, or find someone who knew her and where she was living. The odds were against me. No change there, then.' Lightening with no thunder warning, suddenly he's a man ready and able to kill. 'But when I saw my lovely, sweet girl in that bed, her beautiful face disfigured and police at her side, my family still under attack after all this time, I knew that nothing had changed, and that it was time to fight back.' Bates grins. Accepting that he's lost the game but still looking to conjure up bragging rights. 'I followed you to Brinsworth when you left the hospital. And I watched the big tyrant that I'd seen in the hospital car park enter a house that clearly had you interested. You didn't spot me following you, did you?' Cheeky Mr Butterell merges seamlessly into disturbed Mr Bates: 'after work, I waited in the shadows with a knife and a piece of scaffolding, and I killed him.'

Paul Drury-Smith asks to have a moment with his client, but Donald Bates hasn't finished. He wants this 'on the record.' 'I thought that I would have to wait a long time before an opportunity came along but he walked right passed me on the very first night. I hit the back of his legs with the big metal pipe, and he went down. Then I stabbed him a few times.' A simple, yet to be finished chronicle of what happened. 'I was going to smash his skull with the scaffolding. But when he straightened and I had the knife ready, I slit his throat instead. Thinking on my feet, you see. I've always been good at that.' Bates laugh as he mimes the throat slitting is chilling, and both Colin and Paul have stopped making notes.

Donal Bates and I lock eyes until he breaks the stare and looks away. Then, for a fleeting moment, he has the aura of a man about to salute. With stilted formality, he proclaims,

'I Donald Walter Bates confess to the unlawful but completely justified killing of Anthony Gutowski. I did the deed on my own and no-one else was involved in the planning, or in the act itself. I am far from repentant, and my only regret is that I can only kill him once. I am a good man and a good father, and the proof is lying on a cold, hard slab, in a damp, dark morgue, somewhere in sunny Rotherham.'

35

Louise Bates knows that he can never harm her again, and her relief is verging on overwhelming. She knows that the police have no choice but to punish his murderer. And she understands. Even agrees. But it isn't justice. Locking somebody up for doing a public service might be the law, but it isn't right. She has nothing to fear and everything to look forward to. And it's all because of Anthony Gutowski's killer.

Sam Jardine's unexpected visit - 'Hello, Veronique, or would you prefer Louise?' - triggers tears of joy that fall as if they have a life of their own ... and Louise can't seem to make them stop. Suddenly the patient is having a relapse and Sam is frantically waving for a nurse before, with obvious difficulty, Louise manages to hold up a painfully stiff hand and, faux French completely replaced by authentic, ee by gum Rotherham, can say,

'I'm okay. Honest I am.' Clearly embarrassed, she adds: 'see, it's just that I'm just so bloody happy!'

All three women - the no longer needed nurse, the detective, and the born-again casualty - are laughing, and then every patient visitor auxiliary and nurse on the ward is clapping, and it's all for Louise who starts to cry...again. The nurse affectionately touches her hand and returns to her station, and the ward settles into a relaxed and pleased with itself demeanour.

'Nobody has been as good to me as you have, Sam, ever.' Passions is overflowing but this time both Sam and Louise know to take a moment to gather themselves ... and that's when Louise notices that Sam is nervous. 'What is it, Sam? What's the matter?'

'Bad news should come from someone who cares, and you won't want to hear what I've got to say. You're going to be distressed and I'm sorry.'

'Just tell me, Sam. Whatever it is, it won't be your fault.'

'It's about Mr Butterell,' says Sam, taking a breath for courage. 'Donald Bates. Your dad.' Louise nods. 'I have to tell you that Donald, your dad … has confessed to the murder of Anthony Gutowski.'

Peaks have been rare in a life scarred by endless troughs, and every peak has flattered to deceive. But this latest and best moment in the sun has lasted just long enough for Louise to realise that, despite what she had started to think, she will never leave her crumbling coffin held tight within its sticky black pit. Her fragile air tube is just as useless as she thought. And it really is raining. She's where she deserves to be and there's no point her wishing for better.

The whining is subdued at first but rapidly grows louder, and the kind nurse hurries back to her patient's bedside before pulling round the curtains. She orders Sam to 'grab a coffee,' and returning twenty minutes later with two cappuccinos and two KitKat bars, the curtains are gone, and Louise is sitting up … but her face is horrendously sad. Placing the drinks on a bedside cabinet, the young DC says,

'I'm sorry, love, but there's more … you should also know that Mr Butterell, I mean Mr Bates, is my neighbour.'

This is a new kind of pain and Louise is sobbing again. 'You know him personally? Perhaps he's even a friend?' Sam nods. 'So, you know my dad better than I do' - said with deflated resignation.

'He did a bad thing, Louise,' Sam says quickly, 'but he's the nicest old man you could ever wish to meet. And he did it for you. Because he loves you. I've not known him long, but he's become a kind of surrogate granddad.'

Gesturing for Sam to come closer, Louise hugs her before holding her at arm's length and mouthing, 'sorry.' Then, she declares,

'Get out your pen and notebook, Sam, I need to get something off my chest. You write, every word, and I'll sign it.'

36

Allegedly, only Winterbourne and Roger Huddart witnessed Michael Lloyd exiting the place of Terry Makin's death at the time of Terry Makin's death. I can't interrogate Winterbourne on account of him having been shuffled off this mortal coil by the wrong end of a flathead screwdriver. Conclusion: unless Huddart says that his mate Chris was lying, Michael might have been criminally involved in the death of Joan Burling's disabled older brother.

If I ask Michael directly, he'll deny, whatever the truth of the matter.

I could let sleeping disabled brothers lie and live with uncertainty for the rest of my life. Problem: I've already had a husband who I couldn't trust, and I can't knowingly get involved in such a stupid arrangement for a second time. So, the solution is a proper investigation. And since Sam, bless her, must spend this evening with her Police Federation Rep., and since I'm a big girl now and a detective to boot, I will be doing the investigating on my own.

Huddart whose first name turns out to be Richard - Roger being his middle name - and who now goes by the name of Rick, is quickly found living just down the road in a very ordinary no-frills house in Whiston, one of the more sort-after parts of Rotherham. The ease and speed of my successful search emphasising that I should have done this long ago, my heart in my mouth but still managing to pound in my ears, Big Bag making my left shoulder list thirty-degrees from horizontal and in danger of causing me to spin in ever-decreasing concentric circles, still feeling ill-equipped for knocking on the red-for-danger door, I do so only because I really do now have no option. The exuberant 'oh, thanks for coming, I'm so pleased to see you!' is the opposite of what I expected, and it would leave me even more unsettled if that was remotely possible.

Early twenties, red cried-out eyes and no make-up, five inches below my five-foot-six, and with a bulky symmetry, the young woman with silver tipped geometrically cut purple hair has me over the threshold, in a specific seat, and offered a hot drink, before a word is uttered. And then the pint-sized tornado is instantly off to tackle what sounds like kettle and cups. Almost simultaneously, the Big Ben doorbell bongs loudly and, thinking that I'm helping, I stand and make to see who it is. Returning like a heat-seeking missile, Busy Bee vigorously gestures her honoured guest - me - to sit before making her way to a brief and muffled conversation on the doorstep. Everything happening much too quickly, she's back again, and this time she's accompanied by a just shy of scrawny, conservatively dressed lady, who's sporting a briefcase and a professionally sympathetic smile that evaporates as soon as it encounters visitor number one - again, me.

'Who are you?' she demands as if it's her house. Feeling more done to than doing, I snap right back.

'Detective Chief Inspector Julie Marsden.' Then, turning and directing an exaggeratedly friendly smile to the young woman who's strung out like she has ten kids all under thirteen, and a full washing line, in a hurricane, I say, 'I'd like to talk with Roger Huddart. Perhaps you know him as Rick.'

Both women look confounded, though one of them soon recovers and is immediately ready to rumble. But before she can trigger both barrels, the younger female, who turns out to be Roger/Richard/Rick's daughter, detonates, not bursts or even erupts, but detonates, into hysterical tears. Number Two Visitor is now an emaciated whippet chewing a wasp, her expression alone conveying that this poor excuse for a police officer has, not for the first time, dipped the family gerbil into hot chip fat. I know that I've dropped a bollock. At this precise moment, I have no idea which of the many and varied bollock dropping possibilities I've stumbled upon, or how damaging this dropped bollock will turn out to be; but a bollock has been dropped, and it's a big one.

*

Hit and run! Just days ago! On a zebra crossing! Dying in the ambulance on his way to hospital! Genuinely mortified by Claire Huddart's predicament, I can't get the expressions of regret: 'so sorry for your loss … if I'd known, I never would have …' up out and into the room fast enough. Flowing like lava, each

121

platitude burning my throat more than the last, every utterance awash with eau de heartless bitch who's only contrite because she's been caught with her hand in the poor box, there is nothing that I can say or do to put things right and I know it. What must poor bereaved Claire Huddart be thinking? Heartbroken and at one of those life-defining moments is bad enough. But an uninvited idiot, whose day job is that of detective chief inspector, being so crass as to gate crash a wake and attempt to question the deceased without first checking that he's sufficiently alive to venture an answer, beggars belief, and I can't remember a time when I've felt worse.

No chance now of tipping the balance in favour of Michael's innocence, my own loss feels, God help me, just as terminal as Claire's. I still have a career that affords some sort of compensation for the disappointments of motherhood and marriage, and none of my loved ones have died. But I'd let myself anticipate. I'd started to believe. I'd let my guard down, gone for the knockout, and been floored by the sucker punch that I should have seen coming. I'd opened the door to hope. And while that bastard won't come in, which is fine, he won't go away either. And that's a game-changer.

It turns out that Briefcase has been booked to conduct the humanist funeral of Richard 'Rick' Roger Huddart, and therefore her appointment with daughter Claire was pre-arranged and for a clear purpose. Making me feel even more dreadful, were that a possibility, which it isn't. At her best when divining for despair, every one of her humanistic cells sickened that the police force can be so insensitive, her intention to ensure that I continue to feel like a one-legged woman at an arse kicking party remains as she brandishes her shiny gold pen like a lightsabre and begins taking notes in preparation for the funeral. Exuding the kind of professionalism that this police officer is likely not to recognise let alone possess, and flipping her leather-bound pad like she's beheading chickens, at her prompting, Claire Huddart speaks and sobs and sobs and speaks. And, by osmosis, the gate crasher, as well as the invited guest, learns all about Richard/Roger/Rick.

He was nearing his forty-first birthday, eleven years divorced and single for the last nine of those years. Until his recent plummet from good health, he owned a picture framing shop in

Whiston. He played golf. Watched footie. And was a Whiston Parish Church bell ringer.

'It's just been the two of us since I was eight,' says Claire. 'I've been working in the shop, well, since then really. Officially getting paid since I was sixteen. No other kids, so I'm his next of kin. Mum hasn't spoken to Dad since the divorce.' No longer flitting around like a blue arsed fly on Valium, she's looking exhausted. Still very emotional, a build-up boil-over pattern is emerging. And at the next boil-over, I seize my chance to renew my apologies, mutter something daft like 'I'll be in touch,' and beat a less than dignified retreat into the hallway and then out through the door. Where, blissfully unaware that Michael's mollycoddled Volvo is about to regain full possession of the over-neat but blessedly warm and dry garage, Izzy is waiting patiently for the idiot she has the misfortune to serve.

37

Ever since deciding to set her cap at ex-husband Dennis' next-door neighbour, Rosie has been staying with her dad, so I'm home alone in the only home that my teenage daughter has ever known. The scene of many mother/daughter fights, the location of my icy and loveless bed is living up to expectation, and, oversleeping for the first time ever - the extra two hours of fitful slumber doubling my total for the night - I'm awake but feeling indolent and tormented by what I know that I must do. The one person in the whole world who can provide comfort and reassurance is the one person in the whole world to whom I can never again turn. And my text message to him said that work is piling up and that staying at my own house would be 'easier and less disruptive.' Caller ID is enabling me to avoid Michael's return calls, but I know that it's all just sticking plasters for a gaping gash of my own making. I know. He knows. And soon, we will have to acknowledge the truth, together.

I'm late for work, I'm never late for work, and I couldn't care less. Then Bill Pridding rings to tell me that he's scheduled simultaneous Holroyd and Gutowski interviews for eleven, and to ask what I make of Sam's email. Quickly realising that Sam has sent an email and that the email has a lengthy attachment written by Louise Bates. And that, still bleary eyed and in my jimjams, I stand zero chance of blagging my way through a discussion with Bill whilst pretending that I've read what Louise has to say, I'm burbling and Bill is waiting more patiently than I deserve.

My sergeant closing the call early confirming that I've made a complete tit of myself, again, I begin reading Louise's statement and am quickly enthralled. It tells of a True Dare Kiss or Promise kid's game that left one eleven-year-old dead, another's life in ruins, and a teenager choosing oblivion over a life so out of control that he'd lost all confidence in his ability to live it. Accepting her share of culpability, the woman so recently known as Veronique details how the four: Holroyd, Gutowski, Abigail Hardcastle and herself, came, as they did regularly, to

Holroyd's deserted house. Where, in his mother's rat-infested garage, Holroyd already had a piece of rope hanging from a metal beam. At the other end of the rope, he had fashioned a noose. His house, his game.

'I dare you to put your head in that,' he said, and before anyone could respond, he pulled a long-abandoned bike from amongst garage detritus and grinned, 'while sittin' on the bike.'

Unexpected outrageous behaviour is the Svengali's stock in trade, and each member of the small gathering was nervous but excited, and on the way to being mesmerized. Louise could tell that, this time, unfailingly ballsy Abigail Hardcastle didn't want to be singled out and ushered forward. But all eyes had turned to look at her as she must have known they would, and she meekly sat astride the bike with a smile that carried no pleasure and failed to hide an abundance of fear.

Holroyd extravagantly checked the tension on the rope that was resting on Abi's young neck, and there was some make-believe pushing from big Stephen Gutowski that made Abi jump, the bike wobble, and the group laugh. There was an unspoken guarantee that the threat wasn't real. Just a jolly jape. After all, Gus was holding the bike tightly and his strength was legendary. When he began swaying it, gently at first, Abi's feet touching the floor only intermittently, the increased laughter meant that he was duty bound to step up the pretend risk.

Louise could tell that Abi was feigning indifference, terrified but unable to admit it, so she suggested that someone might think of a different dare, or truth, or kiss, or promise. She even came up with a few edgy and provocative suggestions. But the boys didn't even acknowledge her right to contribute, and, crucially, Abi remained on the bike. It was an opportunity not taken but it was still okay because, even if Abi fell, she wouldn't strangle because strangulation takes time. Time enough for Gus to catch her. Time enough for him to loosen the rope.

Holroyd was encouraging Gus to be more adventurous, and the big lad took up the challenge by holding Abigail's shoulders and not the bike. Louise recalls the hilarity then becoming more tentative. 'It was as if a marker had been reached and then passed,' she wrote. 'It had become more than a dare. It had become a test. A new game. A game for two players. One attacking and one resisting. A battle of egos. Only one winner and me and Abi background scenery for their game.'

Abigail started to ease herself off the seat and the bike ran forward. No more than a half a wheel circumference but enough for it to topple with a crash. Abi fell. Hardly at all. No more than an inch or two. Stephen Gutowski did his job well and he caught her. She would be fine. And, after a moment's heart-stopping silence, there was relieved giggling. But the metal clasp that made the loop, and that was near her ear, had shifted to the back of her head. No more than an inch or two, but an inch or two is, it turns out, enough; an inch or two, it turns out, is plenty. Her head snapping forward had severed the eleven-year-old spinal cord, and death when it came was instant. The lifeless carcase now a dangling doll in Big Stephen's arms, turning to Louise, Holroyd was the first to speak.

'Your fault,' he said with total conviction and absolute certainty. Jealous of Abi because Abi was prettier and more popular, Louise had suggested the game when the girls first arrived and, against their better judgement, Albie and Gus had taken part reluctantly. The boys had opted out long before the tragedy happened and, when the bike fell, it was just the two girls in the garage. One victim and one offender. Appalled when they saw what Louise had done, the two boys were duty bound, for poor Abi's sake, to tell all to the police. Louise's word against theirs, she would be locked up with bad people for the rest of her life.

Terrified and needing her dad, Louise lost control of her bladder and she can still see Holroyd enjoying her shame. She had no choice but to run, and, passing a phone box that hadn't been vandalised, she rang Leather's Farm and, luckily, Big Brother Darren was the one that answered. He was calm and asked her to look for landmarks. And then to describe what she could remember of her journey from Holroyd's house. He told her not to move and not to go back to the house where the boys and Abigail's body would be. Arriving thirty minutes later in his car, he listened carefully to her hysterically garbled story, before taking her back to Holroyd's house so that he could see for himself. Finding the house empty and Abi lying where she fell, the rope still around her neck, Darren removed the rope from the rafters and carefully, reverently, put it and the corpse into the boot of his old car whilst instructing Louise not to look. Her statement tells that, to this day, when she closes her eyes, she can see her best friend's unnaturally bending neck and flopping head. Driving back to the farm, Darren ordered Louise to go straight to bed. And she stood and watched her brother take Abigail Hardcastle's corpse into the night. And with it every scintilla of blame.

When the body was found and Darren was accused, Louise knew that Social Services would move her from Leather's farm. And when they decided on a complete name change, she was too relieved to give the fate of her poor brother a second thought. She would be attending a new school, a school where she wasn't known. Jane Green would be impossible for Holroyd to track down. And she could begin to relax. Begin to forget. Begin her life afresh.

Darren was dead within weeks of her moving in with the Greens. And within weeks, Albie Holroyd was waiting for her on the corner of her new street. He took possession of Jane Green that day, on that street corner, and he took full possession on the day that the Greens emigrated to Australia. She was not yet seventeen, but she had failed Abi and Darren and she deserved to be unhappy. After all, she had survived when they had not. And she was not locked up with bad people for the rest of her life.

38

Big Coat flapping, Big Bag slipping, flustered and arriving at 10.57 a.m., the 11a.m. interviews are about as informative as Prime Minister's Questions. But unlike PMQs, the body language has my juices flowing. Louise's statement is not yet a breakthrough but is a significant development, and, as Colin would say, 'there's fire in the firebox.' For the first time, I can sense fear in the bad guys.

But there's other work that needs my attention and Jim Renavent's report on the state of crime across our patch runs to sixty-two pages. And, after reading it carefully, I have twenty-three points of clarification and in our subsequent meeting I came up with fourteen more. It's time well spent, but there will need to be another get-together, probably as soon as Monday, if I'm to begin to decide upon police deployment recommendations to be discussed with the Super. So, it's 7.30 p.m. and the end of a particularly busy day that picked up after a lousy start, my mind is awash with stats, costings and potential savings, and Big Bag has let me down in my hour of need. I've only managed a Go Bar that's been in Izzy's passenger door compartment for at least four years, and dragging myself back to the scene of my latest misjudgement is taken a lot of willpower.

Leaving Claire Huddart's house after just an hour with no more useful information, the dilemma that is dominating my every waking hour flashing like a gaberdine-macked, septuagenarian sex offender, my next stop is very much the last throw of the dice. But I'm no longer hungry. Tea and Victoria sponge proof that the delightful young woman bears me no ill-will even though this blundering DCI has given her every just cause.

Marie Smart's short-cropped silver hair shaped just like daughter Claire's, gives every impression that the two are close. And she's sporting full red lipstick despite being home alone and the lateness of the hour. Wearing a tight roll neck top and figure-hugging skirt that allow every inch of gathered fat to develop a personality of its own, I'm once again astounded that otherwise sensible and old enough to know better women insist on clothes that fail abysmally to flatter. Surprisingly, Marie appears thrilled to see her late-night visitor.

'Are you the lady who rang this afternoon?'

'Yes, Miss Smart. Detective Chief Inspector Julie Marsden.'

'Detective chief inspector,' says Marie Smart with a flourish, 'I am honoured.'

Soon sitting in a cosy kept for best living room surrounded by ceramic knick-knacks and spotless, pressed to extinction, faux-lace doilies, I can tell that much pre-preparation has already taken place, and even more tea and Victoria sponge soon arrives. It's important for women to acknowledge catering effort and a period of appreciative noise making ensues. Men don't do this. Not because they don't appreciate, but because they don't cater. The ritual complete, I move business.

'I know that it's a long time ago, Marie. May I call you Marie?'

''Course you can, love. All friends here.'

'I really need to know if Rick ever mentioned Michael Lloyd when you were a couple. They grew up together, Rick and Michael Lloyd, in a place called Pottery Street, in Rawmarsh.' Marie thinks carefully, sips her tea, and thinks some more. Seeking to keep my emotions well-hidden but every nerve screaming, I sit quietly, trying but failing to savour my tea. The answer is a long time coming, but when it arrives, it's confident and assured.

'No. Can't say he did.' She hammers the point home. 'Michael Lloyd, you say. Nope. Never mentioned him.'

It's the expected answer, but I'm suddenly empty and wanting nothing other than to bid farewell to the likeable little woman who wouldn't deliberately hurt a fly. It's long past time to climb into Izzy, drive to Michael's house, and tell him of my irresolvable predicament. Getting it all over and done with is now my priority, and, inexplicably, it's my desire. Oblivious to the turmoil playing out across from her, Marie carries on chattering.

'He could talk the hind leg off a donkey about bloody Pottery Street,' she says. 'That's one of the reasons we split up. Just one of many,' she adds with a twinkle that suggests that she and Rick were 'done' a long time ago.

129

She goes on to tell that Christopher Winterbourne, another ex-Pottery Streeter, was Rick's best friend. 'Thick as bloody thieves, the pair of 'em.' Painting Winterbourne as an out and out villain, ex-husband Rick's continued association with him and the regular trips to London and the Lap Dancing Clubs are cited as contributing greatly to the break-up of the Huddarts and their subsequent divorce. 'It became a straight choice between his friend and the wife he said he loved ... and the pillock chose Winterbourne.' It's a snarl, but I can see that the hurt has gone. 'If I didn't know that Rick wasn't gay, I'd swear there was funny business goin' on, if you know what I mean?' She grins. 'I even saw Winterbourne goin' into Rick's house not long before Rick died. Saw me too, the bugger did. Didn't dare say hello. Well, he wouldn't, would he?'

This is unforeseen. Still very much in touch not long before Rick died. Could Rick Huddart be more involved in the kidnap of Joan Burling than I thought?'

*

I hurriedly make my thank-yous for the tea and cake, I leave Marie Smart's house, and I start my walk back to Izzy, still parked outside Claire Huddart's house. Choosing, despite the late hour, to turn away from my lovely little car in favour of marching up the garden path to Claire's front door, I don't hold back on my knock. Not asleep but clearly in the process of preparing herself for bed, and yet still as pleasant as ever, Claire invites me in and waits patiently to see how she can be of help.

And it's then that I realise that I haven't thought this thing through. Uncharacteristically, I start to blather.

'Sorry to disturb you twice in one night, Claire. Your mum is lovely. Made me very welcome. Very nice house. Very cosy.' Claire is beginning to look worried. So, no option, I come straight out with it and hope that Claire doesn't ask why.

'Can I take your dad's computer away with me?'

'Why?' probes Claire.

39

Ninety percent of Sergeant Stan Russell had no doubt that Tammy Alderson had left him forever. And yet one hundred percent of Sergeant Stan Russell constantly planned for her return. He saw no contradiction in this, and his reasoning was sure-fire and astonishingly simple.

First: every other eligible female fancies the pants off him and they can't all be wrong.

Second: now that he's single, the barrier preventing other women flocking to his side has gone.

Third: when she spots the prodigious impact that he's having on the libido of womankind, Tammy will immediately realise what she has lost, and she'll beg him to take her back.

The plan depends upon just one imperative: Tammy must see him fighting off the sexual attentions of others of her sex. Word of mouth just wouldn't do.

A pinch-point, no doubt. But only the one, and eminently surmountable.

Stan gave himself three months to bring about a complete transformation in Tammy's affections. Another month for the formality of removing the tenants from his and Tammy's - well Tammy's - place and moving him and his belongings out of the current rat hole, and back in. And after a renewed commitment, he'll propose, and within days, they will be married.

Samantha Jardine represented low risk bordering on no risk. All the signs that she was up for it were flashing and beeping like Charlie Cairoli's comic car. And with points and signals aligned, his streamlined express would hurtle through unrestricted. It made sense to start with a low bar and then move quickly through the gears, so her rejection was a devastating blow.

But it was Sam's official complaint that caused the God-given sureness for which he is legendary to seep away like damp air from a low-priced kid's paddling pool. He had no Plan B. No need. And so, what to do now has become a conundrum requiring much thought.

Tammy owes him nothing - can't argue with that.

His worries and troubles are no longer her worries and troubles - self-evident.

Telephoning and asking her for help is weak and desperate - every nerd on the planet knows that.

And yet she came when he called, and she is now lying naked beside him, on the bed they'd shared for the best years of his life.

She listened patiently as he explained his predicament, and, while she'd repeated that she thinks that he's been the architect of his own misfortune, she's here for him as she always has been. By her actions, if not always by her words, Tammy is showing Stan that, despite everything, she still cares.

She's right to make clear that he must accept the reality of his situation. She's right to refuse to renounce her declaration of love for Stephen Gutowski and to call it a mistake and not remotely real or significant, even though hearing her say the words would have meant so much. And she's entitled to remind him that Gutowski has had to cope with his own terrible tragedies, particularly over these last few days. But Stan Russell can't agree when she says that her new man needs her more than he does. And, as she lays beside him, his love for her is so intense that he feels light-headed. He knows that he mustn't overplay his hand, but he needs contact, however small, however chaste. And the desire to touch her is irresistible … almost. So, steeling himself to avoid the slightest brush of skin on skin, he carefully reaches across her still body for the iPhone on her bedside table. Scrolling his contacts, he finds Samantha Jardine.

The dull, repetitive tone goes unanswered suggesting Caller ID, and he's extraordinarily relieved when, eventually, the ringing stops, and someone picks up. He hears breathing but, despite a certainty that he should say something, he can't speak.

'You shouldn't be ringing me, Sergeant Russell,' she says, determined and remarkably calm. 'I'm going to ring off now, but I will have no choice but to inform DCI Marsden, Sergeant Pridding, and my union representative about this call.'

'Don't ring off, Sam, please don't ring off.' He wants to continue but speech is controlling him not the other way about. Then Stan Russell is surprised to hear himself say, 'I want you to come to my apartment straight away, please Sam. And Sam, I don't think that you should come alone.'

*

I'm still a gal able to rely on the attentions of plenty of men in the future, but the prospect of flattening grass with any man other than Michael Lloyd no longer holds any interest. And I can't seem to remember a time when it did. Or imagine a time when it ever will again. Until now, my excuse has been that I couldn't meet up with Michael because of my spending time comforting Sam. But it's Saturday, he'll be expecting me home, his home, and my get outa jail cards have all run out. Saturday mornings have become school football followed by hot dogs streaked with custard yellow mustard and blood red sauce, to be consumed from a plate, on a tray, on our knees whilst watching Football Focus on TV. That this ridiculous routine has somehow become so dear to me is proof positive that the change that Michael has brought about is irreversible, no matter what the future may bring.

Last night's unscheduled second visit unsettled Claire Huddart. But a quick phone call to Mum and a dressing gowned, carpet slippered Marie arrived within minutes, and Claire handed over a box labelled 'Dad' full of electronic devises with remarkably little resistance, even offering up the swfcclaire1 password.

So, two laptops and two no longer used mobile phones as well as the current one, pile neatly on my own kitchen table in my own house, and, far from providing a shoulder for Sam's tears or devouring hot dogs with Michael, I'm chasing unrecovered ransom money paid by Leonard Cotterill to secure the release of the kidnapped Joan Burling. I know that real breakthroughs, if there are any, will happen when I take this hardware to the teckies at work. But spotting emails and texts from Chris Winterbourne and texts from Leonard Cotterill has set my pulse racing, and I couldn't resist having an amateur's peak. It could be classed as good police work but I recognise procrastination when I see it, though not eating those bloody hot dogs feels like a point of no return.

The phone rings.

'Sorry to disturb you at home, ma'am.' Sam's voice is quivering. 'I've had a phone call from Sergeant Russell asking me to come round to his flat and to bring back-up.' I can't believe what I'm hearing. 'I checked with senior officers at Main Street and rang Sergeant Pridding at home, and we decided that I should do what Sergeant Russell asked. So, Liz, Greg Pinnock, and I are standing in his bedroom and Sergeant Pridding is on his way. The sarge asked me to ring you.

'I know it's your day off, ma'am, but I'd be grateful if you could come. I can text the postcode and address. Of course, I'll understand if you can't make it. I hope that you can though, make it I mean, because things have just got worse, such a lot worse.'

*

Bursting Chalky White style into Russell's cold and uninviting bedroom. And confronted by barely functional wardrobes, badly cello-taped cardboard boxes, a heavily stained carpet strewn with beer cans, pizza boxes and cold and congealing bread-like material, and an enormous bed swathed in grubby sheets. I'm ready for anything … but not this. Stan Russell is encased in a garishly multi-coloured, still wrapped in its plastic, armchair, and he's immaculately attired in his police sergeant's uniform. Hands cuffed behind his back, he nods towards his boss as if he and I have met unexpectedly by the coffee machine at work. And, serene and above the swell of activity going on around her, Tammy Alderson is lying on the bed, undressed, and despite its state and that of the room, remarkably unsullied. Even in death, she's a perfect specimen of womanhood.

Bill Pridding is standing to one side looking depressed and I know just what he will be thinking … because I'm thinking the same. From this moment on, Bill will become the experienced senior sergeant who suspended a more junior sergeant without recognising him for a killer, and I will be the DCI who was de facto in charge throughout. Picked over like three-day-old Serengeti corpses, by press and within the police force itself, the obvious beauty of the estranged and now dead wife, and the young female DC involved in the bizarre ménage à trois, will add spice to a story that will run, and run, and run.

'I cautioned Mr Russell as soon as Liz Greg and I arrived, ma'am,' says Sam reporting as she has no doubt already done for Bill. 'I repeated the caution, but Mr Russell insisted on telling me that he was responsible for strangling his wife.'

'Ex-wife, Sam.' Russell's intervention sends a shock wave before, self-consciously aware of no longer being part of 'the team' and having crossed a line, he adds sheepishly. 'Sorry. But the decree absolute 'as already come frew and I fought you oughta know. Sorry.' Sam checks her notes before continuing.

'Mr Russell's actual words were, "she looked as beautiful as any woman could ever be. And I knew that I could never love her more than I do now. Even if we both lived to be a hundred. So, you see Sam, killing her and then myself was the only path left for me to take. But as you know, I'm a coward. So, I'm here, very much alive, and ready to be arrested."'

'Did he say anything else?' I'm feeling every bit of Sam's discomfort. And, for the first time, there is a quiver in Sam's voice.

'Mr Russell said that I was doing a brilliant job, ma'am. That he's very proud of me. And that he wanted me to be the one to make the arrest.'

40

Bill is fed up and probably just wants to go home. But he's needed. And he messages Pam to say not to wait up despite being embarrassed and feeling like he's let the team down. I'm equally despondent, but I'm desperate *not* to go home. My home or Michael's. So, I decide to imagine that Main Street Nick can't cope without me.

Settling into Interview Room One with a mug of hot chocolate and a bag of two-day-old doughnuts that, incredible as it may sound, I found in Sergeant Russell's desk drawer. And knowing that Michael will sacrifice his need for answers in favour of my need to work, especially when I drop in the word 'murder' and that the suspect 'is a bobby.' Feeling like a louse for presuming on his good nature, I send the love of my life the briefest of texts. Putting my mind to another superficial scan of Huddart's computers is a poor substitute to dealing with my personal issues, but it'll have to do.

I have proof that Huddart and Chris Winterbourne were in communication until Winterbourne's death. And, whilst there is no mention of Michael Lloyd, Huddart's hardware shows that Leonard Cotterill was a constant topic of conversation between the two. The evidence is circumstantial, but I'm convinced that they were blackmailing Leonard for years, probably from the moment they realised that he had money to burn. And, if there was a swindle, it was likely to be a joint venture from the start. Perhaps the kidnapping of Joan Burling was just taking things to the next level. One big hit to set them up for years, perhaps forever. Joan the perfect target and Leonard the perfect mark. Perhaps this whole kidnap was all about Leonard and his millions, and not really about Joan at all.

'Sorry to bother you, ma'am, especially on your day off.' Top half uncomfortably leaning into the room, feet and legs rooted to the wrong side of the doorway, Colin's tentative approach to his boss is typical. He's a superb police officer and has no need of such diffidence, but the way he interacts when I'm in the room never fails to draw out the maternal side that I'm always saying

I don't possess. Not for the first time, I think he's perfect son-in-law material. Daughter Rosie can bring home a Colin anytime she likes.

'You're not bothering me, Colin. Come in, come in.' I offer what turns out to be an empty doughnut bag before an it's the thought that counts grin, and add, 'isn't today your day off as well?'

'Yes ma'am.' Confesses my DC as if caught cheating in a test. Only Colin could feel embarrassed about doing a shift unacknowledged and unpaid.

'Not just me that needs to get a life then,' I say with what I hope Colin will recognises is a playful wag of the finger. 'Only a matter of time before you start putting on weight, carrying a huge bag, wearing a gigantic coat, and driving a car with its own Christian name.' I gesture towards my size 14 - not big really, I know. But I want to be Sam's size, and only genes, motherhood, work, and eating are stopping me - and I say, 'one day, Colin, this could be you.'

He's still finding the banter with the boss incredibly difficult. So, deciding that I've behaved badly enough for one day, I put on my business face and ask, 'so what can I do you for?'

'Well,' he begins before pausing and blushing because he's just got the 'do you for,' 'I hope you don't mind, ma'am, but I've been looking into Companies House for commercial ventures involving Albie Holroyd and/or Stephen Gutowski.' He pauses again, as if requiring a reply.

'Oh, yes?' It's the best I can do.

'Apart from Gus Logistics, there aren't any.' I smile, knowing that there will come a point when he becomes engrossed in his narrative and his tentativeness will disappear. 'And Gus Logistics is not quite what you might expect. I was surprised, for example, to find that only 50% of Gus Logistics belongs to Gutowski, the other 50% belonging to a holding company in the Isle of Man.' Colin pauses once again. No reply, so he carries on, warming to his task. 'I decided that Holroyd and Gutowski wouldn't use their own names but might register their own addresses. No joy there, so I thought I'd look for businesses registered to premises within a ten-mile radius of Holroyd's or Gutowski's houses.'

'Bloody 'ell, Colin. That must've taken forever.'

'Not really, ma'am,' he says modestly, 'I knew Holroyd's registered business was likely to be to do with property, so I set fields for property rental, refurbishment, development etc. And there are two hundred and sixteen possible companies within the two, ten-mile diameter circles. So, I looked to see how many of the named company directors have criminal records or are in our files for any other reason. There are twenty-eight. Scary, don't you think?'

Colin is now 'in the zone' and enjoying himself. I raise my eyebrows to show I'm in the same zone and that the number scares me too. 'I decided that I needed to dig deeper into these twenty-eight businesses,' says Colin with a knowing grin. I'm enduring the parade before the lord mayor's show, but it's beginning to be a struggle.

'And?' I say enigmatically.

'One of the addresses is a non-descript semi in Thurcroft.' He's now lit like a Christmas tree and his excitement is infectious. 'Ninety-four, Catherine Road. No mortgage and owned outright by a twenty-six-year-old who works at Rotherham Council. She has a relatively low-income job and no obvious other money source and is on our records as a victim of paedophile activity around thirteen or fourteen years ago.

'The twenty-six-year-old is called Elaine Fenell and she employs no staff and has no links to any rental properties at all as far as I can ascertain. And yet, she's listed at Companies House as Managing Director of a company known as Horizon Property Developments.

'I think we stand every chance of finding a connection between Elaine Fenell, and/or Horizon, and the Holding Company in the Isle of Man. And then, between Elaine Fenell and Stephen Gutowski and Albie Holroyd.'

I reach into Big Bag, retrieve my purse, liberate a fiver, and toss it across the desk.

'Vanilla slices, Colin. Three. One each and one to share.'

41

Pushing and pulling when a more rested brain would tell her to lift, she's seriously considering climbing over her garden gate, or moving house altogether just so she can say 'sod you' to the bloody thing once and for all. Then she catches a quickly extinguished light in Mr Butterell's otherwise dark and what should be empty house, and the adrenalin starts to flow in a whole new direction. Furious that looters would take advantage of Charlie's enforced absence, Sam's baton is quickly drawn, her flashlight is held alongside her face, and phoning for back up, she becomes a lioness stalking her prey.

Front door locked, as it should be, and secure, a twist of the handle is all it takes for the back door to give way and she sighs, 'oh, Charlie, what are you like?' Deciding not to wait and risk losing the bastards violating her friend's space, she enters and locks the door behind her using the key that she finds on the inside. She pockets the key and shouts,

'Police officer! I know that you're in here. And you should know that many of my colleagues are within spitting distance and gearing up to charge in mob handed. You won't want that to happen, believe me. Every exit is covered, and you've got minutes, perhaps seconds, before it all gets nasty. Identify yourself and come quietly. Resisting arrest will send you to prison for a long time.'

All the while moving further into a house the inside of which she's never seen but which exactly mirrors her own, she hears a muffled noise coming from the kitchen. Easing open the door and angling her flashlight to where she knows the sink will be, two hugging figures, one frightened and one forlorn, are suddenly in full LED glare. Forlorn says,

'Sorry, Miss. I keep messing up, don't I.'

42

My Stan Russell debacle is so extreme as to knock into a cocked hat our get-together for post-Saturday-morning-school-football, Football Focus watching and hot dogs. Nevertheless, the process of concocting a text to the man I love explaining my absence has taken its toll. He must have known for a long time that there is a truth that wasn't being told, and that the 'looking after Sam' story was always an obvious crock. And I can tell from his replies that he's frantic with worry. So, desperate to avoid being the cause of even more anguish, but certain that I will have to hurt him eventually, I decide that real life is hard, too bloody hard, and that it's time that God gave some thought to cutting me some slack. That this limbo state is worse than coming clean. And that, perversely, telling Michael that we're through has become the kindest thing I can do.

At my own, never really a home, alien house after a long and unexpectedly difficult day off spent at work, I'm readying myself for bed but still wide awake. Aware that my decision will haunt me until morning, and that I have hours of tossing and turning stretching out in front of me, I decide and that at least it's a start … or, more accurately, a start of the finish.

In normal times I would be annoyed to get a work-related phone call at 11 p.m., but these times are anything but normal and I'm ridiculously glad to hear from Sam. And, before any alternatives that would drag me back to my devastatingly sad state can come to mind, I'm soon striding the deserted corridors of Main Street Station and feeling the comfort of being needed. And then, thirty minutes past midnight, I realise that this job has become my mechanism for avoiding life, and suddenly I'm crushed. Deep in thought, I need to be quick on my feet as two bulky, medical looking staff, one man and one woman, clearly escorting a younger woman, burst through like they've got a train to catch. I can't quite put her finger on what is odd about their patient, but odd she is.

*

Stenton is already in secure accommodation in Wakefield and my interview with the little darling about what he was doing in Mr Charlie's house and who was his companion will have to wait until tomorrow/later today. It'll be Sunday but I'm guessing he'll give church a miss, just this once. In any event, Sam has already delivered much of the information that talking face-to-face with the lad himself would have provided, because she was smart enough to ride with him in the police car, another officer taking her Aygo. And, as he always does with Sam, the little tyke talked. None of it is admissible in court, but Sam listened carefully and without interruption and it was a very good use of her time.

'Stenton says that he's been guarding his friend Mr Charlie's house 'to keep it safe,' ma'am. So that Mr Charlie will find it as he left it when he's released. Stenton's been working on the allotment as well. As he says, 'weeds are buggers, Miss.' Sam and I have had better times, but sitting together and chuckling when we should be in our respective beds, Stenton has, once again, weaved his magic and lightened our burdens.

'When he spotted the young woman moving around, he broke in without a second thought,' says Sam. 'Apparently, 'it's his job.' She's about my age and according to Stenton she's called Kitty.' *Kitty by name, cat by nature. Odd doesn't begin to cover it.* 'And she keeps asking, in fact wailing, for Donald. Not Charley or Mr Butterell, but Donald. The lad says that she never ventures out and that she's been living on cat food even though there is human food in the house.'

141

43

Overtime costs rising like the Mekong in rainy season, I'm all too aware that I need to pace myself and my team, and that Sunday is an ideal opportunity to save some dough. But the prison was never going to put Donald Bates up for interview at such outrageously short notice and on the day that God said to rest, and making the application was just going through the motions. Something I should do to be thorough. A shot to nothing. Just doodling. And doodles never produce a Rembrandt. Well, almost never. However, when every duck seems hellbent on lining up - the prisoner insisting on meeting without a solicitor present, being able to call in a favour from a former colleague now working as a senior prison officer and filling in for a younger police officer whose wife had gone into labour, and Colin and me willing and able to respond - then it's destiny. And in the face of destiny, even an overspend bigger than the gross national product of a medium size African republic must be sacrificed for the greater good. Well, that's what I'll tell the Super when he asks.

My ex-police officer friend is clearly pleased to see his old colleague.

'Happy to help, Julie. I've developed a soft spot for the old chap. And I'm not the only one. When you look at why he did what he did, well, he's not a proper criminal, now is he?'

*

All security checks completed and arriving at a contriving to be tasteful, modern hall, that's capable of housing fifty prisoners and their visitors. I'm surprised. I expected a poky little Victorian room, and this is some sort of theatre used for shows and speech-making. Glancing towards the figure lost like a full stop within the pages of an almighty tome, I can't help thinking that little and poky would have been kinder.

My friend nods his permission for the warder standing guard to leave, and all three of us: my ex-colleague, Colin, and me, look down on Donald Bates who belatedly raises his head. No jokes this time. Mr Charlie a distant memory already. We two police officers sit as he makes a washed-out attempt at a welcome.

'Your eye is getting back to normal, detective chief inspector. I'm pleased.' It's an effort and Colin is already moved, especially when the old man goes on to enquire about Sam.

My young colleague is clearly expecting a kid gloves affair, and given what Colin knows, that's understandable. But I intend something very different. My stripped of all pleasantries, harsh approach will probably be seen as needlessly cruel. Nevertheless, it's how I intend to play it, and my two observers will just have to trust that I know what I'm doing. I immediately tell Donald of the sexual harassment that Samantha has suffered at the hands of a fellow, more senior, police officer who went on to murderer his ex-girlfriend, and the old man's reaction is predictably anguished. He's then informed about his friend Stenton breaking into his house, being arrested, specifically by Sam, and finding himself banged up in secure accommodation. And Donald's face disfigures. Captive to my hostility, he's hurting. And Colin and my ex-colleague are demonstrably uncomfortable.

'Stenton is in serious trouble because he was looking out for you,' I assert as Donald recoils. 'In fact, both Stenton and Samantha would be better off had they not met you at all.' The interview must look like planned badgering. A targeted assassination of a vulnerable and defenceless prisoner. And had a solicitor been present, he or she would have put a stop to it. 'Hiding in your house was a distressed young woman about Sam's age who told us that her name is Kitty.' I was counting on a reaction and there's no more than a flicker. 'Who is Kitty, Donald? What was she doing in your house?'

His big eyes are shimmering but remain focussed on mottled, big and bony, cupped hands. He looks too weak to withstand the breeze floating in from a slightly open, barred window, and his voice is thin and unsteady.

'Between them, Gutowski and Holroyd killed my son. And Gutowski's brother badly damaged my daughter. Before long, she would have been dead too.' Donald works to regain composure. It's hard to watch, even for me. 'I lost my wife and with her passing I lost my life. And I had to stand by while bad people hurt my children.' He looks up. Searching my face.

143

Maybe for empathy. Certainly, for sympathy. 'The staff where I was living encouraged me to read Louise and Darren's letters, and I started to see what Gutowski and Holroyd had been doing.' His lips move even when he's not talking. 'You know already what I did to Anthony Gutowski.' The slightest of smirks plays on his face, and then, noticing that I'd noticed, it's gone, and he looks away. 'Well, Holroyd was going to be next. Stephen Gutowski began paying a long time ago.' Unable or unwilling to suppress, Bates' smirk broadens into an unpleasant grin, and I spot Colin's mouth open. Maybe his DCI is not quite so cruel after all. 'I didn't ask her to turn up on my doorstep with all her problems.' Bates is looking less brittle by the second. 'My life was already awash with problems.' He straightens. Bent frail and helpless are being shed as a snake discards its skin. 'But when I looked at her, I saw Gutowski. And then I saw my own children being mistreated and abused. So, I took her in, and I humiliated her. And it made me feel better.

'I bought tins of cat food and started calling her Kitty. Then I told her that she could only stay if she ate the cat food from a bowl on the floor. Like a house cat, a cat that never goes out.' The bastard thinks it's funny, Colin looks ready to throttle him, and my ex-colleague standing guard is no longer pretending not to hear. 'Didn't expect her to do it,' says Bates. 'I thought she'd bugger off to London like they all seem to do. That would have been sensible. But she stayed with me. And even then, I thought that one day she'd storm out and I'd never see or hear from her again. But she never did … and then we got used to each other.

'Inveigled herself into my space, she did. Wanting to be cuddling all the time. Sleeping on my bed and then getting into my bed. Eating the cat food even when I said she could have what I was having. Clever that. But I knew her game. I knew what she was up to.' His voice is cold and bitter. 'It was years before I touched her you know.' It's an accusation and it's aimed directly at me. 'She'd get close and rub up against me, but it was years before I cracked and gave in. And every time I did, she was so bloody happy. She'd won, y'see. Like her dad. Just like her dad.'

This is a surprise to me. I sit back and take stock. Donald sees my reaction and smiles. He's telling me something I hadn't already figured out and he likes it. His tone is now nasty and childish. 'But I always used protection. Always. She didn't like that. Hated that.' He becomes conversational, gossipy, as I've seen him do before. He's Charlie again … almost. 'By all accounts her mother was a nice lady. God knows why she married Gutowski. I went to her funeral you know.' Another segue I wasn't expecting. Again I see enjoyment on his face. It's fleeting, but more than enough to make my skin crawl. 'I wanted to see one of the people responsible for ruining my family and hurting my children. See with my own eyes without being seen.' Bates leans. Deliberately excluding Colin and the prison officer. He's keen for me to see that he's confiding, just to me. Keen for me to comprehend, to appreciate what he's gone through. 'The father was wrapped up in self-importance masquerading as grief and nobody was looking out for the little girl who'd lost her mother.' The irony of dismissing the grief of another man who'd just lost his wife and was fearful for the future of his child, lost on Donald Bates. 'I handed her my address so we could write to each other. Shouldn't have done that. Knew it was a mistake as soon as I'd done it. Telling her where I lived gave her an edge, y'see? Made it easy for her to find a way to make me miserable.'

Spitting venom, I interrupt.

'So, you were overtaken by circumstances and events beyond your control. And the scheming minx used her feminine wiles to draw you in and make you do what you didn't want to do, and what you knew was wrong. Is that what you want us to believe?

'Yes, you've had things happen in your life that would have been hard to deal with. Yes, certain people have done wrong by you and to your family. BUT NOT JOY GUTOWSKI!' I'm shouting and I don't care. 'A lousy father and a clinically depressed mother, finding the dead body of a grandfather to whom she was devoted, and if that isn't enough, she gets abused by you!' Bates is closing like a rangy flower when the sun goes down. The sight would tug at the heartstrings if he weren't playing a part, pretending, using weakness as a shield. Curling his hands onto his head against the physical attack that he seems to believe is imminent, his sleeves slipping to his elbows and exposing withered, not long for this world, wrists, he's creating a pitiful vision, but it isn't working.

145

I'm screaming at him now and Colin and my ex-colleague look to be backing me all the way. 'Why not tell us about Joy as soon as we took you into custody? Why leave her to starve in that dungeon?' There is no answer. It doesn't matter. This needs to be said. 'Louise loves you; Darren loved you; Joy and Stenton idolise you; and Samantha sees you as a kindly old granddad who she's grown to love. But you're just a self-obsessed shit, aren't you Bates? A loathsome excuse for a man who never once considered that his motherless children needed their father. A man who Social Services separated by as many miles as possible from the desperately unlucky poor wretches who shared his DNA. A man they deemed the last person on earth to be a parent.

'Gutowski and Holroyd didn't ruin Louise's life and force her into prostitution. They didn't kill innocent, sensitive, lovely Darren. YOU DID BATES! YOU DID!

44

The opportunity to root through Rick Huddart's hardware is Christmas come early for hard to demotivate Colin, and I'm in no doubt that he will spend the rest of Sunday happy as a pig in muck. I on the other hand, will remember today as the worst day of my life.

Standing in front of Michael who's listening patiently and very unhappily, and saying the words I've long been thinking, this is turning out to be even more tragic than I feared. His riposte is alarmingly concise.

'So, you think that I'm capable of executing an innocent, defenceless, disabled boy?'

'Of course not. Not the Michael I know and love. And I do love you, Michael. More than I ever thought possible. No matter what happens in the future, I will always love you.' I should leave it there, but I don't. 'But ten-year-old Michael? The Michael who is certain that his best friend in all the world would have her life ruined by having to provide twenty-four-hour care for a brother who wouldn't even know let alone appreciate the sacrifice being made? For a teenager who, for all anybody knew, may even have been silently praying to be released from the straitjacket that his body had always been?

'You care about people, Michael, and Winterbourne ...'

'A dead kidnapper.' The interruption is clipped and moody.

'Said that he and Huddart ...'

'A dead kidnapper's dead best friend.'

'Saw you come out of Terry's house at about the time that Terry died.' I can't seem to stop myself arguing the case for the prosecution. 'And I can't think why they would say it. Why of all the people that they could accuse, they would accuse you ... unless it's the truth.' The silence hangs like a poisonous fog, and eventually, Michael, whose six-foot sturdy athletic body is visibly hurting. Whose bright blue grey eyes are conspicuously losing transparency. Whose straight and strong mouth is now crooked and ailing. And whose once defiant and confident demeanour my accusations have soured into a defeated and dejected bearing, simply says,

'I wasn't where they say I was. I didn't kill Terry. And until you just said what you just said, like everybody else, I believed that he died of natural causes. We all assumed that his body had just given in because we all knew that one day it would.

'I thought the world of Joan's mum and dad, Lilly and Les, and Terry's death destroyed them. Les was happy-go-lucky. Always joking, always ready to play, and all the kids loved him. And Lilly was the kindest person I've ever known. They never got over Terry's death. And even as a ten-year-old, I couldn't have done that to anybody, much less to people I loved.' He sighs deeply. 'But, innocent or guilty, you would expect me to say exactly that, wouldn't you, Julie? And until you can be certain that I'm not a murderer, you and I can't be together.' I've heard the words in my mind many times, but they still manage to shock. 'At this moment you look at me and you see an assassin. So, there is no way back for you and me, is there?'

Standing as if carrying the world on his shoulders, and walking slowly out of his own front door, Michael doesn't look back.

I'll remember this instant as the point at which I began my journey through life alone. I've been alone before, but this time it will be so much harder. Because this time I can visualise the life I would have lived with Michael, and this time I will know that not living that life is nobody's fault but my own. This time I know that if I can't have Michael, I don't want anybody else.

45

'I've been going out with the same lad since we were teenagers together at school.' Not at all the beginning I was expecting. 'We never actually broke up. But we drifted apart, and we hadn't spoken, well properly, for a good eighteen months. So, I guess that us breaking up is a bit of a given.' Sam is trying but not quite succeeding to appear philosophical. 'According to Facebook, he's started a relationship with Elaine Fenell. Who was also my friend at school. My friend, not his.' Coincidence? I don't believe in coincidence. And the mention of Colin's Thurcroft link to Holroyd and Gutowski - a possible moving rapidly to a probable - has my pulse racing. As I'm running Colin's findings and hypothesis through my head, Sam shrugs an easy come easy go shrug that she doesn't look like she feels. 'They've moved in together which is pretty clear cut.' Then: 'you've met Elaine, boss. She was the girl that said hello to me in Costa.' I nod and smile as Sam carries on. 'I thought, well mutual friends had said, that Joss, Joss Rawlin, that's the lad I was involved with, was working in a call centre. I didn't know for certain because, as I say, neither of us have bothered to get in touch for ages.

'The thing is, ma'am, Joss phoned me. I thought that he just wanted to tell me that he was pleased that me and Elaine are friends again - we'd met up and had a nice meal together - but he really wanted me to know, I mean really wanted me to know, that he wasn't working at a call centre and that he's now a kind of 'fixer.'' Sam's expression is suddenly deadly serious. 'A fixer for Albie Holroyd and Stephen Gutowski.' Bingo! The 'advise me about my love-life' talk has become something very different, and there's more to come. 'As soon as he said the two names, he became kind of formal. In fact, at one point he said that he was talking to me in my capacity as a police officer.' Suddenly, Sam is desperate to fill in some gaps. 'Joss is not a thug, ma'am. And he's not violent. If anything he's a bit of a powder puff.' She grins, despite herself. 'His job seems to involve doing all the legwork, smoothing over cracks, and keeping things legitimate and legal for Holroyd and Gutowski.

He won't have done anything bent himself, even though he says that he's worked for them for quite a while.

'The real reason for ringing me was so that the police would know that he's picked up a lot of information, and that there are lots of dodgy practices that are running alongside the legit stuff. He says that he knows a lot about things that the police would also want to know about. And this is the main bit, ma'am: he's desperate to see the two of 'em locked up.'

Sam is worried about the involvement of her ex-boyfriend but also excited about the prospect of nailing two villains. But, to me, this has the feel of something that Holroyd would concoct to divert me and my team. Sam's a smart cookie. Nobody's fool. But she has a history with Joss, and in this instance, she may not be as objective as I need her to be.

'So why now?' I ask. 'Why would Joss Rawlin risk everything, including perhaps his own freedom, or worse? And why would he do it now, just when we're closing in on Holroyd and Gutowski?' Sam has an answer. A good sign.

'Well, Elaine is in the early stage of pregnancy.' The way that Sam says the word 'pregnancy' more than suggests that not all her Joss Rawlin baggage is forgotten and forgiven. And there's a finality about pregnancy that starts me thinking about Michael, and, to my shame, tears begin to form. Luckily, Sam is deep in her thoughts and her tale, and she doesn't notice. 'She's twelve weeks, and Joss was adamant that they both can't stand the idea of the little 'un being brought into their world. His exact words on the phone were "it's not the kid's fault that its parents are fuckups." He wants it all sorted because, as he said, "that's what good dads do."'

Sam goes on to talk about brown paper parcels periodically left on Elaine's doorstep. Parcels that are taken in by Elaine, kept in her spare bedroom, and picked up from time to time by Holroyd's minder, Marvin. Elaine doesn't know what's in them, but she's certain that they're something she can get locked up for having in her possession. There are currently over thirty packages in her house.

'Joss says that Holroyd's property portfolio is pretty much legit, but that Holroyd is a lousy landlord and penny pinches like you wouldn't believe. Gus Logistics transport business also seems genuine. However, Holroyd has a network of drug suppliers and pushers. And a man called Bubbles Stevenson, whose real name is Ben and who was until recently a trusted drugs deployed lieutenant, blotted his copybook and got busted to the ranks. It must have been a big blot because Marvin beat him up and cut off some of his fingers.' Sam mimics my reaction and adds, 'yeah, I know! These buggers don't play nicely and there must be a lot of money involved.

'Joss also suspects that there's been dodgy deals involving Rotherham borough councillors and even bent police officers. Something to do with very cheap, illegal cigarettes in eastern European fronted grocery stores all over Yorkshire. Polish, Slovaks, and Czechs work in the shops, but the owners are mostly Asians and Turks. Joss thinks he can find out more, and that Holroyd has a plan to get involved in a big way.

'The cigarettes are sourced and somehow brought into the country and Joss is going to find out if Gus Logistics' trucks are providing, or thinking about providing, the transport.' There's a short pause before Sam adds 'Joss also thinks that Holroyd was the brains behind the attempted murder of Louise Bates. And the word is that Holroyd regularly abuses underage girls.'

Suddenly, Sam's haunted look has returned. I give my young colleague space to gather her thoughts before she says, 'years ago, I knew that Elaine got herself involved in all that white girls and Asian men stuff that we had in Rotherham at the time. But I didn't know until Joss told me, that, as a fourteen-year-old, Elaine was used to entice Henry Thompson so that he could be blackmailed out of his transport company. Henry Thompson committed suicide because of the shame of it and Stephen Gutowski took control … all because of Elaine.'

46

It's the everyday things that you miss most. Things like going to bed at a time of your choosing, eating what you fancy, and soaking in a hot bath just because you can. Nevertheless, his physical size and a determination to keep himself to himself are all that he needs to survive. And when everything is said and done, the regimented regime in this place gives Kevin 'Red Beard' Caldwell's life a much-needed structure without which he would be dead and soon forgotten. Not only coping in prison but thriving, he'll plead guilty when his court date comes through, and he'll continue to focus on doing his time until his time is done. He expects no visitors, and he has no regrets. And, even if he was on the outside and looking after her, he'd already proved that, on his own, he couldn't keep Sandra safe.

Persistent slaps to the white tiled wall interrupt his long anticipated hot shower, and Kevin knows instinctively that they mean trouble. Shutting off his water flow, he turns, ready to fight if he must. Coming face to face with a nervous man wearing only a towel thrown over one shoulder, Kevin waits. The man's statement is stark.

'She's dead, Kevin. Sandra is dead.'

Bodychecked into unforgiving tiled walls, the bad-news-bearer is severely hurt but has the look of a man who attaches no blame to his attacker. And before the left sprawled and disorientated supervising warder hits the alarm button, naked and out-of-control Kevin Caldwell has run the length of the shower block without thought or design, direction or purpose, until a uniformed avalanche of blue hits, as it was bound to do. He's wrestled to the ground, hefted one officer on each arm and each leg, and thrown into a cell. Ands ten minutes later, he stops screaming and starts to think.

Crack cocaine deliberately contaminated with chalk, flour, and various other dross will quickly do the trick. Sandra is dead, not because he wasn't there to check on her, but because he wasn't there to check on her supply. Holroyd promised to look after and rehabilitate, 'no matter how long it takes or how difficult it is.' He promised to wean her gradually off the drugs. To do things that Kevin couldn't do. And to save her life. Promises that have turned out to be hogwash. Always the equivalent of attempting to climb Everest in flip-flops and a kaftan, Kevin knew that, for Sandra, recovery was unlikely. But he'd fulfilled his side of the bargain and Albie should have done more, much more. Sandra is dead. And Kevin has been taken for a fool.

They'll allow time for his aggression to dissipate before, looking to talk but ready to fight, they'll enter the cell mob handed. So, he leans against the metal door and says,

'I'm sorry for causing trouble and I won't do it again.' The spyhole cover moves slightly. Someone is listening. 'I know that I'll be up before the Governor and I'm sorry for what I did to Mick Smedley and Mr Johnston. I didn't mean to hurt either of them. All Mick did was tell me some tragic news, and Mr Johnston was only doing his job. I should have behaved better and I'll try as hard as I can to make it up to them both.

'I know I'll be punished and it's only what I deserve. But can I request a meeting with my solicitor, please? And I would be very grateful if you would also allow a visit for Detective Chief Inspector Marsden, or one of her team.'

There's no reply.

It'll take time.

And he has nothing but time.

47

Misery means weight loss and weight loss is good. It's the law. But my weight only seems to decrease when I don't care if I'm heavy or not. So, it's fair to conclude that my world has turned to shit, and there is not the merest hint of an upside. On stakeout, and, because I need to be alone with my despair, opting not to join my team in their car, Izzie and I are nearby and watching the object's movements on my iPad. I'm hoping that I'm wrong but certain that I'm right. Again, no upside.

Our search has revealed five of what Rosie would call 'seriously uncool' wooden lockers, each with a long part for hanging a jacket and/or shirt, and a smaller, boxed shaped bit presumably for keeping shoes or trainers. Their paint has flaked badly. And three of the five doors of the smaller boxes are unlocked. The other two are missing altogether. The long bits all have locked doors with no keys. Four are of the original design. And the fifth is without an integral keyhole and is looking recently fitted. This door has a heavy-duty metal clasp screwed from the inside and folding onto a metal ring through which curls a code operated, rolling wheel padlock. Using a kind of x-ray gismo that thankfully is simple enough for a four-year-old to operate, me and the team have already shown two of the long cupboards to be empty, one to have in it what looks like a screwdriver, and another a pair of gardening gloves that appear to have turned to concrete. The image exposed within the one with the new lock attests beyond all doubt - well almost - that my guess was right. Events might show that to break in to check, retrieve the contents, and put said contents somewhere safe, would have been the sensible action. But I want the bad guys caught in the act and I've judged the risk acceptable. A judgement that I'm hoping against hope I don't live to regret.

After a mercifully short surveillance, the gloved hand removing a holdall that could well be bright red from this locker, and the careful counting of what is clearly cash before, surprisingly, returning much of the cash to the holdall, is clear and no doubt recorded. My phone rings. It's Chalky.

'Ma'am?' he asks, and with a sad heart, I give permission to move in.

*

Paul Drury-Smith leans over his client and whispers. She looks uncomfortable but nods. My sense is that everyone in the room, including Paul Drury-Smith, knows that she will talk eventually. Because being personable is what defines Claire Huddart, and so, in this interview, personable is what we'll see.

'You kindly gave us permission to interrogate your dad's computers and old mobiles. And my DC has found many emails, going back many years, to and from Christopher Winterbourne.' Claire is listening to me, but in all other respects she's lifeless. 'I want to ask you about Elsie. There are repeated references to Elsie running from the beginning of the laptops and iPhones, old and new: "Elsie will come through,' 'ask Elsie,' 'stick with Elsie,' 'trust Elsie,' and sometimes, just plain 'Elsie.' The messages often contain numbers or number comparisons such as 'double' and 'more than last time.' Belatedly Claire realises that I'm waiting for a reply, and she jerks back to life just long enough to whisper, 'no comment.' I continue. 'It's our belief that Elsie is LC or Leonard Cotterell. Mr Cotterell grew up living in the same street as your dad and Winterbourne. And he was eccentric. Some would think him a bit odd. Especially at the time.

'As a young boy, Leonard had a passion for antiques, and that was enough for many of the other boys and girls to laugh at and bully him. But, as he got older, he became a very successful dealer in antiques, and he made a great deal of money. In fact, he became a multi-millionaire. So, perhaps he had the last laugh. We think that your dad and Winterbourne were just two of the many children that bullied Mr Cotterell. And we think that they knew that he had gone on to become very rich.'

'No comment.'

'Not very long ago, Leonard Cotterell was found dead in his penthouse apartment in Sheffield. He had committed suicide.' Claire is not shocked. Hearing this for the first time, she should be shocked. 'Mr Cotterell's dead body was found wearing women's clothing.' I wait. Surely, this bit of information should have sparked a reaction. Curiosity at least. But I see nothing. 'Further research showed that he had lived a secret life for many years, and that he went to great lengths to keep his alternative existence secret. He would routinely leave Sheffield and go to another apartment he had in Manchester so that he could dress as, indeed try to be, a woman. We think he believed that, should this become public knowledge, it would have made him a laughingstock, just as he had been as a boy. And the very thought of this miserable existence returning would horrify him. It would also have damaged his credibility in the business in which he had been so successful, and where he was so well known.

'We think your dad and Chris Winterbourne discovered Leonard's secret when they and Leonard were just young men, and together they began to make Mr Cotterell's life difficult. Referring to him as Elsie was all part of the intimidation.' Claire Huddart is uncomfortable and clearly anxious to see where this is going. 'This then led to blackmail and there is bank account evidence of Elsie paying your dad a lot of money over many years. £1000 every month rising to £3000 every month. Leonard's own bank transfers coincide completely in timings and amounts with the money going to your dad, and they go back as far as we've been able to trace. The money was paid into an account your dad called SW, or Sheffield Wednesday, the football team he supported, and it kept your dad's fundamentally non-viable business afloat. We think that your dad and Winterbourne were sharing the money 50:50.'

'My dad wouldn't do that,' snaps Claire, surprising everyone in the room. Paul touches her arm to remind her to say nothing, and I carry on.

'But both Winterbourne and your dad recently found themselves in need of quick money. Winterbourne because his wife was divorcing him, raiding his bank balance, and determined to get every penny that she could; and because he was desperate to move back to London. And your dad because his business had never really been strong enough to survive, and because he'd begun to doubt his ability to look after you.' Claire Huddart hangs her head. 'So, they decided to go for one big hit.

'Leonard Cotterill was a tremendously lonely man, and Michael Lloyd and another friend from school called Joan Burling were the only people that he could call his friends. He loved both Joan and Michael dearly and your dad and

Winterbourne knew it. They decided that he'd pay a lot to keep them safe. Michael Lloyd represented a hard target, but not so Joan Burling. So, their once and forever 'big hit' became the kidnapping and short-term detention of Leonard's vulnerable and relatively defenceless, female friend.

'In their mind, Cotterill was good for a million pounds, but I think that they'd have settled for less. I also think that they were surprised when Leonard could get such a large amount in used notes at such short notice. 'Claire's eyes are darting from side to side as keeping herself in check becomes and obvious struggle. 'A masked motorbike rider took the red holdall containing the ransom money from Leonard Cotterill on a dark street in Rotherham.' My words are hitting home, and Claire is increasingly distressed. 'And that rider we believe was Winterbourne, not your dad. However, Rick was the bell ringer, not Winterbourne, and we found the money still in its red holdall, in a locker, in the bell ringer's room that your dad had access to. We have every reason to believe that your dad stashed the red holdall with all but £39,000 of the original £1 million ransom money still in it. But you know that, don't you Claire?' I give Claire more opportunity to defend her dad before continuing. 'Small amounts of money have been taken, we think as and when needed. And we think that, since your dad's death, you're the one who's been taking it.' Claire is fighting with herself and, expecting Paul Drury-Smith to request a recess so that his client might recover her composure, I wait once more. No intervention comes, so I carry on. 'Your dad and Winterbourne needed other partners to successfully pull off the kidnap, and those people murdered another woman as well as kidnapping Mrs Burling. We think that Rick, and probably Winterbourne, knew nothing about the murder and that they would never have signed up to anything as violent as that. The whole thing was starting to get out of control. And then Chris Winterbourne himself was killed. Your dad must have thought that he, or you, would be next, and he must have been terrified. And then he died … and that to me is very strange.'

Claire, Drury-Smith, and even Sam, are suddenly looking perplexed. And so, I add: 'perhaps I should explain. The other kidnappers are now dead or in prison with no reason to volunteer any information. Leonard Cotterill committed suicide. Found alive but ill, Joan Burling has yet to utter a single word, and she would know nothing of your dad anyway. Rick had a lot of untraceable cash and, because he was very much background support, he wasn't linked and was unlikely to be linked to the murders or the kidnap. To put it bluntly, he was home free. And yet a freak accident brings it all tumbling down.' I take a deep breath. What I'm about to say will tear this young woman apart. But it must be said. 'I think somebody figured out that Rick had all the ransom money. That person wanted it and was prepared to do anything to get it. When Rick wouldn't or couldn't hand it over, that person had your dad killed.'

*

Sitting on the pavement and cautiously touching the back of his head, he feels blood and the side of his face hurts. Checking his back pocket, he finds his wallet where he left it and his seventy pounds and credit cards untouched. His expensive laptop is still laying by his side in what Julie calls his 'manbag,' and he thinks, 'so who hates me enough to knock me senseless just for the hell of it?' The thought throws up such a ridiculously high number of possibilities that, damaged as he is, Michael can't help but laugh.

48

A cocktail of pills grouped in fives and in time and date order in front of her, Louise has just said goodbye to Sam and she's sitting alone in her soulless but clean kitchen in the women's rescue. She's suddenly emotional and, from nowhere, the tears start to flow. Throughout her life there have been tears. Tears of despair. Tears of dread. Rare tears of happiness. Rarer tears of optimism. And she now knows beyond all doubt that she has a shit for a dad. She knows him to be a man who seems to have always been a shit. And a man who used the very act of losing his wife, her mother, as the perfect excuse to be a shit. Despite no longer being in Anthony's clutches and having her own place to live and call home, she's still in mortal danger from Holroyd and/or Gutowski, and her self-esteem has never really left base camp. But, out of the goodness of her heart, a young police officer who barely knows her, has sorted bed sheets, stocked the fridge and freezer, and promised to treat Louise to a drink and cake 'sometime soon.' Having a person to call 'friend' has, just for a moment, made her wonder if a normal life might, just might, be possible. Then, her mobile rings, and she's instantly terrified.

'Hello?'

'Hello, Veronique?' The use of her slave-name turns her blood to ice. 'It's David. David Smith. You might have heard me called Marvin.' Louise can't speak, can't think, and can't press the off button. Marvin's tone is serious. 'You need to change your mobile number,' he says. 'Holroyd will use it to find you.'

49

It's late, the hiatus caused by Claire Huddart first hyperventilating and then collapsing into a full panic attack looked anything but short lived, and we decided to call it a day. However, before we've summoned up the energy to get our backsides into gear and go home, out of the blue, Paul Drury-Smith opens the door and waves for us to follow him back to Interview Room One. Surprised but keen, we stride at pace to the door, but once there, Claire's solicitor turns and says with some force:

'My client is in no fit state to continue and what she's about to do is against my professional advice. You need to know, Julie, that if you carry on with the interview now, you will almost certainly jeopardise your case. You'd be well advised to decide to let Claire rest and for us all to come together again tomorrow.' He's doing his job and doing it well. And I know that he's right. 'However,' he carries on with a sigh, 'Claire says she wants answers and that you have them. And she's determined to make a statement, now.'

Paul, Sam, and I join Claire in Interview Room One, and immediately and on tape, I strongly advise her to get a good night's sleep before saying another word. But this is a different girl to the one we left earlier. This Claire is more than capable of ignoring advice from anybody. It's almost midnight and she must be exhausted, nevertheless, she begins speaking fluently and with authority.

'Dad knew Chris Winterbourne and Leonard Cotterill when they were all kids. They grew up together in the same street. Uncle Chris told Dad that Leonard had made a lot of money selling antiques … and that he was a multi-millionaire, like you said.

'Dad's business has always struggled because people don't pay their bills on time, and in some cases, they don't pay at all. When times are tough, nobody's interested in framing pictures, and we could never really afford two salaries. But having a business for me to take over was important to Dad, and Uncle

Chris was doing well and driving a big car. I think my dad thought that he should have done better in life. I think that he thought he'd let me down.

'Extra money somehow always seemed to come through when we were short. And when I got older, I started to wonder where it was coming from. I didn't know then about Mr Cotterill, and I assumed that the money was from Uncle Chris sending us loans that my dad paid back once we were doing a bit better.' Her voice begins to falter. 'But, when I got old enough to understand the books, I realised that a fixed amount of money was coming into the business every month, and I couldn't see what we were doing to earn it.

'Dad didn't try to stop me looking and getting a feel for the finances of the business. In fact, he encouraged me to do it. I think he knew that one day I'd ask where this money was coming from and who Elsie was, but it was a long time before I felt able to do so. I thought that perhaps she was a woman he was seeing and didn't want me to know about. So, I didn't ask. Until the not knowing became too much. When I finally found out, it was a shock.

'He said that he'd done a big favour for a man called Leonard Cotterill when they were kids, and that Leonard insisted on paying him back.' Claire's tone has become timorous, and I feel the need to repeat my earlier advice. The admirable young woman's response is to sit up straighter, square her shoulders, and to carry on. 'Twenty or so years ago, when it all started, the amount involved was £1000 every month. A lot of money for anybody, particularly in those days, but for us it was a Godsend. It carried on coming until it stopped a few months ago.' Thoroughly ashamed, she says, 'by that time it had grown to £4000 per month. And without it, the business would have gone bust years ago.

'I still had a vague idea that it was Uncle Chris' money and that there was no Leonard Cotterill. And I thought that, if Uncle Chris could afford to have a house in London, he must have a mega job. Then Uncle Chris moved up from London to live near us and I couldn't understand that at all. Why would he leave London? Why would he leave such a great job that paid so well? It didn't make sense.

161

'At first, I was pleased, even though I thought that the money would stop coming because Uncle Chris wouldn't be earning as much. I always liked Uncle Chris, and Dad always cheered up when Uncle Chris was around. But this time was different, this time my dad snapped at me a lot more than he'd ever done all the time I was growing up. He was always moody, and it was like I couldn't do right for doing wrong. He started going out and not telling me where he was going or what he was doing. And that wasn't like Dad, not like him at all. He even stopped going to Hillsborough to watch Wednesday, even though he had a season ticket and season tickets are expensive.

'Then the bellringing started to be an issue.

'We'd been bellringing ever since I was a kid. Mum never cared for it, but I used to like to watch. And as I grew older, I started to help with the teas and sandwiches. Made me feel grown up. Now, as far as refreshments are concerned, I'm it. The ringers pay upfront, I buy the food and take it up to the church when I go. And I make up a spread downstairs in the kitchen that I take up at a specified time.

'Me and Dad had the same routine for years, and it was more fun than you'd think. Then he started missing practices without telling me. And one ringer not turning up is enough to spoil it for everybody. The other ringers started asking me where he was and why he wasn't there, and I didn't know. And then they started asking me to take his place as a ringer, and I'm hopeless. So, I didn't want to. Ringing was my dad's thing, not mine. He was the only reason I went to the ringing in the first place, and it was embarrassing to keep having to say no. It was my dad that was letting them down, not me. But it felt like it was me and I didn't like it, so I told Dad that, if he wasn't going to bother, then I wasn't either and somebody else would have to do the teas. And that's when he started crying.'

There's a catch in Claire's throat but she's determined to get this said. 'Dad doesn't cry, ever, and seeing him sobbing broke my heart and frightened me. He blurted out that Uncle Chris was dead, killed, and that frightened me even more. Then he grabbed my arm and dragged me back up to the church. It was like he'd gone mad. He was behaving like a different person. Not my dad at all.

'When we got there, he insisted we went into the bell pull room, even though it wasn't a ringing night and there was nobody there. He kept repeating '8664'. It was like he was having a breakdown. He was crying, I couldn't understand any of it, and I didn't know how to help him. He suddenly grabbed my shoulders and looked me straight in the eye. And he started making me say '8664' until we were chanting it together. Then he stopped and he pulled me into a hug. We both stood there for the longest time with the tears pouring out. I could tell that he knew that he was scaring me, but he didn't seem able to stop. Suddenly, he pulled out of the hug and dragged me towards one of the lockers. He told me to put into the lock the number I'd memorised. And he stood and watched as I did it. The padlock opened and he pushed me out of the way and threw open the locker door. And pulled out a big red bag, which he dropped onto the floor and then unzipped. And that's when I saw more money than I'd ever seen in my life. Then he sat me down on one of the benches and told me all about Leonard Cotterill and Joan Burling, and him and Uncle Chris.'

Sad and exhausted, Claire is slumped, but she carries on. 'After Dad died, I couldn't let his business go under, I just couldn't. I always intended to hand the whole lot in to the police, anonymously, and I probably would have eventually. I wish I had.'

It's well past the time to stop and I'm even more convinced that Paul's advice had been correct. I should stop now. Indeed, I should never have started. But I must know.

'Did your dad ever talk about somebody called Terry Makin? Or Leonard's other friend, Michael Lloyd? It's important, love. Very important.'

163

50

'POLICE IN THE DOCK.'

The Stan Russell story is front-page of the Rotherham Advertiser and has made the nationals, so things are not going well. But what's really bugging me is that Claire can't or won't tell precisely what her dad and Winterbourne had over Leonard Cotterill before the kidnapping. I can feel in my bones that it must be more than Leonard's cross-dressing, but I'm struggling to see much light at the end of a long and lengthening tunnel. And then Bill Pridding's call sends me into a blind panic.

Bursting into Ward A4 in Rotherham General and immediately spotting Michael sitting up, telephone to his ear, it's a race to get to him before a posse of nurses get to me. Realising that he's at the epicentre of converging women, and that he's in no position to take evasive action, Michael holds up his hands in the universal gesture of surrender, and the avalanche subsides but continues to seethe. Obviously bruised and clearly mithered, but otherwise looking well enough to be out of bed and at school, he says,

'Before all or any of you say or do anything, I want it understood that I'm fine. If I was unconscious, it can only have been for a second and I should never have gone to A&E in the first place. I know that I don't have concussion even if people who studied medicine for squillions of years can't seem to grasp that the danger has passed. In fact, the only things that are aggravating my ailments are that I've got a mountain of work piling up that need doing, I'm stuck waiting for a doctor who can't find twenty seconds in his or her hectic day to sign my release form because he or she also has a mountain of work piling up that need doing, and nobody seems to hear me when I say that I'm fine!'

The gathered hordes are not for budging, so, throwing off his bedsheets, the patient hops out of bed to an audible gasp from the blue corner. And then, backside hanging out of a gown barely big enough for an eight-year-old who's small for her age, he strides towards me - something of a victory - and, throwing one arm around me, - an even bigger victory - he marches me out of the ward. And then my personal, non-business, mobile rings.

'Hi, Mum, it's Rosie. Now you're not to worry.'

*

A doctor sighting occurs within minutes of Michael's decision to discharge himself, and all 'you can't sue us' documents are pretend read and quickly signed. Ten minutes later, the frosty atmosphere is left behind, and he, me, and Izzy are racing to Rosie's boyfriend John's apartment before anyone can say 'relapse.'

The hug is, I must admit, worthy of two falls or a submission, and I quickly receive confirmation that somebody has made an, admittedly half-hearted, attempt to put a burning accelerant-soaked cloth through the letterbox of the apartment occupied by my only daughter. Only a Persian rug that was a much-treasured family heirloom handed down to John by his mother has been damaged. But it could have been so much worse. And while, despite taking arson-dwelling very seriously, scene of crime people, two of whom are still present, are seemingly certain that the intent was to scare and not to kill, my apprehension and fury are not assuaged, not one jot. Describing John, who has opted to remain at work, as 'taking it all in his stride' translates as Rosie hasn't told him. Contacting her dad, who lives in the next-door apartment, has clearly never entered her head. And she's Queen Bee loving every minute of the drama. I've gone from being terrified for my daughter's safety to wanting to strangle her myself.

'And why aren't you at school?' I bark.

'And why isn't he?' Rosie points at my boyfriend, her Headteacher, and barks right back. Michael's head must still be pounding, but he just stands and laughs.

*

Having declined my tentative offer of a lift, Michael leaves by taxi to pick up his car at the hospital. Back at Main Street Station and feeling dreadful, in the face of Bill and Colin anxiously waiting with tea and sympathy, I'm once again inexplicably tearful. First the partner and then the daughter, Holroyd is telling me to back off. A line has been crossed and

165

this is now personal. Sensibly, Colin decides just to crack on and deliver his report.

'We ended up, ma'am, unwrapping, photographing, and cataloguing the brown parcels that were left in Elaine Fenell's house. We wrapped them all again and returned them to her back bedroom and nobody but Ms Fenell, Mr Rawlin, and each of us will know that they've been touched.'

'Well?' I ask.

'The contents all look legit, ma'am. There are luxury designer watches. Lots of gold in high carat rings and ingots. All types of expensive looking jewellery and some uncut diamonds. The odd original painting. Rare vintage wines that I'm told are worth an awful lot. Logbooks and ownership documents for nine cars and two motorbikes. Even a kind of puffer jacket complete with proof of provenance worn by Princess Diana. We think that he's been buying stuff confiscated by debt collectors, and he's bought cheap, very cheap. And because he can take his time to sell, he'll turn over a big profit on each sale.

'However, for a little while now he's not been selling. And the stuff that Marvin retrieves from time to time is being sent over to a four-bedroom villa, proudly trumpeting bougainvillea and swimming pool, situated near Yerevan in Armenia. Holroyd owns the villa, keeps an always taxed and insured but never driven car in its garage, and pays a house cleaner to clean and a gardener to garden for a day each fortnight. He also has a 4-berth yacht moored at a posh marina on the Karpas Peninsula in North Cyprus. Holroyd himself has never been out of the country, let alone to Cyprus or Armenia.'

'So, he's getting ready to run to the sun?'

'Looks that way, ma'am. We have no extradition treaty with Armenia, and, once there, he could still operate most of his business outlets.' Colin starts to develop that 'I'm coming to the best bit,' look. 'I've been talking to Inspector Glover who's based in Lincolnshire and who heads up all things to do with duty free contraband - particularly cigarettes - coming into and leaving Yorkshire and the East Midlands. It's apparently a multimillion-pound trade and, while he didn't mention Gus Logistics or Holroyd, he did say that they have their eye on several dodgy police officers, local politicians, and council workers.' Colin grins. 'And somehow, more than once, in our casual conversation, Councillor Jeff Chapman's name cropped up.'

*

The 5 a.m. call from Marvin found Stephen Gutowski wide-awake. Now 6.30 a.m. and standing in Holroyd's corrugated steel roofed icebox of a garage, his escape route blocked by a man who dwarfs even him, Gus couldn't care less about what might be going to happen next.

'If he wants me to jump,' he says, too loud and with unnecessary hostility, 'just tell me when and how high and I'll jump. Like I always do. Good old Gus. Good old reliable, fucking Gus.'

He needs a response, but Marvin looks in no mood to oblige.

Spittle flying, eyes about to pop, suddenly Gus has had enough. 'Listen you big bastard. I loved my mother and she died. I've loved just two other women in my life, and they are also dead. And the love I feel for my daughter is a constant ache that won't go away because her mind is ruined. She's twenty-three, has no future, and it's all my fault!' He gives a grin that he clearly doesn't remotely feel. 'My life isn't worth …' the finger click is unsuccessful, but it doesn't seem to matter. 'So, fuck you, Marvin, and fuck Holroyd. Do your worst, it'll be a relief.'

Alarmingly quickly, Marvin's massive hands lock, vice-like on Gus' shaking shoulders … and he pulls him close. And, as the bigger man holds the big man's quivering head to his gargantuan chest, Gus sobs, and sobs, and sobs.

51

Convinced that Joy will only completely withdraw from her aberrant, cat-like behaviour once she has escaped the influence of Donald Bates - no shit Sherlock - bizarrely, the medics think that Stenton Cornthwaite could be the one substitute-Donald that could affect that change. Jess Simcox and I are pleased that they don't intend to fill Joy up with pills. But Stenton replacing Donald feels like banking on successfully threading a needle whilst dangling from the top of the Shard. And who's to say that it is even legal, let alone ethical? Not surprisingly, our thirteen-year-old recidivist is keen to have a crack, and Kylie, his mum, thinks it's a 'beltin' idea.' She's already told the doctors that she'll 'do a deal on her son's fee.'

So here we all are - all but Kylie who, though invited, failed to turn up - and we're looking through a one-way mirror at a feline Joy Gutowski sitting alone in a very un-hospital room. Before long, Sam Jess and I see a casually dressed woman about Joy's age lead Stenton in before skilfully blending into the background. It's like watching a scene from a badly conceived acted written and directed daytime soap, and Joy's constant cat-like affectations are so ridiculous that they would test the patience of any audience. We're all expecting the scenery to wobble.

Stenton begins reflecting Joy's movements, and, quickly aware of and seemingly amused by what he's doing, Stephen Gutowski's daughter joins his game. The two of them in cahoots, the young woman neatly cast as a figure of authority who is non-the-wiser about what's playing out behind her back, it's kids versus adults and Joy looks to be enjoying herself. After a few minutes, she is looking towards Stenton who continues to mimic everything she does. A few minutes more and she is looking at Stenton. And fifteen minutes into the session, the two are making sustained eye contact. The nurse on the periphery but needed, she's playing her part well. At some point, Joy begins copying Stenton rather than the other way round, and when she does, she becomes Stenton. And when she's Stenton, she is no longer a cat.

The doctor standing next to me says something into his mouthpiece and the young nurse responds by looking as if she's forgotten to do something important, before leaving the room. And what happens next is remarkable. As soon as there is no adult present, Stenton and Joy openly acknowledge each other. They move close enough for Stenton to reach out and hold Joy's hand. Draping an arm around her, he begins to talk softly about 'Mr Charlie.' And there is a communal melancholy that eradicates all sign of cat.

Stenton Cornthwaite has done it again.

52

People-watching in Clifton Park whilst out shopping for
groceries twice a week, and the warmth of Rotherham Library,
are her luxuries. Clothes shopping is high on her 'to-do list,' and
she's confident that it will happen. One day. Perhaps soon.
Careful to vary the days when she ventures out. Head-to-toe
covered and as incognito as she can manage. She finds ignoring
the winter weather easy. To her, even at this time of year, Clifton
Park is a riot of colour. She wants to tell the gardening staff that
they're doing a fantastic job, but she can't. Being always vigilant
is vital if she's to remain safe, but it takes its toll and makes
Louise sad. She's taken Marvin's advice and changed her phone
number, staff at the shelter collect her gyro for her, and, until
now, she has talked only with 'insiders.'

However, today is a red-letter day in her road to recovery.
Today there will be no safety net and she will be outside, with
company.

The stone built former home of the South Yorkshire pottery
magnate whose garden Clifton Park used to be, has columns and
statues and is exquisite. It has long been a council run museum
with its own Tea Room, and Louise finds the prospect of entering
such a grand building and ordering a coffee and a coconut slice
daunting, but tremendously exciting. Her coat is threadbare but
clean and her face is still that of a victim. But she has put on
much needed weight, her hair has returned to its natural chestnut,
and the cut - carried out by one of the other women in the
sheltered housing who used to be a hairdresser - is simple and
tasteful. And for the first time in her life, Louise has had a
manicure. She agonised over its cost, but at this moment, it's
worth every penny. Her ice-blue nails almost match her lightly
applied eye shadow and slightly heeled shoes, and, most
important, the Thai girls from the beauty parlour came to her
apartment specially and made a fuss of her.

Louise is as ready as she can be. The Tea Room is clean bright
and cosy with an array of luminous cakes and the lovely smell of
fresh coffee, and the staff are cheerful and chatty. Nevertheless,

she still feels the need to pick up the free copy of the Advertiser to give her hands something to do, and to calm her nerves. Giving and paying for her order is as thrilling as she anticipated, and as she sits, she begins to fiddle with her coat before, despite the state of the dress beneath, plucking up the courage to unbutton. Eventually she settles, and since the newspaper is there and available, she starts to read. The lead story is of a local man fined for not controlling his pit bull, and she learns that the dog has been destroyed. Suddenly she's crying. She knows that she's drawing attention to herself and that's the last thing she should do. But no-one seems to care about the injustice, and she wants to shout: 'put down the owner, not the pet!' Then, a giant sequoia is towering above her and its presence is a tap that instantly turns off her tears. How long has he been there? She would run away but, like that poor, dead dog, she's trapped and powerless, and bereft of options. Defeated and not bothering to wipe away the tears and mucus from her nose, she sinks heavily into her chair. Things don't change. She should have known better.

When she realises that he's not going to speak, Louise peeks up at his face, and she can tell that he's nervous. He could snap her like a twig and yet he's scared. He seems to be still standing because he feels he needs her permission to sit. Hesitantly, she gestures for him to join her, and he makes a clumsy attempt to push his massive legs under the table. And that's when they notice that they have each chosen the coconut slice and, inexplicably, the tension evaporates.

'You look lovely,' says Marvin. She doesn't, but she can tell that he means it. And, if this enormous man who needs to fear nobody says that she looks lovely, who is she to argue.

53

The contraband investigation is just getting started, and four serving police officers, six council officials, and six councillors across Yorkshire and Lincolnshire, have all discovered an urgent and immediate need to 'spend more time with family.' His return to greeting the well-healed outside the Hilton Hotel was always going to be difficult. But Jeff, the former member of the decision-making elite, needn't have worried. Redundancy came swiftly.

Even though he's denying all wrongdoing and has no family to spend time with, Jeff decided to stand down. Officially because 'the story has become a distraction to my public service.' But, in truth, because the hounds were determined to catch and kill their quarry, and when the time to fight back came, he found that he couldn't be arsed. And so, the once in-demand and busy Bishop now has nowhere to go, nobody to meet, and no status to protect. But he does have a future as well as a past, and even though for him politics is over, high calibre manipulation and high stakes power play have only just begun.

*

I'm already having a good day, even before the lovely Colin pops his head around my door.

'Morning, ma'am.'

'Yes, Colin? What can I do for you?'

'Well, I've been talking with Sergeant Pridding, and then with Sam, who squared it with Joss Rawlin, who agreed to send me a list of tenants in Holroyd's properties and of people who work for him.' It's like the start of a joke. 'I also asked for people who still owe Holroyd money with no hope of paying it off, and the names of people who, in the last couple of years, owed a lot of money and *have* managed to pay it all off. As you might expect, the paid off list is much shorter. In fact, it's a list of one. A lady called Carol Peach.' His smile is fixed and broadening as I ask,

'And you're going to tell me that this Carol Peach is linked to Nick Peach?'

'I'm going to say that this Carol Peach is the mother of Nick Peach, ma'am.' Colin is very pleased with himself, and rightly so. 'Nick Peach, the CCTV expert recruited by Christopher Winterbourne to provide a fake alibi to cover up a murder and to keep us in the dark about the kidnap of Joan Burling, and who's still on remand in Armley Prison.'

'We don't believe in coincidences, do we Colin?'

'No, ma'am, we don't.'

'So now the only question I need answered is: how much was Mrs Peach in hock to Holroyd?'

'The original amount borrowed was £10,000,' says Colin. 'But just fourteen months later, it had grown to approximately £27,000.'

In my mind's eye, I can see the pieces slotting into place.

'Bill Pridding always said that Nick Peach had a bigger pay-off than the £10,000 he admitted to. And I think we now know that he had at least £27,000. Peach said that he got involved with Winterbourne because of an urgent and unexpected need for quick money resulting from his girlfriend being pregnant; but that was all rubbish. He needed the money because his mother was in the power of Holroyd, and she needed to be set free from a debt that was rising by the hour. No less than a complete break would do. No less than £27,000 would be enough.'

Colin goes on to explain how he and Bill Pridding have already met with Peach at Armley Prison and the young man looked relieved to admit that his share was £35,000, not the £10,000 he'd sworn to many times. He even volunteered that about £5000 of the cash should still be buried in his garden. Colin is quick to let me know that Bill's already taken steps to get that back. Apparently, when Bill spoke with Carol Peach, she said that she just thought her lovely son was 'helping her out of a spot,' and she insisted that she didn't know that the money was stolen.

'Bullshit,' is my response to that. 'Mrs Peach would have taken money from a blind eight-year-old begging in the street if it meant getting out of Holroyd's clutches. And speaking of the odious little man, his sensors would be doing summersaults the minute a debtor, any debtor, paid him back in full and in one go. He'd make it his business to find out where the newfound brass had come from, and then the Carol to Nick connection would have been easy to make. The link between Peach and

173

Winterbourne was public knowledge. And so, joining Winterbourne to Huddart would have been the logical next step.

'Holroyd would have every reason to think that Rick Huddart - very much backstage backup - was the team's banker, and that he would pop under pressure before spilling almost £1 million notes into the nearest fedora. Huddart the sleeping partner that the police would never find, a million in untraceable notes to play with, Holroyd would be home free. The perfect crime.

'But Holroyd was squeezing and Huddart wasn't popping. And Rick Huddart's road traffic accident was murder!'

Colin is grinning like a Cheshire cat, and I can tell, God bless him, that there's more to come.

'Kevin Caldwell, the man who claimed he was contracted by Holroyd to kill Louise Bates, has had a visitor in prison, ma'am.'

'Oh, yes?'

'Ben Stevenson, aka Bubbles Stevenson. He was Holroyd's top drug dealer until a recent sudden and dramatic fall from favour that cost him his senior role in the organisation and a couple of his fingers.'

Now wound like a coiled spring, I'm all action and pinging commands.

'Get uniform to collect Stevenson, Colin. Then talk with Bill before bringing in Holroyd. I want Stevenson and Holroyd interviewed at the same time. And this is very important Colin, I want Holroyd to see Stevenson here at the Nick. Not talk to Stevenson, Colin. Just see him. Time to jab an arse cheek and see which way it flinches.'

This time DCI vulgarity doesn't provoke a young detective's blush ... and that is a breakthrough.

54

Asking permission from Joss Rawlin is these days the same as asking Holroyd himself, and Ben Stevenson guessed, rightly as it turned out, that if Joss bothered to mentioned it to his boss, Holroyd would just assume that asking to visit Kevin Caldwell was Bubbles' way of trying to toady his path back into favour. Ben should be pleased. Getting one over on Holroyd is rare as rocking horse shit. But, sitting in Main Street Police Station reception, his satisfaction is swamped by fear.

A big operators' runner aged nine, and Bubbles because of a teenage perm that didn't go according to plan, a ducker and diver happy to serve and not lead, and well known for living off the crumbs dropped from the high table, the move from Foot Soldier to Management - sending others to make deliveries and take money, his back covered by Holroyd's muscle - never felt right. But he got used to it. And then he got soft. And then he got careless.

He'd proudly resisted the temptation to regress from pusher to user when most didn't. He'd worked hard to earn the kudos that came with being Holroyd's drug lieutenant. And he was in the privileged position of knowing the business inside out. He had rank and creaming off the top was a perc and was overlooked. For the first time in his life, he was secure and making good money. And still he wanted more. It should have been obvious that using Holroyd's product and infrastructure to develop his own rival drug business was suicidal, but it took being strung up by his wrists at midnight in a cold and dusty garage for Bubbles to finally understand. Hanging with one foot barely touching a cordless drill carelessly left on the rough concrete floor, several ribs already broken and one eye closing, he was certain that Marvin had orders to kill. And everybody knew that Marvin carried out orders to the letter. Ben Stevenson begged anyway. But an example had to be seen to be made. It was his own fault. He'd become cocky. Gone too far. Marvin was only doing his job. Bubbles should have been content to do the same.

Holroyd turning up in person seemed to confirm his worst fears. And being lowered so that manacles could be removed could only mean that he was nearing his end. But the clump hammer swing. The thud caused by striking the wide blade chisel that removed index and middle fingers on first the left and then the right hand. And pain the like of which he's never come close to feeling. Brought, of all things, relief.

Why bother to maim? Why not just kill me? I'm bleeding like a stuck pig. Too much blood. Too risky for Marvin. Unacceptably risky for Holroyd. It's a reprieve. But why?

Back to Foot Soldier and the streets. A task to carry out, no questions asked, no choice. He'd dodged a bullet already grazing his skin and it was no less than a miracle; and yet he's fucked up again.

A bump to show intent. A few days in hospital. A broken bone or two. The task to be completed with Huddart getting the message, and without the need for him, or his daughter, to get too badly hurt. But deformed and still throbbing hands make driving difficult. Pumping adrenalin makes for a heavy right foot. And Huddart turning and dipping at the last moment to offset the impact. All connived to create an outcome that nobody wanted. Amongst the bones broken was a hip that caused severe internal bleeding. Just bad luck, and Bubbles wouldn't have known the extent of the injuries even if he'd climbed out of his car to check. But he didn't climb out and he didn't send for an ambulance, the bleeding did lead to cardiac arrest, and Huddart did die. Holroyd will decide that his underling hadn't followed orders, had panicked and made a mistake, and, instead of rectifying his error, had driven off. Now, Bubbles' only chance is to find Huddart's daughter and pray that she knows where her father stashed the money … and to hope that the Huddart killing trail doesn't lead the police back to him.

Who does he think he's kidding? He's been in the business long enough to know that even these unlikely outcomes won't save him. He's the link. The link to Huddart's death. The link to the cash. The link that the police can follow all the way to Holroyd. And the link that, whatever happens, Holroyd can't allow to live. The threat from Holroyd far exceeds that from the police. And so, to survive, Bubbles must eliminate Albie Holroyd. No less will do. And to do that, he desperately needs an edge.

Knowing what Red Beard knows can only make a slight difference and he's clutching at straws. But a weapon is a weapon, even when it's a pea shooter. So, enduring the 'it's not worth spending good money on the bus fare home' sarcasm of screws and the pity of prison inmates who remember him as he used to be, was a small price to pay because his appointment with co-op funerals is already booked and paid for, and he's got nothing to lose.

*

Bubbles is no stranger to this place, and whatever the police want, even if they have connected him to Huddart's death, it can't make matters any worse than they already are. The local criminal fraternity will have clocked his police car escort, boosting a street cred that needs all the boosting it can get, but officers chatting with him and referring to him as 'mate' and 'pal,' and being left unattended in Main Street Police Station reception, have made him ridiculously nervous. He's an old hand at this game and none of this feels right. It ought to make sense, but it doesn't, and it's like being back in that garage waiting for what should have happened then to happen now. He's the dog crap that they scrape off their size elevens. All he ever gets is a perfunctory sign-in before being whizzed straight through to avoid contaminating the pure air needed by the law-abiding public. So, something is going on, he can smell it, and with his luck, it'll be the final nail in a coffin that already welded down. Then a hunting orca wearing a mohair long coat and fedora sweeps in with solicitor Paul Drury-Smith in tow and spots the daydreaming seal. Holroyd's frown standing out like a third nipple, The Man can't have failed to hear the desk sergeant shout: 'Kelvin, can you rustle up a nice cup of sweet tea for Mr Stevenson, please.'

Bubbles first thought is 'how can I throw myself on the boss' mercy. Here and now. Police station or not.' But thankfully a complete lack of hope provides space for the reasoning function to kick in.

This is Marsden pulling strings. She's determined to get Holroyd and so me and her are on the same side. I'm not here for Huddart, I'm here because she wants Holroyd to be asking himself all the questions that I'm asking myself. She wants him rattled. She thinks that I can do that. I've found my edge, and it's me!

55

'Let me remind you, Mr Holroyd, that you're under caution and that this interview is being recorded.' I'm smiling, Holroyd isn't. 'I'm going to ask some questions which I hope you will find in your interests to answer as fully as possible, but to start with, I'd like to explain why you're here.' Business-like, no sugar coating. 'We think that you play a leading role in the supply of drugs and prostitution in the South Yorkshire area.' Paul Drury-Smith immediately springs into action.

'My client refutes that assertion completely, furthermore . . .'

'Duly noted, Mr Drury-Smith. We also think, Mr Holroyd, that you make money from the sale of contraband items such as duty-free cigarettes.'

'Again, my client knows nothing about such illegal activities, and I would ask you to provide some evidential proof for these unfounded allegations.'

'You knew Louise Bates when you were both children, Mr Holroyd, and Louise says that, when she was eleven and you were fifteen, you covered up your causal contribution to the manslaughter of Abigail Hardcastle. And knowing Louise's teenage brother, Darren, to be innocent of any involvement in the death of Abigail Hardcastle, you made no attempt to prevent him being charged with her murder. We say that your decision to withhold information and evidence from the police contributed to Darren's subsequent suicide, and so you bear significant responsibility for it.' Drury-Smith stirs again, this time like a man wary of asking a question with no clue as to what the answer might be. Like a don't mess with me lollipop lady, I hold up a hand before he can speak. 'And Kevin Caldwell, who carries the nickname of Red Beard, contends that you recently paid him to murder Louise Bates. A failed attempt, I'm pleased to report.'

'Innuendo with no actual proof, detective chief inspector,' says Paul who's lawyering his heart out but looking shocked.

'And that brings me to the death of Rick Huddart.'

As expected, Drury-Smith is now at the point where to pull his man out of the fight before he's thrown a punch is the only sensible course to take. But Holroyd's twitches - a movement equivalent to a facial earthquake for a normal person - and I can sense that beneath the fedora lies a face that is keen to know more, and he's bound to be doing mental gymnastics about what Bubbles Stevenson was doing talking with the police. I carry on quickly. 'We know that a £1 million ransom for the kidnap of a woman called Joan Burling was taken from a man called Leonard Cotterill by a team of people that included a man called Christopher Winterbourne. Happily, Mrs Burling was found safe and well. Unhappily, the money was not. We say that finding the whereabouts of that amount of already laundered money would be irresistible to you, Mr Holroyd. We think you figured out who knew where it was stashed, and that you felt capable of persuading that person or those people to tell you and to step back whilst you took it. You were not involved in the original crime, so the police would be unable to prove a link between the money and you, even if they suspected one, and the money would be untraceable, so, you could spend at will.

'Somehow, you made the connection between Winterbourne and his childhood friend Roger 'Rick' Huddart' - it's important for me not to mention Peach - 'who you believed to be the custodian of the money, the gang's banker.'

Drury-Smith is on his feet packing up papers and mumbling. It's a dramatic intervention and getting himself and his client out of the game to regroup is exactly what I would have done in his shoes. But his client is 'in the zone,' and wants to hear what the police have to say just as much as I want to tell. With Holroyd refusing to budge, Drury-Smith has no option but to sit back down. 'You put pressure on Huddart believing that, through him, you could get your hands on the money. And then forty-year-old Rick Huddart is found dying on a zebra crossing.'

'Is a question coming any time soon, chief inspector?' Paul Drury-Smith is showing signs of frustration.

'Mr Holroyd. Did you kill or have someone else kill Rick Huddart?'

The slight tilting of the fedora is only the second sign that Holroyd has heard let alone understood any of the interview, and the effeminate but strangely intimidating, high pitch, squeaked 'no' comes as a surprise.

'Does a man called Ben (Bubbles) Stevenson know who drove the car into Rick Huddart? And does Mr Stevenson know whether that person was under orders from you?'

There is no answer, but the mention of Bubbles Stevenson has hit home, and I now know that I'm on the right track. 'Interview suspended at 3.33 p.m.,' I say as I switch off the machine.

Standing and exaggeratedly pulling together papers before hoisting Big Bag onto the table, I pointedly look away from Holroyd and at Paul Drury-Smith, smile and say, 'nice to see you again, Paul. I hope that Melissa and the girls are doing well and continuing their mission to bully Daddy at every opportunity.' Paul also smiles, hesitantly, unsure where this is going but knowing it to be aimed at his client. 'Did you know that someone threatened my family recently?' I'm still pokerfaced, and Paul is still uncomfortable. I don't like using him in this way, but I carry on regardless. 'My partner was attacked and the apartment where my daughter was staying was fired.' Paul is shocked and I turn my glare onto Holroyd, my voice now a thug-seeking missile. 'The piece of shit responsible has made it personal, Paul, and that's a mistake, a big mistake.'

*

The police knock was the first for twenty years and Marvin was elsewhere. Funny that. Choosing not to enforce his 'no days off' rule when the big man asked, even though Albie could have easily done so, is now looking foolhardy. The rancid smell of rat is all too unmistakeably, and proof that no good deed goes unpunished. Fumbling in one filthy plastic bag and then another, and then in the glove box, all the while trying to make Albie feel uncomfortable enough to walk away leaving the change as a tip, the cabbie is working his client for all he's worth. If he could see beneath the Fedora, he'd realise that, far from uneasy or embarrassed, the little man dressed in the stupid clothes is bloody furious. Albie is outside and exposed and it's all Marvin's fault. He should get inside where he'll be safe … but eight pence, is eight pence.

56

The London conferences, especially the discussions in the tearoom and then the pub, were a mistake. He knew that their schemes were dodgy - not in and of itself a problem - and a massive risk, as it turns out, too massive a risk. His instincts told him not to get involved and he should have heeded the warning. But everyone seemed to be 'at it' and ego and greed took over. He never could stand to be the one missing out.

Meeting Holroyd just days after one such conference was, of course, anything but 'by chance,' but at the time it seemed like a fortuitous opportunity dropping neatly in his lap. As if the God Jeff Chapman didn't believe in was telling him to dip his wick. Holroyd had the criminal knowhow and the contacts and the oven-ready scams, and all Jeff had to do was speak in favour or against certain planning decisions and vote accordingly. At most he would be required to have quiet words in powerful ears and be ready to comply with any reasonable request that The Man might make. Some of the things he would be doing were crimes, technically speaking. But if they were crimes, they were victimless, and it wasn't as if he was agreeing to kill, or even hurt, anybody.

It's a damned shame! All his years of public service should count for more than a state pension and a mortgage that he can never pay off. He'd more than earned a little something for himself. Perhaps temptation winning through was inevitable. But he knew it was stupid, as it proved to be, and now jumping before being pushed is the only course left to navigate; though he bloody hates not being the decision maker. Better than anyone, he understood that sermonising had votes in it, and he accepts that his style and reputation, and yes perhaps, his arrogance, has made his fall from grace more painful than it might otherwise have been. However, when weighed against a lifetime of good works, his offence ranks as no more than uncharacteristic recklessness. And the feeding frenzy of retribution his resignation has unleashed is, he thinks, up there with burning witches and lynching. And it has left Jeff wanting some retribution of his own.

No actual evidence of wrongdoing exists because all was at the planning stage. But the talk, the nasty and malicious tittle-tattle, that has been and is still being vomited, has meant that influential people all over Yorkshire are disowning him to the point that there are things that he wants to do that he now can't do because he is who he is, and amongst them are things he could do before because he was who he was. And that's not fucking fair! Jeff has grown used to being a somebody and he's not about to grow used to being a nobody, not any time soon. He warrants status, and if he can't have status linked to selfless service, then he's determined to grasp it some other way. He's doing the time, he may as well do the crime, and the days when he needed the good opinion of others have gone forever ... and they're never coming back.

57

Desperate not to be spotted leaving, he made sure that only sheep witnessed him tying his pedal bicycle to a fence, and, after walking for forty minutes, a 2003 registered Toyota Rav 4 rust bucket pulls up alongside. And without a word, he climbs into the passenger seat.

'Could have set off sooner and saved you a bit of foot action,' she says, 'but love handles aren't a good look.'

'Now listen 'ere, little miss skinny ...' Eyes glued to the road, Louise reaches for Marvin's massive hand, places it on her thigh, and smiles contentedly. Her face will never fully heal, but to Marvin she's a game-changer, and she knows it.

All too soon, they're through Dinnington and pulling up at Gutowski's big house in Bawtry, and as he spots Gus the Puss waiting between two ostentatious, fake columns either side of an expansive white mock-marble doorstep, Marvin makes no attempt to hide his disgust. In navy blue deck shoes, light grey slacks, canary yellow polo shirt and V-neck sweater, and looking like a male model from a 1970's 'woman's' magazine, Gus will be thinking 'smart casual,' but Marvin only sees 'aging prat.' Deciding there and then that this visit will be even shorter than planned takes no effort and little thought.

Mein host gives Louise a hug like the one Marvin gave him in Albie's garage not that long ago, and once released, Louise graciously allows her coat to be taken. No attempt is made to separate Marvin from his leather jacket and both visitors are guided through to a front room big enough for four sofas. Several men and one-woman stand as they enter, and Marvin immediately strides towards Bubbles Stevenson who takes an involuntary step backwards, his scrawny legs only halted by a sofa. Towering over the man whose fingers he removed one night in a dank garage not far from where the two are now standing, Marvin nods and says, 'just business,' and Bubbles gives an 'another professional doing his job' shrug.

Returning to sit next to Louise who takes his arm, for the first time, Marvin notices an older man sitting quietly next to the never played and just for show Baby Grande. Acknowledging that he's been observed, and that his presence is a surprise, the man stands and moves forward.

'Counc … ex-councillor Jeff Chapman,' he says, holding out his hand. 'I'm grateful to have been invited.'

*

A decision regarding the 'what' is quickly reached, but the 'how' is taking much longer. Fundamentals are being skirted, and finer points are being debated to death, until a deep and mellow voice brings sufficient menace to gain immediate silence and attention.

'You're all people who've had ups and downs in life,' says Marvin, 'but none of you know Albie like me and Louise do, and none of you have had to deal with what Louise has had thrown at her.' He's talking slowly, safe in the knowledge that no one here will dare to interrupt. 'Getting Albie out of our lives can be done in one of three ways.' They wait. 'We can have him put away for a long time by making sure that the police have the kind of proof that a smart lawyer won't be able to get round. This'll mean that one or more of us will end up going down with him. And we can be sure that Albie will still be able to run his businesses from jail, and that he'll figure out a way to get his revenge.' The meeting now has the look and feel of a court with Hanging Judge Marvin passing sentence.

'The second way is that we let him know that we have the proof, and we give him enough time and space to get out of the country. No Albie, no court case, and none of us ends up in legal trouble. The downside is that he can still get at us from wherever he ends up, and we can be sure that he will.'

Marvin falls silent and his audience begins to shuffle. Eventually, Elaine Fennel asks,

'And the third option?'

'We kill him,' says Holroyd's bodyguard.

185

58

The last thing I want is a party, and having to wrestle with Sam's wreck of a garden gate doesn't help. Fed up before I even arrive, I must remind myself that tonight I'm the DCI, and as such, I'm duty bound to put on a show. So, holding in one hand a bottle of red and a bottle of white by their necks, and leaning on the doorjamb, feet crossed Stan Russell style, when Sam answers my knock, I say,

'I'm not going to find Stenton behind me with a bike chain, am I?'

It could have backfired, but it doesn't, and we laugh even though we know that we shouldn't. And, looking at so youthful and seemingly optimistic Sam, I decide there and then that it's time to buck up and pull myself together. And, after a hug, I stride into the cosy semidetached determined to do better for everyone's sakes.

Stonewashed jeans and trendy trainers take years off Bill, and wife Pam, who is understandably ambivalent as to whether the DCI is a good friend or the wicked witch of the west, gives me a genuine and heartfelt embrace. I spot Jim Renavent and smile. His smile back is tentative. No surprise. Jim is known for hating parties. And yet he's here. And when I see that, not only is he here but he has brought his nearly grown-up daughter, Anya, I realise what this 'party' is really for. It's a 'be kind to the sad lady' party. Up there with unwanted matchmaking and slimming advice. And serving to emphasise what a pathetic specimen of womanhood I've become.

The doorbell rings before I can dwell on my situation, and in walks a typically diffident Acting Sergeant Colin, wearing a tweed, granddad jacket and tie. He's followed by a beaming Sam who announces,

'Everybody, this is Amanda.'

Colin has a girlfriend! She's a vision in pale lilac. And she's a stunner!

A collective intrigue immediately seems to put paid to the game plan, and it turns out that Amanda or Mandy is of Cuban extraction but brought up in Doncaster, and she likes nothing better than getting oily and burned at the model railway track. She teaches maths at Michael's school - something I might have known if ...

The group agrees not to talk shop and that lasts less than a minute, and I'm amused to see Pam and Mandy exchanging knowing glances. And as the red wine goes down and I can smell Sam's gammon and turkey, it doesn't take long before I resolve to swap Izzy for an alcohol fuelled, going home 'merry,' taxi. A weepy drunk is anything but funny, but it's what the pre-Michael Julie would have done, and even though post-Michael Julie is past caring, I am the DCI, and I must treat my colleagues and their partners with the respect they deserve.

The doorbell rings again and the restored tension in the room, dissipated by Colin's unexpected private life and Mandy's beauty, becomes all too apparent. And when Michael, who looks more frightened than all the others put together, appears, my suspicions are confirmed.

'The food's ready if we're all ready to eat,' announces Sam with a shade too much jocularity, and there's an in stereo response of 'I'll help, Sam' from Pam and Mandy. Before Michael and I can react, the room has emptied, leaving the pair of us alone. It's a ridiculously transparent manoeuvre and we look knowingly at each other. Michael looks dreadful, even ill. I want to hug him and tell him that it'll be alright when we both know it won't, but it's Michael who speaks first.

'We eat. Have a nice night. We don't embarrass ourselves or our friends. And then we talk.' My reply is so on the button that it scares us both.

'Yes, Michael,' I say. 'We can't go on like this.'

*

Ex-councillor Chapman keeps saying that killing Holroyd will be his final act of public service, that he has no more to lose, and that any further decline will be as nothing compared to the fall he has already taken. It's a fine speech delivered with appropriately placed inflection, and he doesn't mean a word of it. Jeff couldn't hit a barn door with a bazooka and everybody, including Jeff himself, knows it. When he finally stops talking, Elaine Fenell rescues a room drowning in embarrassed silence.

'If we're looking for a pecking order …' She waits for a moment, gauging Marvin's reaction. 'Of the people in this room who are most guilty and therefore should step up and attempt to kill Mr Holroyd, I think I should put forward that Louise is the least at fault. And so, she should be the last one of all of us to be asked to risk going to jail.' Before Louise can protest, Marvin barks,

'Agreed. Go on, Elaine.'

Louise looks troubled and uncomfortable, but Elaine stiffens. It's clear that each one of them must get the same treatment, that there can be no exceptions, and that she must take the lead.

'I think Joss has done nothing terrible either,' she says, 'certainly nothing to put him in line for a murder charge.' Already holding her hand, Joss raises it to his mouth and kisses it. Marvin remains silent but Elaine looks to him for strength to continue. He nods. 'Then comes the councillor. He's done bad things and he's an unprincipled fraud.' She takes a beat. 'He's a scumbag but he's not a killer.' Jeff Chapman has a skin like a rhinoceros but even he has the decency to look hurt and embarrassed. He scopes the room. Nobody speaks but he knows that the votes are in … and he isn't.

'I come next,' says Elaine. 'Mr Gutowski, Mr Holroyd, and me, three of us, killed Mr Thompson. It's true that I was young, but I knew what I was doing, and even though I really liked the old man, I still went through with it. I played my part well. Really well. Too well.'

She's sad and for a moment she hangs her head. Then she looks up and says, 'but that doesn't make me more guilty than Mr Stevenson.

'Mr Stevenson is a lifelong drug dealer, and I'm sorry Mr Stevenson but that puts you in a different league of wickedness to me. I was a fourteen-year-old used to tempt older men, and you're close to pond life.' Elaine is unexpectedly blunt and aggressive, and the ferocity of her words takes everyone by surprise. Marvin is impressed. 'People like you ruin lives, Mr Stevenson,' she continues, 'and in my book, you're so low that you could crawl under a snake with a top hat on.'

Deformed hands hidden beneath crossed arms; Bubbles Stevenson is nodding vigorously.

'So, it should be me,' he says. 'I'm such a shit that nobody'll miss me.'

'No, I don't think so, Mr Stevenson,' Elaine interrupts. 'You've suffered a lot. And while you deserve all of it, Mr Gutowski's guilt comes higher than mine and yours because of the damage to Louise and others that he's allowed to happen over so many years. And because he and Mr Holroyd as good as killed Louise's brother, Darren.' Louise looks shocked and then miserable, and Marvin puts a big arm around her and hugs her close. 'He's been as well placed as anybody to do something about all the hurt that Mr Holroyd has caused, and yet he's done nothing except make himself a lot of money. Like you, Mr Stevenson, he's suffered, and we can only imagine the trauma that any parent would experience when they see such a terrible thing happening to their only daughter. But Joy's mental state has a lot to do with his parenting, and that only adds to his guilt.'

Elaine pauses again. 'But she's recovering and she's going to need her dad to finally step up the plate. So, our killer will have to be someone else.' Gus, who had been holding his breath, now folds like a cheap suit, begins to blub, and Marvin is disgusted.

'And the winner is me!' he shouts. Elaine sinks back into her seat, the effort of bringing rigorous analysis to the proceedings having taken its toll. Louise makes a frantic attempt to stop the man she adores talking, but he strokes her cheek and says, 'I love you, and I want to be with you more than I've ever wanted anything. But we all know that Elaine is right. As long as Holroyd lives, you and me have no future.' And, looking around the room, he roars, 'and none of you useless buggers would know where to start!'

*

In my own mind, I'm not sozzled, just a little tipsy. The tingle is there but dizziness and nausea aren't, and I'm certain that I'm capable of driving. A truly absurd conclusion that in my present state seems logical, as it must do to all drunks about to get behind the wheel of a car. Luckily, Michael, who has sipped lemonade throughout the evening, takes charge once again.

Izzy left parked outside Sam's house, he silently pulls his Volvo into his driveway, and I wait meekly for him to open the passenger door before clambering out and following him inside.

189

Soon slouched and watching Michael busy himself lighting the living gas fire that I hated but now love, my hot chocolate prepared as if I've never been away, he moves to sit beside me, and we both two-hand warm containers and sip in silence.

It's late and we both have work in the morning, but we need to talk, and, true to form, Michael grasps the nettle.

'I've missed you,' he says, gazing impassively at the fire.

'And I've missed you.'

'I love you.'

'And I love you.'

'I love and have missed you more than you love and have missed me.'

'Now wait a minute ...' We're both laughing. 'You're a wind-up merchant, Michael Lloyd.'

'Wind-up merchant I may be, Detective Chief Inspector Marsden, but I'm your wind-up merchant. And don't you forget it.'

59

Holroyd is a man who rarely goes out and yet on Marvin's day off he's chosen to meet at a place that is not his home. This smells off. And fool that I am, I've put civilians in the firing line. Joss and Elaine are waiting for Holroyd and Gutowski in the Crusty Cobb Café and they will suffer if I've made a mistake. I should have known better.

Colin and two out of uniform PCs are parked fifty yards from the back emergency exit and Chalky Sam and I are in a white Renaud van sitting approximately fifty metres from the front door. We have the place covered, but to say I'm nervous would be an understatement. Nevertheless, like 007's long lost love child, Joss is showing no hint of concern and a definite skill for this undercover caper as he pretends to talk into his mobile so that the agreed sound equipment checks can be made.

'Yeah, I'm good thanks. Just sitting with Elaine in a lovely café and I'm having the best coffee I've tasted in a long time,' he says, no doubt flashing a winning smile at the lady who made and served that coffee. 'How's Aunty Carol? Oh, I am pleased. Isn't it amazing what doctors can do these days?'

Grinning despite the tension, I'm satisfied that the electronic gear is working perfectly. Then, suddenly, Joss' phone is engaged, not simulated, and he's having a proper conversation only one side of which I can hear. Sam's ex sounds stressed.

'Now? Yes. Yes, okay. Whatever you say Mr Holroyd. Not the Crusty Cob. Got it. Elaine and I will set off for your house in a couple of minutes.'

Irrationally, I'm relieved at the last gasp change of location. Moving everyone back to his house will be a scramble, but this is more like the Holroyd that I think I know. And I'm instantly more confident that, when he makes his move, and he will make his move, I'll be ready.

*

Both police vehicles make their way to pre-arranged hidey-holes near to the new venue, Holroyd's house, where Holroyd, Gutowski, and Gary - the stand-in bodyguard, with luck not

Marvin trained - are waiting, and we're able to watch Joss and Elaine's mini pull up. A lot is riding on the foam torso cover under Joss' tee-shirt that's secreting the listening device. If Gary is a pro, he'll find the device, and, saving civilians always the priority, I'll pull the plug and we'll pile in mob handed. If the new bodyguard's search is superficial, we might just get away with it.

Joss knocks, the door immediately swings open, and Gary is looking anxious, a good sign. As Elaine and Joss enter the house, reaching the 'no way back point,' trigger-happy detective chief inspector Julie becomes 'how will I live with myself should this go terribly wrong?' worried sick mother.

*

In the event, both searches - Gary searches Elaine as well as Joss - turn out to be not worthy of the name, and a relieved Joss can feel his blood pressure drop to just below life threatening. Trying to look proficient and professional but only managing ungainly and awkward, Holroyd's new protector is just drafted in muscle. And after he ushers Joss and Elaine through into the front room where Gus stands, grins, and gestures that they should join him on the three-seater sofa, Gary fades into the seclusion of the small kitchen and closes the door behind him.

It's Holroyd's house and Holroyd's meeting, so a greeting from him would be reassuring. But he's a cleverly constructed facsimile of a real person that just happens to be glued to a Parker Knoll, high-backed, disability armchair. A fairground machine that does tricks, badly. And from where he sits, there is no visible movement or sound, or for that matter, life. So, it's left for Gus to perform the duties of host, and this he attempts to do until, from under the fedora, a high-pitched question leaks like Zyklon B and wrong-foots everyone.

'So, Joss Rawlin, who is biting the hand that feeds?' The twitching toothpick is hypnotic, and hearing his own assured reply, Joss wonders where in Hell that came from.

'Well, we know that somebody is passing information to your enemies, Mr Holroyd, and I think that that person must be someone close to you, one of us in fact. Either Mr Gutowski, Marvin, Elaine … or me.' Joss knows that he's no better than toilet paper and is just as easily disposed of, and that The Man uses silences to generate a razor blade atmosphere. The voice in his head is telling him to cut and run and standing his ground is proving difficult. Stating his view with a conviction that he does not feel is going to be a mammoth undertaking. 'We can assume that Louise Bates has told the police all that she knows, and that her information may well have given our enemies leads to follow that will prove damaging. Forgive me Mr Holroyd, Mr Gutowski, without knowing what happened between Ms Bates and yourselves, I can only guess how damaging Ms Bates information might prove to be.' Neither Gutowski nor Holroyd offer to enlighten him, and so Joss continues. 'Kevin Caldwell is telling everyone that Mr Holroyd paid him to kill Louise Bates. And even though he's in Armley Prison and therefore quite vulnerable, if that's shown to be true, Ms Bates information might prove to be dynamite. Whether it's verified or not, we should assume that people will listen and use it against us. And if one or two would-be tough guys start to see it as a weak spot and begin thinking that they can take over, a movement might start, and then we're in big trouble.'

Sensing that his words are receiving a frosty reception, Joss feels he must ask, 'do you want me to carry on, Mr Holroyd?' There is no hint of a reaction from The Man, but Gutowski gestures that Joss should finish what he's started. In for a penny, Joss says, 'I could be the turncoat in the organisation. I know names, places, and amounts, and I'm in a position where I can keep my information current. I would be even more use to the police than Ms Bates because I could give chapter and verse on what's happening now.' There is still no reaction from Holroyd, though Elaine's face is covered in a sheen of sweat. Joss hates being the cause of her discomfort, but it's vital that she's here. 'I know it's not me,' he says, 'and I know it's not Elaine.' Holroyd moves slightly in his seat, but Joss presses the point. 'Elaine doesn't know enough to cause both or either of you any damage. For her to be a threat, I'd have to tell her everything that I know, and then she'd have to go running to the police without me knowing about it. I know that I've said nothing to Elaine, and I can't see her going to the police even if I had; and if she did go to the police, I'd know.'

'Joss is saying that it's me, Albie.' Gus is looking more amused than afraid and Joss' heart feels set to explode. 'He's saying that the traitor is me.'

The fedora brim lifts unnaturally slowly but surprisingly completely, and Joss sees his boss' face properly - a rare event. The intention was that the two men, whose partnership began before either was shaving, would lock horns. But the battle looks to be arriving sooner than Joss anticipated, and the body language on display is strange and unpredictable.

'You see, young people, Albie and I are not equal collaborators at all,' sneers Gus, 'and it's been a long, long time since we could call ourselves friends. That's right, isn't it partner?' Gus' lack of concern has Joss' anxiety levels skyrocketing. He wanted to make them both angry so that they would say things that they wouldn't say if calm, but this feels out of control. Holroyd is remarkably animated but it's Gutowski who shrieks, 'nearly thirty years ago I killed a little girl called Abigail Hardcastle and dear Albie has never let me forget it!' Holroyd is radiating fury but remains silent. 'Louise was my friend,' growls Gus, 'but she hates us both because South Yorkshire's very own Al Capone over there persuaded me to let her and her brother, Darren, take the blame. The records will show that Darren Bates committed suicide, but what really happened is that me and Albie killed him, just as we killed Abi.' It's like watching a slow-motion car crash with only one possible outcome and Joss is starting to worry for Elaine's safety … and his own. An effeminate anaconda stalking a lackadaisical rabbit, Holroyd gives Gus an order.

'You have said more than enough … partner.'

'What are you going to do to stop me … pal,' shouts Gus. 'Send for your minder?' Comically and terrifyingly, Gus unexpectedly begins prancing, shadow boxing, swinging at an unseen assailant. 'Send for him!' he yells, 'go on, get him in here! I'm ready to punch somebody and it may as well be him.

'Joy's life is damaged forever, and I did that, her father did that, her own father!' He's bellowing at Holroyd but finger pointing, his arm stiff straight and horizontal, at the woman that Joss was forced to live with to consolidate debts and to alienate Sam. 'We pimped Elaine!' We pimped her to an old and lonely man whose only crime was to be my father-in-law. We did that, Albie! You and me. You and me, you bastard!

'Had to be a girl under sixteen, you said. And you like 'em young, don't you Albie old boy?' Body unnaturally twisted, face contorted, disgust overflowing like lava. 'Between us, Marvin and me, we can bury you.' He's laughing, too loud, too long, and too frenzied. 'Forget Louise, just us two can send you away for a long time, little man, and I hear that prison can be just a tad difficult for your average, run-of-the-mill kiddie fiddler.'

The shouts have finally reached Gary, and as he sees him enter, Gus is on his toes, fists balled and ready. Joss jumps up, anxious to do something but clueless as to what. Trying hard but failing miserably to assess the room, it's clear that Gary knows that tackling his boss's partner is a high-risk strategy, and it's also clear that, like Joss, the big bruiser has no idea what to do.

'Mr Holroyd and I are having a falling out, Gary,' says Gus, his body still boxer parodying, his voice now eerily calm. 'So, it's your move, old son. You should know that it'll be untidy, things will get broken.' Like a man with zero spatial awareness stuck in a hall of mirrors, Big Gary is frozen to the spot and looking to Mr Holroyd for instruction.

'Fuck off, Gary,' snaps Holroyd whilst still staring at Stephen Gutowski. 'The boy scouts might need a lad for bob a job week and that's about your mark.'

Glad to be anywhere but where he is now, Gary leaves the room and then the house without a backward glance. His departure seems to open an air lock permitting Gutowski to crumble and to sink back onto the sofa, and Joss and Elaine, face grey and weeping, also sit. Gus turns to Joss and whispers, 'we killed my daughter's granddad, Albie and me. Another one who committed suicide because of what we put him through, just like poor Darren.' Suddenly, Gutowski grabs Elaine's hand, and she jumps. 'I'm so sorry, Elaine. Try to forgive me, please,' he begs. Then, turning back to Joss, he says, 'yet another victim, you do know that don't you? Albie planned the step-by-step destruction of Henry Thompson and I stood by and did nothing. Elaine was just the weapon we chose to use.' He pauses briefly, then, appearing to come to a decision, he straightens. 'I think I should give myself up to the police.' And, standing and leaning over

Holroyd, his big hands on the arms of the Parker Knoll, high-backed, disability armchair, he adds, 'And, old friend, I'm taking you down with me.'

'Where are you going with Mr Holroyd, Mr Gutowski?' shouts Joss. 'Why are you dragging him outside?'

*

The drama has played out in textbook fashion, and we've recorded every syllable. Nevertheless, I know that I have much to do before we can deliver the goods in court. And the ferocity of the encounter means that I need to batten down hatches, quickly. Joss still has his wits about him and that's a bonus, but there was anxiety and fear in his warning, and this will only be over when it's wrapped up tight with no civilians injured. So, I give the order for the two unmarked cars bulging with bobbies to move in, take control, and calm things down.

As I leave our vehicle, the sight that greets me is bizarre. Gutowski is dangling what looks like a navy-blue, double-breasted boiler suit with red pocket square, black shiny shoes with tan spats are barely touching the ground, and what I know was a once immaculate white shirt is ripped and pulled shapeless. The red tie and Fedor are gone. The 'occupant' of the boiler suit is as inert as it's possible to be. And Gus, the partner who's finally running the whole show, is looking incapable of deciding what to do next. A drained and ready to collapse Joss and Elaine are standing nearby.

As always, Chalky is trailblazing, and, walking steadily behind other equally pumped-up constables, I'm taking my time and already beginning to plan Holroyd's back at the station interview. Then, seeing Chalky begin CPR, I too start to run.

60

Well into her eighties and living on her own, Margaret McCracken's part demolished fence and overgrown back garden suggest no family, or family that are unwilling or unable to help. And it's easy to imagine her convincing herself that her ancient brick outbuilding, with its malfunctioning toilet and twenty-year empty coal shed, still has its uses, and that, unlike the Collingwoods next door, she has no need to knock down and build on. He's seen but never met Mrs McCraken, but he's come to like the old girl whose outhouse has proven so integral to his plan. His expectation of avoiding captivity is he accepts no better than almost non-existent, but that 'almost' is down to the useless eyesore that Margaret McCracken has seen fit to protect.

The quiet brother never destined to make their parents proud, he wasn't the good at school, liked by teachers brother, the one that the neighbours knew the name of brother, the one whose future was talked about and planned for. This brother was cast as audience and never performer. For him, whatever turned up would be fine because it would be 'for the best.' He made stuff and that defined him, and the fallback position became: 'good with his hands' - a euphemism for being a bit thick. In metalwork he produced an elaborate poker even though their house had no coal fire. In woodwork a dovetail-jointed box to hold unspecified and, as it turned out, imaginary things. And in the shed that became his go-to place, he made a crossbow to murder a monster.

Hidden behind the seventy-year-old outbuilding and turning without checking if his target is dead or just wounded, he walks quickly but calmly and hops over Mrs McCraken's broken fence and into an adjoining garden. Making his way down the side of that house, he's soon into a parallel street and relieved to see his pedal bike still secured against a streetlight. Taking his time so as not to draw attention, he unlocks before fastening the robust cable around his seat and putting on his safety helmet. His veins are throbbing and his limbs are like lead, but an observer wouldn't know that accomplishing a leisurely pull away is any more difficult today than such a very big man balanced on flimsy, lightweight wheels, would normally experience. He's trying for local resident doing mundane things in a mundane way, and his backpack is showing no sign of the crossbow that has just done its job.

He has successfully planned, recced, and completed, and Kevin and their parents would be astounded by how competent he's been. And, just for a moment, he's saddened that no-one, including Kevin, can ever know. And then he thinks: that's how it should be because Karl Cardwell is a quiet chap who's good with his hands. Audience not performer, all he does is make stuff - a euphemism for being a bit thick.

61

His 'I don't care what happens to me' phase well and truly over, Stephen Gutowski has surrounded himself with the best legal advice that money can buy. He's refusing to repeat confirm or contradict what he was recorded as saying in Holroyd's house, and his high spec team are claiming that their client had guessed that Mr Rawlin was wearing a wire, and was merely helping by trying to rile Holroyd into talking. The Crown Prosecution Service have let it be known that they feel that this could add up to reasonable doubt and I'm furious, mainly because I know that the CPS is right.

Hard on the heels of the Stan Russell debacle, 'The Crossbow Killing' has also made the national press, and the Great British Public are no doubt characterising Rotherham as the crime capital of England, and perhaps Europe. I'm under pressure and my bosses are fretting, but not I think unreasonably, I'm enjoying being distracted from my up and down love life. And Joss Rawlin has let me know that, in Gutowski's absence, he's been promoted to day-to-day operational control of Gus Logistics; and that's pleased me no end. Sam's ex has already decided to change the company name back to Thompson Transport, and that's a good start. Nevertheless, Joss will have his work cut out and adverse publicity will not be diverted by a simple name change. Local jobs are at risk, and notoriety clings for a long, long time. It saddens me that the wave created by Holroyd and Gutowski is still set to drown many that have had no part whatsoever in wrongdoing, and victims like Becca Gutowski, Henry Thompson, the fifteen-year-old Elaine Fenell, Tammy Alderson, AND the ruined life that is Joy Gutowski, are everywhere. Stephen Gutowski is the villain yet to be punished. So, it's horses for courses. Joss will do his best to support sufferers that I can't begin to help, and I will do my best to ensure that Gutowski is locked up. Not this time according to the CPS. But Big Gus is a broken man. He's vulnerable, and he'll make a mistake. And then I'll pounce.

Michael is out at Saturday Morning Literacy Club - like Saturday morning football but with books coloured pens less mud no cuts and only the odd bruise - and I'm home alone at Michael's and plotting Stephen Gutowski's downfall. When Michael comes home, he'll rattle on about how keen the kids were, how much progress is being made, how dedicated the staff are and how lucky he is to have them, and I'll listen and smile. We've settled into a pleasant enough routine that's better than many couples have or hope for. And that's fine. At least that's what I'm telling myself. But that word 'settled' is ever-present. Like a sticking plaster that doesn't quite stick and is just shy of big enough to cover a still visible if not quite gaping wound. The constant nag doesn't need to do anything other than exist to pretty much spoil everything, and I just know that I'll never really learn to live with a marriage of three – Michael, me, and it. So, my love and I are temporary, and, short or long term, that's just not good for either of us. The knock is a surprise, but seeing the frail and instantly recognisable woman standing quietly at the door is, almost, heart-stopping. I just about manage a cheery greeting.

'Joan. What a lovely surprise. How are you? Come in. Come in.'

Ridiculously conscious of the mess in the living room, as if it matters, I rush ahead and begin a two-minute tidying blitzkrieg, and Joan Burling, who hasn't spoken a word since her kidnap and release, is expected to follow. But she doesn't. And I suddenly have an awful vision of Michael's lifelong friend deciding that this breakthrough visit is much too complicated after all and hightailing it back to the safety of her sheltered housing. Charging back to the hallway and anticipating Joan gone, I almost crash into the poor delicate woman waiting patiently with her back against the closed door, hands crossed at the wrists and pressed into her grey woollen skirt, and eyes fixed on the dusty faux oak flooring. This time, I notice that the heel on one of her shoes is missing, and I realise that Joan would have had to hobble all the way. And it's then that I begin to understand that this visit has a purpose, a purpose that Michael's childhood friend is determined to fulfil.

Full of questions and now wondering whether the sheltered housing care staff know where Joan is and if I should call and ask, I escorts Michael's visitor through to the living room where, still self-contained and mentally shut down, Joan sits.

'Sorry about the mess,' I say, 'would you like a drink? Tea? Coffee?' Joan's silence is predictable, and I agitatedly fill the void. 'I'll make us a nice pot of tea and we'll have some biscuits. Biscuits are always a good idea.'

In the kitchen and resisting the urge to check that Joan hasn't scarpered, I'm cursing myself for not keeping up with developments, not that there have been any. When she was first found and rescued, Michael and I regularly visited Joan in hospital, and we've all three met up several times since. On each occasion, at hospital or in her small sparsely furnished apartment, I've been a fifth wheel while Michael talked across Joan who showed no sign of recognising either of us. Michael still sees his beloved friend once or twice each week without fail, but I quickly abandoned the task, pleading pressure of work. In hindsight, it was an unforgiveable thing to do. And it's come back to haunt me because I'm now so ill-informed that I didn't even know that Joan was now considered well enough to go out on her own. Perhaps she isn't?

Carrying in what I hopes is a warm and welcoming tray, I find Joan now standing at Michael's 'shelf unit,' and she has a framed picture of her daughter Emily in her hands. I can still see the girl in the mother. But Joan's hair, so neat and cared for in the 'have you seen this woman' flyers and posters, is now a rarely washed unkempt mess that flops around deep-set, dark and sad eyes, and she's concentration camp thin. Interrogating the poor woman would be cruel and I shouldn't say anything. But just imagining how I would feel if Rosie was dead at sixteen is tearing me apart. So:

'Michael still loves Emily very much, Joan.' Words that are well-meant are clearly spears through Joan's heart, the already broken woman begins to shake, and once again, I'm kicking myself.

Michael describes her as strong and decisive, even commanding, and he often declares that she is one of the most caring people that he has ever met. But the fall of this empty shell is never-ending and I'm shocked when the much-imagined voice is deeper and more authoritative than Joan's feeble body gave reason to expect.

And there are a few seconds of delay before my jaw drops as I realise that elective mutes don't talk!

Her tone is flat and emotion free, I'm immediately full of questions, but this time, thankfully, I keep my mouth shut. I want Michael to be here. He deserves to hear what his friend has to say. It's just not right that I'm the one favoured to witness this tremendous breakthrough. And I'm struggling with the weight of the responsibility. And yet again I start to blather.

'Michael will be home soon, about one, you're welcome to stay and wait until then. Join us for lunch. Michael would love that. We would both love that. Michael really wants to see you and to talk with you, Joan. He'll be so excited.'

As soon as the wave of words has subsided, I'm furious with myself … again. I'm not handling this well and I can't for the life of me understand why. Despite the headless chicken sitting across from her, Joan's seemingly prepared speech continues: cheated on twice and losing the two men she's ever loved to the same woman; meeting a kind and generous man from a past that she'd shared with Michael and Leonard; the prospect of a new life in London; openings for Emily that she could never hope to have in Rotherham; and all far enough away to prevent her cheating husband following.

'He was called Chris Winterbourne,' Joan's voice remains flat but steely and I can see glimpses of the woman she once was. 'Even though I hadn't told him, Chris seemed to know that Leonard had already said that I could have £50,000 as a gift. He said that even this amount of money was nothing and that it would be nowhere near enough, and that I should ask Leonard for more. Ten times more. He said London was terrifically expensive, thousands more than Rotherham, and that £50,000 wouldn't last two minutes.' Joan's eyes begin moving side-to-side, but there is no pause. 'Chris wasn't different after all. He didn't get mad and shout like Simon, my husband, but he wasn't the man I thought he was. I love Leonard and I could never hurt him. I'd made another mistake and I'd put Emily in harm's way … again.' Joan stops abruptly, gulping air before attempting to continue, applying some sort of speech technique. 'My brother, Terry, died when we were all children. Terry was disabled, and Chris Winterbourne said that Leonard was a horrible person and had smothered Terry.'

Her words are suddenly coming from the end of a long tunnel, and I must fight to tune back in. I need to hear this. I need to filter out the sense from the white noise.

'... his apartment, face to face.' It's still a droning chant, and, sure that I've missed the one thing that I needed to hear most and thought that I'd never hear at all, I'm frantic ... but Joan is still talking. 'I started to think that perhaps I could still leave Simon even if I didn't go with Chris. That Michael would take in Emily and me. Give us time to look for a house of our own to rent. Michael could keep Simon away better than anybody, and perhaps Emily and me could stay in Rotherham.'

I want to shout, 'SO DID YOU CONFRONT LEONARD ABOUT KILLING TERRY?' But I've learned my lesson, and it's suddenly clear that Joan has come to sort out her affairs, to say goodbye to those that she loves. She must do this in her own way and in her own time. And I must keep my mouth shut!

'Leonard had come back from a business trip,' she says. 'He didn't want to tell me at first, but then he said that Chris and a boy called Roger Huddart had been blackmailing him because they knew that he had put a pillow over Terry's face.' *MICHAEL WAS TELLING THE TRUTH!* Joan is still talking. 'I could always tell when Leonard was lying, even when we were children. Michael I sometimes got wrong, but Leonard I always knew.' *OH, GOD, WHERE IS THIS GOING?* 'So, I made Leonard tell me what had really happened.' *Final proof of Michael's guilt? Final proof of what, deep down, I've always known?* 'Leonard did go into Terry's bedroom, and he was ready to kill Terry ...for my sake. But someone else was already there, and my poor brother was already dead.' Joan stops. Gulping air. Working her technique. 'My dad had already smothered his first-born son to protect his only daughter and he made Leonard swear that he would never tell. My dad went to his grave with the pain of knowing that he'd murdered his son and ruined the life of my lovely mother. And he'd done it for me. Always me. All this heartbreak starts and ends with me.'

203

I know that Joan is waiting for Michael, and no more is said for the next two hours. And, within seconds of arriving home and my telling him that the childhood friend who has always been like a sister is here in his house, he is immediately on his knees, at her feet, and rocking her back and forth.

'Here where you belong, Joanie. Here where you belong.'

But Joan's slight flicker of recognition is ruthlessly shut down before it can gain purchase. She won't allow herself to be vulnerable, and she won't talk, ever again.

62

We've let Joan's care workers know that she's with us. They are relieved that she's been found and, panic over, they're both amazed and pleased that she's talking. They give permission for Joan to stay for a little while and be looked after by us.

I only have his number and he mine because of our collaboration around the needs of Joy Gutowski, and Joan Burling is unlikely to be one of Dr Hafeez patients. So, not going through appropriate channels and ringing Dr Hafeez personal mobile to talk about a friend of mine who he doesn't know professionally, will violate entrenched, never to be broken, medical protocols, and I'm pushing my luck. Nonetheless, Joan deserves a highly trained and competent clinician who cares more about making people better than the rules of the game. And having royally cocked up everything else, I'm determined to pull every string that I can reach. The good doctor is waiting as we enter Middlewood Hospital, and he's owed an explanation.

'I know that this is an imposition, Dr Hafeez, but …' He's holding his hand aloft and grinning.

'Just means that I come into work a couple of hours early, and, truth be told, I'm grateful. It's a rare chance to catch up and grab a bit of peace and quiet instead being surrounded by grunge music, whatever that is. It's a bonus, trust me.' He's laughing and I'm relieved. But noticing Joan, his relaxed demeanour changes dramatically. Now very serious, he takes charge. 'I think we'd better go through to my office.'

After Michael struggles to answer Dr Hafeez' questions, and Joan presents an impenetrable front, Dr Hafeez bluntly tells the patient what her options are.

'You may not have suicide in mind, Mrs Burling.' Michael stiffens and I take his hand. 'And if that's the case, I apologise for even suggesting it.' The doctor is taking his time, letting the words sink in. 'But I think that you are contemplating bringing about your own death, and I'm duty bound to advise you whether you want my advice or not.' I can't believe that he is being so matter of fact. 'And my advice is that you should reconsider.

'There has already been so much death amongst your immediate friends and family and none of the dead wanted to die. And that means that to bring about your own death would be to insult their memory.' Joan moves her head. Her face is still expressionless, but she's looking at the doctor and it's clear that she's listening. Dr Hafeez carries on as if nothing has changed. 'Given the opportunity, don't you think that people who are unfortunate enough to have a terminal illness would choose life? I think you know that they would. Life is a precious thing that all of us must protect.' The doctor moves his chair nearer to Joan and takes both her hands in his. 'I think that the people that have shared your life would be hurt beyond endurance if they knew what you are planning, and I think you're too good a person to do that to them, or to their memory. To reject what life you have left would be the act of a callous and selfish person, and I think that you are anything but callous and selfish.'

He turns to speak with Michael, and I'm astounded to see Joan turn too. A teardrop is forming in the poor woman's eye. Her kidnap finally over, Joan Burling is coming home.

63

Just an hour later, Joan has agreed to an emergency, voluntarily section under the Mental Health Act, and she will remain, twenty-four hours supervised, in a room in this hospital until she is diagnosed as able to cope independently, and she will remain under Dr Hafeez care. It's a lot for me to take in. But Michael looks ecstatically happy, and I decide to put off telling him that poor misguided but fundamentally good Leonard Cotterill chose to pay blackmailers rather than devastate one of his dearest friends by telling her that the dad she loved killed the brother she loved just as much. And that I know beyond doubt that he didn't kill Terry Makin. And, most important, that I'm so sorry that I doubted him.

I love Michael and I know that he loves me, but I didn't trust him, and I could picture him as a murderer. Neither Joan nor Leonard would have let their friend down so fundamentally, and, while I'm certain that Michael would forgive Leonard or Joan anything, I don't know if he'll forgive me. The possibility that he might reject me, as I rejected him, is chilling.

'Detective chief inspector! Julie!' Abdul Hafeez is walking quickly in the way that people do when they want to run but feel that they shouldn't. Michael and I turn simultaneously and wait for the doctor to catch up. 'I've just been told that Stenton is here,' he says, 'and that he's visiting Joy.' There's a smile on his face that for some reason has me worried. Well, perhaps not worried but wary. 'And I've had quite a high-risk thought.' Now I'm worried. 'The timing feels right, and if you're up for it, I think we ought to give it a try.'

*

Abdul Hafeez, Michael, a female nurse, and a man clutching a computer who seems to be doing clever things including filming the whole thing, are with me as I watch Stenton and Joy, again through a one-way-mirror. I'm relieved and astounded at how recovered and 'normal' Stephen Gutowski's daughter looks. Nevertheless, my pulse jumps when Abdul says, 'it's time.'

'This is Miss,' says Stenton as I join them in 'their' room. 'And Miss is my friend.'

'Hello, Miss,' emphasising 'Miss,' Stenton's other friend is clearly making fun of the older lady and the kid, and I take that as a good sign. Still a little too cat-like but so much improved, she gestures for me to sit in the armchair across from their shared couch before saying, 'Stenton tells me that you want to talk to me about my dad.'

I've discussed Stephen Gutowski as well as Donald Bates and Joy's granddad with the medics, more than I should, and I suspect that's why they feel that this meeting would be beneficial. However, I was wrong to do so, legally, and the proverbial could really hit the fan if it becomes widely known. Gus' daughter continues to play host.

'Stenton says that you're a police officer. That must be an interesting job.' Told that Joy sees lies as a declaration of war, my reply, I'm relieved to say, is calm and assured.

'Yes, I am, and I'm investigating your dad who I think did things to harm your mum and your granddad.' My assertion is blunt, but the caustic finality of the reply: 'he killed them both,' makes me sit back in my chair.

Joy is set on prescribing the questions that I will feel compelled to ask. Not my style at all. But I can sense that it's what the good doctor was hoping to see, and to that extent I'm pleased.

'Why do you say that?'

'Granddad told me that Dad wanted to take over his business and wouldn't stop until he got it. Granddad said that Dad wanted him out of the way and that he'd have to keep his wits about him to stop Dad getting the better of him. "Keep his wits about him," that's what Granddad said. His exact words.' Joy's anger is growing, and as it does, she looks increasingly feline. 'So, I kept a watch on both Granddad and Dad, and after a few weeks, Granddad started to behave funny. He wasn't interested in anything, and the business didn't seem to matter much anymore. And granddad's business was granddad's life.

'He started to go missing. Always a Friday afternoon. So, I told my mother what Granddad had said and she agreed that Granddad wasn't himself. But she said that he was just getting old and that my dad wouldn't harm him, and that when Granddad retired, she, not Dad, would take over the business.

'One Friday, I bunked off school with a lad in the sixth form who had passed his driving test and could get his mum's car. We followed Granddad to a house in Kiveton Park. The door of the house just opened when Granddad's car pulled up, like the person in the house had been watching and he was expected.' The cat is dwindling, the young woman more to the fore. 'A big black man with a shaved head and dressed all in black, let him in. The sixth form lad fancied me.' Joy grins mischievously, another good sign. 'So, he didn't mind waiting and, about ninety minutes later, Granddad came out and drove off.

'I decided that we wouldn't follow Granddad and we waited to see what would happen at the house. And a few minutes after Granddad left, a girl about my age came out and walked around the corner. We followed her and got where we could see from a safe distance. The girl walked about 200 meters to where my dad's Bentley was waiting, and she got in. Her and Dad sat talking for about fifteen minutes and then they drove away, and we followed. After fifteen or twenty minutes more, they pulled up outside of another house and she went in. I knew the girl because she was in some of my sets at school. Her name is Elaine Fenell, and at school she was always flashing money and we all knew what she did to get it. Some of the other kids thought she was cool. I didn't.' All cat has gone. What I'm seeing is all Joy Gutowski.

Joy goes on to describe how her dad, not her mum, took over Granddad's business when Granddad died, and that her mum changed overnight. She became depressed and took to drinking, and not long after, a taxi driver in Leeds refused to let a drunk into his taxi; and that drunk ended up being fished out of the river Aire. The dead drunk was Becca Gutowski and Joy believes it to be a tragic accident, but one caused by her dad's behaviour. And from the moment of her mum's death, Joy says that she has hated him with a passion.

Having decided that I'm sufficiently shocked, Joy's venom disappears as she starts to find something hilarious. It's clearly a joke at Stenton's expense, and the lad is already blushing. When Joy asks how I damaged my still marked eye, what she's up to is instantly clear, and the need for a reply is superfluous. Joy is laughing and pointing, and then Stenton starts to grin. And at that moment, I know that Gus Gutowski's daughter will recover, I know how to build my case, and more significantly, I know how I'll win it.

64

Despite a long desired but held at arm's length sex-life that every fibre of his being is telling him to keep theoretical, that would be meat and drink for tittle tattlers, and for which he holds such contempt that he would never dream of voting for himself, local celebrity but now former local politician Jeff Chapman has determined to tough it out. Coming clean to the world would be seen as absolute proof, not that it's needed, of his engrained, long-term hypocrisy, but more than that, his inability to justify his new and different lifestyle would make him look stupid. And while he can cope with most things, being thought a fool is the stuff of nightmares. He's determined to follow his heart and he will ... but he's so conflicted.

His early sexual encounters left no room for him to become the man of his ambitions, and stepping away from such thrills so soon after their launch to save the career he craved was a mind-blowing feat of self-discipline that to this day remains his proudest achievement. He has no regrets. Indeed, he believes self-discipline to be the single learned attribute that has enabled him ... almost ... to fulfil his destiny. However, the demand for never ending and all-consuming self-restraint no longer applies, and he's finally begun to accept that control has long been his addiction, and that it's now a trait that poses significant additional problems at a time when he already has plenty to contend with. Their new business enterprise requires a very different persona if it is to succeed, and he's determined to become what is needed no matter how alien and counterintuitive it feels.

He and new partner each have their own dwelling house and they have never ... yet ... been seen together in public. No family and no friends other than each other, they are completely ignorant of and separate from each other's professional lives. They have both recently realised that the pursuit of rank and status is as irrelevant as it always was. And now that the shackles are no longer required, they both sense a once in a lifetime opportunity. Only a lack of readily available working capital is standing in the way. And astonishingly - in their collective mind's eye at least - the timely prospect of lots and lots of Holroyd dosh has suddenly become a reality.

All Stephen Gutowski's energy will be devoted to staying out of prison and looking after and making amends to Joy, so he's out of the game for a long time. Holroyd has been sin-binned … permanently. The Gus Logistics driver that Albie used to bring the goods into the country, and that Gus Albie and nobody else except Jeff's new partner knew about, has agreed their revised pricing structure and he and the customised truck will be available whenever needed. The Croatian contact was awkward at first but the need to quickly find a buyer, any buyer, proved decisive. And the predictably pragmatic Netherlanders figuratively sucked on their spliffs before shrugging their agreement. So, any success that they have from now on has already been hard-earned and Jeff is apologising to nobody. For once in their lives, each of them is in the right spot at the right time, and all is set for the unlikely pair to reap what Albie has sowed.

*

Thin, yellowing, grey hair pulled back to cover an expanse of shiny skin and caught in a cobweb bobble, despite ineptly gloved hands, and with embarrassed difficulty, he rings the bell even though he has his own key. Only after the door closes behind him does he reach up and kiss Jeff - old habits die hard.

This will be a challenging meeting. Ben Stevenson has done things that Jeff knows nothing about, and yet would make a marble statue twitch. But if Jeff is to lead the wide ranging and complicated business, and Bubbles is to be a competent relied upon and respected right-hand man, a simple clear and workable strategy must be talked through and decided upon. And that means that the ex-councillor must be brought up to speed about everything, including the drugs empire. No secrets. Not anymore.

They both recognise that bringing in talented outsiders with ambition will be essential, but they are under no illusions that to do so will create exploitable fault lines that will be very demanding to manage. The troops, and not just the new ones, will have to be kept compliant and that means keeping them fearful.

Put simply: they know that they need Marvin ... and Louise because the money generated selling sex is second only to the narcotics, and controlling and sourcing the girls, and boys, that do will be like herding eels.

But Louise wants out and Marvin wants what Louise wants and that gives rise to a conundrum. A conundrum that that only five people on the planet can solve. Luckily, Ben and Jeff are two of that five.

They know, not suspect not surmise but know, that Marvin killed Albie. And they have no doubt that the threat of informing the police of that provable certainty will be the nose ring that will keep their bull very much in and consistently meeting requirements. And since Louise loves Marvin, she will reluctantly, which is a pity, become the experienced Madame that they need, and she will, with no need of Anthony's strong-arm tactics, follow instruction to the letter.

And that just leaves the man currently running Thompson Transport. Joss Rawlin is young, he's fundamentally honest, he was DCI Marsden's right-hand man in the downfall of Albie Holroyd and Gus Gutowski, the new venture cannot be made to work without him, and he's a tough nut to crack. Indeed, there was a time when they each would have run for the hills in the face of such an insurmountable problem. But not anymore. Because this time they have a solution, a solution in the same vein as the first one. Around Holroyd for years, kept in the loop and remaining the weapon of choice should Gutowski rally, Elaine Fennell wants the best for her family, and she's programmed to follow the money. And Joss Rawlin will follow Elaine.

They say that love makes the world go round. Well, who knows. But it can bring much needed leverage, and it will be love that will keep the money to flowing. Ben knows that Jeff is the only man capable of exploiting every loophole, and he has long been the man who can make all his fears disappear. From here on in, they will each need to keep a strong hold on their nerve, and an even stronger hold on each other.

65

Elaine was damaged goods aged twelve, she has been damaged goods ever since, and Joss knows just what he's undertaking. Nonetheless, being informed that she was pregnant before even discussing whether they were ready and should try for a child was a shock. And her stark and non-negotiable command that the future for their kids - evidently there will be more than one - must be 'infinitely better than either he or Elaine herself have experienced thus far,' is weighing heavy. Apparently, the expense is irrelevant - Albie provided, and so will Joss – and there are times when Elaine reminds him of an aging Russian liberated by the collapse of the Soviet Union: overjoyed at having self-determination, but still expecting a job for life and to get a doctor within seconds of feeling the slightest bit unwell. Like the Russian, Elaine has no concept of the psychological harm that has been done by her forced exclusion from day-to-day decision-making, and, despite appreciating the lack of a money tree, she still seems to think that something will turn up, because it always has.

Joss has shared his worries and fears with Louise who understands and sympathises because Marvin and Elaine are similarly challenged. But Louise is emotionally wedded to the all-consuming force for good, that will conquer, and mend all hurt, and that is love. And she's already solved the issues that Elaine and Marvin have in common for Marvin by moving with him to somewhere far away and where no one knows them. She's spread the rumour that they've gone to North America whilst letting Joss, and only Joss, know that Jane Green and David Smith have opened a buy sell and repair motorbikes garage on the Isle of Man.

He really hopes that their escape and business venture will work but he's certain that neither will. Seven people - seven! - Joss himself, Elaine, Louise, Marvin, Jeff Chapman, Ben Stevenson, and most of all Gus Gutowski, know that Marvin murdered Albie Holroyd, and one of them, maybe all of them, will talk. And then Marsden will find Marvin no matter where he goes. And yet, Marvin and Louise, who are far from daft, seem unconcerned. Perhaps they know something that Joss doesn't. Perhaps he should just ask them straight out. Perhaps the answer would help him to square his own circle. A circle that is beginning to resemble a shark's mouth.

No will was written so all of Albie's known assets: his house, his car, the house and goods abroad, Elaine's house, and the brown paper parcels delivered to Elaine's house by Marvin, have gone, either directly to the state or by being compounded pending a profit from crime enquiry. And pound to a penny, Gus Gutowski is at this moment brokering an information for leniency deal. A fraction of the worth of the contents of the parcels alone could have delivered a six-figure sum and a lot of money has already slipped through Joss' fingers. And that matters because, ever since he fell for Elaine, he's known that no less than Holroyd's pot of gold will be enough.

It's a mess of his own choosing, it's his own fault, and like the baby already on its way, there's no going back. So, constantly trawling through possible future scenarios to get his hands on that pot, when Holroyd was alive and especially now that he's very dead, is his duty as a loving husband and father, and has been increasingly exercising his mind. And as such, the summons dressed up as an invitation from Jeff Chapman was expected. And despite the arrogance of the approach and the fact that he will need to disappoint, Joss is pleased, even excited, to see the two middle-aged men of whom he's become surprisingly fond, together and so happy. The lofty politician and low-life drug dealer love match was a shock, it would be a surprise for anybody, but the tea and crumpets are a nice touch, and letting them down now, before things have progressed too far, is a kindness of sorts. Josh can hear Loise: 'don't worry boys, your love is worth more than gold.'

Jeff takes the lead, again expected, and Joss is flabbergasted that the ex-councillor and Ben ever thought that they could lever Marvin or Louise into the roles of Enforcer and Company Madame. He quickly tells them that there will never be sufficient money in all the world to convince Big Marvin and Savvy Louise to stay. And that, while Ben and Jeff are right to say that bringing in new people will necessary but dangerous, and that an omnipotent, ruthless, not to be crossed supremo very much in the mould of Holroyd will be needed, with or without Marvin, Jeff cast as The Man and Ben having big enough balls to pull off running the drugs side where uncontrolled violence is as common as raindrops, are ideas that not only will not fly, but will very definitely see them both dead.

'I've spoken with Joy,' he says, 'and she's going to make sure that her dad goes to prison with a whimper. So, we're all safe in that Gus will not drop any of us in it. And I'm satisfied that I'll continue to run Thompson Transport pretty much on my own for many years to come.' The two older men are still looking glum. Worse, they look ready to argue. 'I also think that there can be a future in Holroyd's businesses that can leave you both comfortably off,' says Joss quickly, hoping to appease but girding his loins to brook no argument. 'But out in front and leading requires certain skills and a level of mercilessness that you two don't have. You just don't have what it takes, lads, sorry but you don't.'

The ex-councillor and the drug pusher are still determined to make a challenge, but Joss is having none of it. 'You'll be eaten alive. And if you think about it, really think about it, you know I'm right. All Albie's contacts responded positively to your advances, Jeff, but they were bound to. It doesn't mean that the deals are done, or even that you've spoken to all of Albie's contacts. There may be some you don't know about, and some that could be trouble going forward because they have plans of their own. It doesn't mean anything really. They said yes to you, but they were bound to seek better alternatives.' Joss waits, daring them to come back at him. Then he says, 'they were bound, for example, to touch base with the person now running Stephen Gutowski's haulage firm.'

This has alarmed his audience, and he can feel the room grow cold. 'Of course, I'll step away from all forms of criminality in a few years … and Elaine will ask no questions because she'll just think that my legitimate local businessman role is paying incredibly well. Joy will enjoy a life that has been denied her and she'll be delighted to leave everything to me. Marvin and Louise will stay well out of it … and I've already recruited their replacements.

'You two will be my trusted lieutenants and it'll be my job to make you happy chappies.' There is a sudden steeliness. 'But there will be one chief and the rest Indians. You hear me? It's important that you do, because I'll destroy anybody that says different.'

A twinkle appears in Joss' eye. 'Perhaps I'll get a fedora, what do you think?'

The laugh is terrifying and the twinkle in Joss Rawlin's eye has become a lifeless, ice-cold vision. He is The Man, and The Man is evil.

Questions that a Book Club might ask.

1.Are the main players sufficiently well drawn and believable and are the twists sufficient of a surprise?

2.The main character is Detective Inspector Julie Marsden, and she believes her lover to have committed murder when he was a young boy. Despite having no hard evidence of Michael's guilt, she can't seem to let the thought go, even though it promises to destroy her life. Does it fit with what we know about the character traits of the DCI? Can you see yourself reacting in this way?

3.Joan Burling is a foil for many of the other characters, but we only meet her briefly and near the end. Do you think Joan is a well enough drawn character given that she is so pivotal?

4.Is Stenton loveable, irritating, or dangerous, all three, or none of these? You might like to develop your answer.

Missing Joan

1

Friday, 15 November - Morning

Her brown-rooted, bottle-blonde hair is pulled ragged and her bony back lies uncomfortably on his wife's bed. Breasts teeth-marked and sore, the crick in her neck is hurting and getting worse. Just a slab of meat deemed insensible to feeling and incapable of injury, and yet the ending of human contact saddens her. Pain beats thinking ... at least since Brian left.

Her craving for affection is heightened at moments like this and, despite Simon Burling's irascibility and pathetically desperate not to upset him, she reaches over his naked back. She knows that she's breaking the rules—his rules—but she can't stop herself tenderly kissing his shoulder. Burling pulls away and the duvet is flung back in one hostile motion. Vaulting out of his marital bed, he leaves her cold and exposed. She has transgressed. His women must never initiate. Rule number one. His reproach is typical.

'You knew the score when we got together, Sue. You listenin'? Look at me. You knew the score. Never told you different.'

Their couplings leave her consumed by hopelessness and Burling doesn't give her a second thought unless he's between her legs, and often not even then. But without a man to share her journey, she's a ship adrift in ice-cold waters; and if she can't have companionship, she must have contact. Emptied of emotion and thus incapable of forming the new relationship that she so desperately needs, she will let this despicable human being have her until he decides to dispose of her. She has long since accepted that it will be his choice.

Grabbing her head in his two hands, he directs her eyes towards his ever-open mouth.

219

'Look at me. Listening ears on. Odours are a dead giveaway. Bedsheets pulled all the way back. All the way back, Sue. You listenin'? All the way.' He instructs because he's in charge and that's what people who are in charge do. And Sue does listen. She does do as instructed. She plays her role exactly the way Simon has decided. And she never argues.

Leaving this school caretaker's house marks her return to her own sixth floor flat and she has come to dread this moment. Her flat was once her home, but it has become a cold coffin from which she constantly looks, or thinks about looking, down into what she surmises is the bedroom that her soon to be ex-husband now shares with his new love. Unable to turn away, she watches and imagines … and injustice clings like a flesh-eating bug.

Brian's death would have been kinder. But he's not dead, he's an instant Daddy, and he'll have to organise the school run around work and shopping for four; and balancing tender shepherding with energetic play. It will be a challenge and gorgeous eleven-year-old Luke and India a little blonde girl of eight will keep him busy-busy. But it's his fresh-start and he has so much to look forward to; and nothing to regret. Sue was going to have children. Lots of children. A whole football team according to Brian. But later, Sue. When we can afford it. When we're on our feet. Taking her daily pill became a non-thinking routine that she can't even remember discussing … and now it's too late. Brian Redmond has treated her badly, but she can't bring herself to hate him. She's a one-man woman that knows that that man could never have liked, let alone loved, her. Even now, despite everything and given the slightest encouragement, she would run into his arms or fall at his feet.

Only the despair of staring out of her bedroom window awaits and she knows that she will not sleep; but Burling has made clear that she must go and go she must. Listening to him urinate noisily in the elegant white en-suite bathroom, she eases painfully to a seated position. He doesn't flush and she watches as he roughly forces his still wet penis into hastily thrown-on work trousers before grabbing a T-shirt from the floor and cigarettes from the bedside table. He is quickly gone from the room, and, as instructed, she dresses hurriedly and silently. Minutes later, she apologises for having to squeeze past his wiry and immovable body leaning against the back patio doorframe. He's pulling hard on his it's all right because it's only low strength and I don't inhale anyway filter-tipped cigarette. He makes no eye contact. He fails to acknowledge her departure.

She will dawdle and turn the solitary five-minute walk ¬into a fifteen-minute meander. Then, sitting and watching in her bedroom, with nothing to lose because everything is already lost, she will take a blade to her upper arms and inner thighs. Sue Redmond is dangerous, and she knows it. She knows and she doesn't care.

2

Saturday, 16 November - Evening

Julie can't decide if she's mad at herself, at life in general, or just plain mad. It's far enough away from home to give her a fighting chance of anonymity, but thirty-nine-year-old divorced single mothers, even those whose social life has become terminally tedious and entirely work-related—and whose sex life is more endangered panda than Debbie Does Dallas—should know better. No way in hell can she claim to be alluring, and the last time she actually needed a man, she was six.

There's no getting away from the fact that she's stuck at a crossroads with no sense of which way to go; and she is increasingly certain that 'lost cause' status is not only imminent, but also inevitable. Her friends don't agree, and they seem confident that she's out on the razzle with a different Adonis every night of the week. They bang on about 'envying her freedom'; that she should be 'careful not to get hooked'; that she is 'quite a catch'; and that she has 'big, dark, and hypnotic Disneyesque eyes;' and they all seem to think that having too much choice is Julie's only concern. She's pleased that her friends are being nice—they are her friends after all—but the only thing those Disneyesque eyes see is mounting flesh and everything going south faster than geese in winter. And she's terrified that the deadline for accepting that Chief Inspector Julie Marsden is hurtling towards old age, and is destined to do so alone, has already passed.

If that's the case, she needs to stop craving something better and begin to play the cards she's been dealt ... and she will ... but not yet.

If she could claim stunning good looks and Elle Macpherson's body, then putting herself through the cutthroat grinding mill of gatherings such as this would make some kind of sense. But Elle wouldn't need to be here in the first place. And Julie knows only too well that her chance of success is slight at best. Truth is, plain and simple pig-headed determination is what's keeping her in the game, and, if there is still a chance, however slim, even a full-frontal assault on her dignity is a price she's prepared to pay. Thanking God and Auntie Phyllis for tummy tightening tights, she straightens her knee-length turquoise dress, flicks her bobbed chestnut hair, and leaves her self-esteem somewhere under the offside rear tyre of the Mazda RX-8 she's named Izzy. The sparkly white marble light-festooned steps of Doncaster's Holiday Inn are this evening's personal Everest, and she's ready to climb.

'Hello, you must be Julie,' beams an overly made-up stick-thin woman in white trouser suit and nametag. 'I'm Freda.' Then, surprisingly sheepishly, she says, 'your host.' Bubbling with efficiency, perky Freda bounces Julie on to what turns out to be courteous Dean, who escorts her out of the hotel reception area and into the ornately decorated but unimaginatively named Red and Gold Room. The prominently positioned sign promises Speed Dating: The Experience of a Lifetime.

Corralled clients are already present. Like Julie, they are unlikely to have eaten much before coming. Nevertheless, the complementary wine and nibbles are under only polite and restrained assault because, at this stage of the game, nobody wants to be guilty of a social gaffe. Julie estimates that there are about fourteen rival females, all years younger and pounds lighter than she is. Eventually, professionally excited Freda announces that the women should choose a table at which to sit. 'If you could all sit with your backs to the centre of the room please, ladies. Feel free to bring your drinks with you.'

Each table bears a big, black-on-white, numbered and laminated card, and a personalised pink form upon which each woman is expected to write their name, the Christian names and surnames of each man already having been entered. There is an aide-mémoire space for comments—critical or otherwise. In bold against each man's name there is a bordered box big enough only for a tick (like to see again), or a cross (not for me). Julie is well aware that all of this and the excessively sharp pencil provided is meant to show personal preparation for them that very evening by Freda and Dean, because they care. She knows that it is just business and that significant money has changed hands, but she's still touched. If they intended to create an emotion charged atmosphere, then at least in that, they've succeeded.

Freda announces that a man will sit across from each woman at the appointed time and will chat for no more than ten minutes and, upon hearing the whistle, he will move in a clockwise direction. She stresses that 'like in golf' participants are personally responsible for completing their own—blue for the man and pink for the woman—scorecards. Despite her anxiety, the mention of golf starts Julie thinking about clichés such as big driver to carry the green or pitching wedge to lay up and hope to get close on the next shot; or, please God, hole-in-one! She's chuckling and people are beginning to notice, and she tells herself to take it all more seriously. For reasons she can't explain, she's ashamed to admit that she's already attended five similar events with two different agencies. Once in, she's usually found everyone to be nice and friendly and just like her: looking for love and not just searching for sex. She's even managed a couple of pleasant but ultimately unproductive dates with men who matched her tick with theirs. All the agencies seem to have a strict policy of only sharing a man's details with women who have expressed an interest in that man. It's then up to the woman, and always the woman, to make or not make the call. All very sensible as far as Julie is concerned. Her fourth man sits down as she's still writing 'nice but dim' alongside her cross for the third and, as Julie looks up, she sees her worst nightmare.

'I think we know each other,' he says.

'Mr Lloyd?' Bugger! Julie recognises him and, annoyingly, he seems to recognise her. Typical. You come all the way to sunny Donny to avoid bumping into people you know, and you run into your daughter's teacher. He knows all about Rosie and he knows that she's Rosie's mother. It's a car crash already.

'It's Michael. Please. Call me Michael.' Julie can only manage a wet-lettuce-leaf smile and she finds herself tittering. Julie never titters. She hasn't tittered since she was thirteen; and then only when she was drunk. Here she is, talking to a schoolteacher and acting like a schoolgirl.

'Julie,' she says. 'Call me Julie.' He's noticed her discomfort.

'I suppose, Julie, that, on an occasion such as this, whether I'm a teacher and you're a police officer doesn't really matter,' he says, trying to help. Bravado always her bolthole of choice, she declares,

'I thought you were the head teacher, Mr Lloyd. Am I to understand that you've been demoted?'

'I won't tell anybody if you don't, Inspector Marsden,' Michael grins. Julie affects exasperation. Not difficult in the circumstances.

'It's Chief Inspector, I think you'll find.' ¬

'Both very important people then,' he says. 'We already have so much in common. We're dedicated and skilled practitioners from the caring professions, and we both have our own pencil.'

He's handling this well, but she knows all about his no-nonsense tough-guy reputation from the slanderous outbursts of her 'I already know everything' daughter who describes him as a cross between a gabardine-wearing pervert flashing women in bus queues, and Vlad the Impaler … and who's never once mentioned his lovely smile. Enjoying this conversation comes as a surprise and the ten minutes go by far too quickly.

Michael Lloyd and Julie Marsden part awkwardly and—for her and she senses for him too—it's a reluctant parting. Moving on to her next man, she finds that she can't begin to concentrate, and she's consumed by a nervousness that is hard to explain.

*

The disparate gathering of embarrassed and awkward individuals has become a homogeneous group of friends ambling to the exit with relaxed and relieved chatter, and the organisers are very careful not to rush the departures. There's no tapping of feet theatrical sighs or exaggerated looks at watches, and every completed form is handed in—pink to Freda and blue to Dean. There's the usual last-minute unplanned and daring group agreement to go on together to a nearby pub, and Julie is loudly invited. She declines, as she always does, flattered by the clear disappointment shown by many of the men and some of the women. She's acutely aware of, and surprised by, the depth of disappointment that she felt when she realised that Michael Lloyd had already left.

Harnessing herself into Izzy, Julie finds herself imagining Freda and Dean carefully interrogating pink and blue piles whilst tucked up in bed. When they do, they'll find that she's ticked the boxes of three men; and that Michael Lloyd is not one of them.

3

Saturday, 16 November - The same evening

Pandora's Nightspot has long represented Emily's best shot at peer group popularity and this was to be her debut night of adulthood. She's just two hours in and already her heaven-on-earth dream has turned to a hell-in-Rotherham nightmare. All she wants is to find Rosie—who claimed to have had it all figured out—and go home.

'It's a game, Em,' she'd said. 'Over eighteen's ID is only a problem for lads. We're just pretending to fool door staff who pretend to be fooled. Showing plenty of cleavage and lots of leg is all that's needed for the likes of you and me. And once in … well, you'll see.'

Rosie never mentioned getting shit-faced being compulsory, and while Emily's seen no pills or powder—just lots of alcohol thrown down throats—something illegal has to be responsible for all the semi-comatose retching; and if this is what she's meant to 'see,' she wants no part of it. A pinball bounced from one pinhead to another, Emily has had enough. It's time to find Rosie and not ask but tell her that they're going home.

Last seen all over a thirty-five-year-old bloke who had made clear that two was company and three was unacceptable, identifying Rosie's bloke again presents little difficulty. However, he's now giving big wet sloppy kisses and feeling up another girl who is propped, barely conscious, on his knee; and there's no sign of Rosie. She's wasted twenty precious minutes searching dark and deeply unpleasant corners and the loud unremittingly repetitive music that Emily loves when sitting in her bedroom is vibrating her brain and making thinking almost impossible. She has to steel herself not to faint. She doesn't want to abandon her friend, but eventually Emily has no choice but to get away from the thud thud thud, and out into fresh, cold air.

Trying to be confident and casual but managing only lost and helpless, she catches the eye of the door attendant.

'Excuse me. Have you seen the girl I came with?' One of the two men wearing a long black coat, immaculate black shirt, and white tie, barely acknowledges Emily's existence; but Derek, the older and shorter of the pair—who looks like he just wants to be at home with his wife and kids drinking nothing stronger than decaf tea—seems to soften.

'What does she look like, love?'

'She's wearing a green sparkly dress and her hair is a kind of ginger colour, and ...'

'Oh, you mean Rosie,' he laughs. 'She was 'ere not long since. We tried to call 'er a cab but she took a swing at Vinnie 'ere.' Emily looks at Vinnie and sees Satan, minus the charm. 'She called us a lot of names and set off up Masbrough Street. She 'ad 'er shoes in 'er hand, so she won't 'ave got far.' Responsibility is sitting heavy on Emily's frail uncovered young shoulders.

'I've got to go and find her,' she says.

'Now 'old on, love. You're going to get into a mess an' all. Let me call you a cab so at least one of you'll be safe.' Derek is a kind man. Emily can tell that he recognises a kid out of her depth.

'But I've got to find her,' she repeats forlornly causing Derek to give his partner an enquiring look.

'No way, José!' growls Vinnie. 'You can forget it. You're not leavin' me 'ere on me own. It'll be ten minutes before Clive comes out to relieve you and this is a two-man job, matey.'

Derek turns to Emily with a 'what can I do?' gesture, and Emily smiles her appreciation before beginning her lonely walk away from the bright lights of Pandora's, and into the dark winter streets of downtown Rotherham.

*

The prone figure lying in John Street is surprisingly visible from the better-lit main road and, anxious to put things right and get home as soon as possible, Emily is quickly at Rosie's side. She has often listened from the back as her role model has held court, and she's long coveted Rosie's 'man-trap mane' make-up and defiantly outrageous choice of clothes. But the hair is sprawled like its owner over the damp pavement and matted with beer sweat and vomit; and the green sparkly dress—always too

228

short and failing miserably to cover a now desirable-as-diphtheria pink frilly thong—that just four hours ago looked spectacular, is no match for cold and filthy concrete. The contrast with the mature elegance of earlier in the evening is glaring and, for the first time, Emily sees just another little girl like her, playing at grown-ups.

Phoning for a taxi just emphasises that it's too late and too dark for any cabbie to venture anywhere near this particular Rotherham backstreet and Emily keeps being told to get back to Pandora's, and that they'll do the pick up from there. Self-assured pack-leader Rosie Marsden can't move an inch under her own steam and Emily can't lift her. She's out of ideas, cold, and close to breakdown.

'You all right, love?' A disembodied male voice comes out of the darkness and she wants to run. But, when the man appears, she just stands, dejected and defeated, arms down and shoulders hunched, and she bursts into tears.

'I can't move her and I don't know what to do.'

Striding towards the horizontal lump, the thirty-something looks first at Rosie and then at Emily, and he sniggers before bending down and, with supreme ease, manoeuvring the drunk sixteen-year-old into a sitting position. Shocked by how dreadful her friend looks, only the wrath of Rosie's mother is preventing Emily ringing for an ambulance to take Rosie straight to A&E. However, she can now see a way out of this mess, and she can't tell the man quickly enough what needs to happen.

'We have to get back to Pandora's or to a street with more lights, so we can call a taxi that'll come.' The man looks again at the slumped and exposed girl.

'I'll sort you out, darlin',' he says. 'Don't you worry. Got this covered.' Then, squatting on his haunches and smiling, and never taking his eyes from Emily's, he slides his hand down the front of Rosie's green sparkly dress. Emily can tell that it's important to him that she's watching. She doesn't want to, but somehow she seems to have no choice. It's his fee. Clasping Rosie's breast as if a kind of handle, the stranger then raises her in one motion into a standing position before half-lifting and half-walking her towards a more populated area. Emily follows, mesmerised. At one point, and all the time looking back and grinning at Emily, the man hitches up Rosie's skirt and strokes her exposed backside. Just because he can. The incapacitated girl has become an inanimate object used to harass her sober and very frightened friend.

Soon they're under bright streetlights, a few cars are passing, and there's faint but audible people noise. The car park of Pandora's is visible, Rosie is again flopped on the pavement, and the man is gone. The three of them had been together for a matter of minutes and, still dazed but glad now to have a plan that might work, Emily snaps out of her self-imposed stupor and, once again, she rings for a taxi. This time she's called madam and is told that they will 'be there in a tick.'

Milton Keynes UK
Ingram Content Group UK Ltd.
UKHW020634170824
447045UK00011B/676

9 781917 293730